HOOK, LINE AND SINGLE

PHOEBE MACLEOD

Boldwood

First published in Great Britain in 2025 by Boldwood Books Ltd.

Copyright © Phoebe MacLeod, 2025

Cover Design by Head Design Ltd.

Cover Images: Shutterstock

The moral right of Phoebe MacLeod to be identified as the author of this work has been asserted in accordance with the Copyright, Designs and Patents Act 1988.

All rights reserved. No part of this book may be reproduced in any form or by any electronic or mechanical means, including information storage and retrieval systems, without written permission from the author, except for the use of brief quotations in a book review. This book is a work of fiction and, except in the case of historical fact, any resemblance to actual persons, living or dead, is purely coincidental.

Every effort has been made to obtain the necessary permissions with reference to copyright material, both illustrative and quoted. We apologise for any omissions in this respect and will be pleased to make the appropriate acknowledgements in any future edition.

A CIP catalogue record for this book is available from the British Library.

Paperback ISBN 978-1-83533-360-0

Large Print ISBN 978-1-83533-361-7

Hardback ISBN 978-1-83533-359-4

Ebook ISBN 978-1-83533-362-4

Kindle ISBN 978-1-83533-363-1

Audio CD ISBN 978-1-83533-354-9

MP3 CD ISBN 978-1-83533-355-6

Digital audio download ISBN 978-1-83533-357-0

This book is printed on certified sustainable paper. Boldwood Books is dedicated to putting sustainability at the heart of our business. For more information please visit https://www.boldwoodbooks.com/about-us/sustainability/

Boldwood Books Ltd, 23 Bowerdean Street, London, SW6 3TN

www.boldwoodbooks.com

To Richard

1

The sound of the front door closing with a bang surprises me, and I glance automatically at the clock on the wall. Seven thirty. Given that it's a Friday night, that's way too early for my flatmate Sam to be coming home. In fact, I wasn't expecting her home at all tonight.

'Everything OK?' I call.

'No, of course it fucking isn't,' her voice replies in a snarl from the hallway. A moment or two later, she bursts through the sitting room door with a crash, startling Samson awake. I wince as he drives his claws into my thighs before leaping to the floor ready to make a quick escape.

As soon as I see her, it's obvious that something is very wrong. Her eyes are bloodshot and there are tear stains on her cheeks, delicately framed by the last vestiges of the mascara she applied so painstakingly before she went out. She's clutching a bottle of wine and has a manic expression on her face.

'Jason?' I ask.

'Yup.'

'What's he done?'

'You know, Ruby, I never thought I'd say this, because I don't want to turn into an embittered old woman, but it's true. All men are bastards.'

'What happened?'

'Usual bastard stuff. I need a glass of wine the size of a fish tank and then we can play bastard bingo if you like. Want one?'

'Yeah, why not.'

I follow her into the kitchen. Samson, having realised that he's not in immediate danger, also saunters through, evidently hoping for some kind of treat. When we don't immediately pander to him, he begins winding himself round Sam's ankles and purring loudly.

'It won't work,' she tells him sadly as she reaches down to stroke him, increasing the volume of his purring to road drill levels. 'You may be the handsomest cat in Margate and named after me, but you're still a boy and therefore firmly in the bastard camp today. Sorry, Samson.'

He seems totally unfussed by her pronouncement and continues rubbing his cheek against her ankle as she fights to remove the foil from the bottle.

'Here, let me,' I offer. 'If you carry on like that, you'll slice off a finger, and that won't improve your mood at all.' I gently prise the bottle out of her grip, remove the foil carefully and open the drawer to find the corkscrew.

'This is a bit posher than our normal screwtop stuff,' I observe as I ease the cork out with a soft pop.

'You need expensive wine for break-ups,' she remarks simply. 'The cheap stuff is fine if you're in a good mood, but tastes like vinegar when you're upset.'

'Have you eaten?' I ask after I've handed her the open bottle and a glass, watching her fill it to the brim before taking a large mouthful.

'No. Fucker didn't even have the decency to buy me dinner before shitting all over me. Bastard.'

I sense this is going to be a long evening, so I pour myself an equally generous glass, taking a sip rather than the glug that Sam took.

'I've got a cottage pie in the oven. I expect we can stretch it between us if I add enough vegetables.'

She sighs. 'I'm not really hungry.'

'I know, but you need to eat something to soak up the wine, otherwise you'll feel like shit in the morning.'

'I'm going to feel like shit anyway. Might as well do it in style.' She takes another large mouthful, half emptying the glass.

'Do you want to tell me what happened?' I ask gently.

'No. Bastard bingo will be more fun. You give me as many cliché break-up phrases as you can think of, and I'll give you a point for each one he used.'

At least she hasn't lost her sense of humour. I smile. 'How many points do I need for bingo?'

She considers for a moment. 'Four. No, five that I can remember. What's your first guess?'

Now it's my turn to think. '"It's all moving too fast,"' I say after a couple of seconds.

'Strong start. One point to you. Next?'

'Umm, he could go one of two ways here. "I'm confused" or "I think we need a bit of space."'

'Which one are you going for?'

'Can I have both?'

'Of course. He used both, so you're up to three points.'

'Oh, God,' I exclaim, getting into the game now. 'He didn't try "it's not you, it's me", did he?'

'He absolutely did. Four points. One to get.'

I wrack my brains, but I'm coming up short. Sam is watching me over the rim of her glass.

'Come on,' she prompts. 'You've got the hard ones. This is a total no-brainer. Stop overthinking it. This is Jason we're talking about, remember?'

I stare at her, willing inspiration to come, but my mind is blank. After a while, she sighs expressively. 'Are you seriously telling me you can't think what it might be?'

I've played bastard bingo with her several times before; unfortunately, Sam has a bit of a track record where choosing useless boyfriends is concerned. I try to cast my mind back to the previous game, after Kyle dumped her, and inspiration finally strikes.

'"I hope we can still be friends!"' I exclaim triumphantly.

'Bingo! Give the woman a prize.'

I step forward and wrap my arms around her. Hers come up automatically in return, and I can feel her ragged breathing as her mood plummets again and she begins to sob against my shoulder.

'Why is it always me?' she moans indistinctly into my T-shirt after some time has passed.

'I don't know.' I do have a suspicion, but she's in no fit state to hear it. One of the many things that I love about Sam is that she throws herself wholeheartedly into everything she does. She's enthusiastic almost to a fault, and that applies to her relationships as well. I secretly wonder whether this 'all-in' approach to life actually intimidates the men she meets, causing them to back away, usually after a couple of months. Jason's typical of the breed; I try not to track it, but I reckon they would have been going out for eight weeks on Sunday if he hadn't dumped her.

I hold her until she gently starts to release me.

'Are you OK?' I ask carefully.

'No, but you know me. I'll live. Maybe I'll finally take a leaf out of your book and swear off relationships forever. How do you do it? Don't you want to fall in love?'

'What for? I've got Samson for cuddles, and who needs all the hassle and faff of disappointing sex with a man when vibrators exist? Simple, efficient and get the job done reliably, unlike a bloke.'

'Jason said he didn't think I was as "in" to sex as he was,' Sam remarks sadly. 'I did at least have a decent comeback for that.'

'Which was?'

'If he had the faintest idea how to please a woman, and didn't come before I even had a chance to get going, I might have been more in to it.'

'Nice. Hit him where it hurts. I read somewhere that men take it very badly if you criticise the way they make love or drive. There was a third one as well, but I can't remember it.'

'Shame. I'd have thrown that in too if I'd known. He's a terrible driver.' She giggles. 'He thinks he's so cool with his pimped-up Fiesta, but I hate that car. It's noisy, uncomfortable and you can't hear yourself think over the thudding of the stereo. I won't miss that. Maybe I'll creep round there in the middle of the night and scratch a motivational message into the custom paint job that he paid so much for.'

'What would you write?'

She ponders for a minute. '"If I look like an arsehole and I sound like an arsehole, chances are I'm an arsehole."'

'I like it.'

'On the other side, I'd write "I fuck like I drive. Badly."' She takes another swig from her glass, draining it completely before reaching for the bottle to refill it.

'Why don't you go and have a hot bath?' I suggest. 'I'll call you when dinner's ready, and then we can watch a weepy on Netflix if you like. That always cheers you up.'

'I love you, you know that, right?' she says.

'Of course I do. I love you too. Now go.'

I watch as she potters off in the direction of her bedroom, carrying the glass of wine. Sensing that she's not going to meet his demands, Samson switches his attention to me. I pick him up and put him over my shoulder, causing a fresh outbreak of purring so intense it feels like my brain is vibrating.

'All right,' I tell him as I reach into the cupboard. 'One treat. That's all though, remember what the vet said about your weight.'

Samson nuzzles my neck with his cheek. If he could talk, I reckon he'd be saying, 'Screw the vet, what does he know about anything?'

Having dealt with the cat, I turn my attention back to dinner and start rummaging through the vegetable drawer in the fridge to see what I can use to bulk out my cottage pie for one. Samson watches me hopefully for a minute or two, clearly wondering if he can con another treat out of me, before giving it up as a bad job and stalking off in the direction of the sitting room with his fluffy ginger tail held high. I know I joke about him meeting my emotional needs, but he's just affectionate enough without being needy, which is perfect for me. Sam and I got him as a kitten from a rescue centre when we first moved into our ground-floor flat in Margate. We ran through hundreds of possible names for him before settling on Samson – the joke being that he's Sam's son. Despite him being named after her, we both absolutely dote on him and he takes full advantage whenever he can. We did have a conversation a year or so ago about who would keep him if one of us moved out but, thankfully, it wasn't prickly. Sam had been typically generous.

'The only thing that would make me move out, Ruby, would be if I was madly in love with someone and we were going to live together,' she'd said. 'If that happens, you'll miss me so terribly that you'll need another redhead in your life to cheer you up. Samson fits the bill perfectly.'

I'd laughed at the time, but she had hit a nerve. I know we won't be flatmates forever, but she's my best friend and I would miss her horribly if she moved out. We've known each other since primary school, where she was bullied horrendously by a couple of the boys in our class for having ginger hair. I found her crying in the girls' toilets one day after a particularly vicious attack, and the injustice of it just tipped me over the edge. I was into Judo at the time, so I used a few moves on the boys, and it worked. The fact that they'd been humiliated by a girl was too much for them, so they steered well clear of both of us after that, and Sam's and my friendship hasn't wavered since.

I can hear the bathwater running as I chop some carrots and add them to a pan of water. I've got a head of broccoli as well, and I was stunned to find a tub of Ben & Jerry's in the freezer that we somehow must have forgotten about, so we've actually got enough for a reasonable feast. It'll be nearly nine by the time it's ready, as I was distracted by my book and lost track of time earlier. It's a whodunnit with more twists and turns than a rollercoaster, but that's actually worked out well. Normally, I'd have eaten and cleared up by the time Sam got home, but that would have meant she'd have had most of a bottle of wine on an empty stomach, and I have enough experience with her to know that wouldn't have ended well.

'How are you feeling now?' I ask when she pads in a while later. She's changed into her pyjamas, with her fluffy dressing gown over the top.

'Bruised and battered,' she replies. 'Angry, disappointed, like I've had my time wasted. I'm not getting any younger. Do you think I should freeze my eggs, just in case I can't find the one decent man in the world before I hit the menopause?'

'We're twenty-eight,' I remind her with a smile. 'I don't think you need to worry about the menopause just yet.'

'You're probably right,' she sighs as I dish out and carry the plates over to the table. 'I've made a decision though.'

'Oh, yes?'

'No more men. Not for a while, anyway. I'm going to come off the apps and just enjoy being me.'

I smile at her but wisely say nothing. This is also a familiar refrain, and I'd be prepared to bet my bastard bingo prize money, if there were any, that she'll be back in the saddle before Samson has caught his next mouse.

2

Two weeks have passed and my prediction has been proved wrong. Samson has delivered the heads of three mice to the mat by the cat flap, but Sam appears to be sticking to her guns. She's deleted the dating apps from her phone, although I know that doesn't mean much. I'm pretty sure her profiles are still there, so all she needs to do is re-download them when she changes her mind, as I'm sure she will.

It's a glorious summer morning as Samson and I make our way to my bookshop. I say it's mine, but I actually co-own it with another friend from my school days, Jono. The main part of the shop, which is my domain, has all the new releases and bestsellers that you'd expect to find in an independent bookshop, and Jono rigorously curates our small second-hand section when he's not serving drinks in our instore coffee bar. If you're after the type of cheap and cheerful fare you'd find in a typical charity shop, Jono's second-hand section isn't for you. If you're after something esoteric or a first edition, he'll either have it or take your details and do his best to find it for you. It wasn't easy persuading the bank that our business plan was viable to begin with, especially as bookshops aren't known for being massively profitable enterprises now that most people seem to buy books online, but we were eventually able to persuade them that there are enough customers who still love to buy from a real store. Our coffee bar was a last-minute addition to the business plan, but it was comparatively cheap to install and has proved to be a real money-spinner.

Samson started following me to work pretty much as soon as he was old enough to be allowed outside on his own. He doesn't walk alongside me, and sometimes I can't see him at all, but I know he's there, either sauntering along the top of a fence like a high-wire artist or trotting along the pavement a few yards behind me. Sometimes, he gets distracted by something and doesn't turn up until an hour or more after we've opened, but usually he dashes ahead as the shop comes into view, settling himself by the front door to wait for me and adopting an expression that I swear translates to 'What took you so long?'

This morning is a dash-ahead morning, and I've barely opened the door a crack before he's pushed through the gap and hopped up into his favourite armchair to begin a lengthy spell of grooming. Samson likes to look his best for the customers and most of them will detour to give him a stroke at some point during their visit. Jono wasn't at all impressed the first time Samson showed up, but he's actually good for business too. Lots of people call by regularly to see him and, once they're inside, the new releases table and the smell of fresh coffee are pretty much guaranteed to part them from at least some of their cash.

I've just finished switching on the lights when Jono arrives. He has what is best described as an eclectic sense of fashion; his long moustache is always immaculately waxed into points, giving him the air of a 1920s cad, and he owns an impressive array of floral shirts. Today's example has large purple roses on it.

'Morning, Ruby. Morning, Fleabag,' he trills as he closes the door behind him, bolting it to stop any over-eager customers from trying to sneak in before we open. 'It's Tuesday, the sun is shining and I can smell money in the air.'

'Samson doesn't have fleas, do you, darling?' I coo as I reach out to stroke him, interrupting his grooming regime. 'Anyway, all the fleas in this shop have probably been frightened away by Uncle Jono's shirt.'

Jono leans in to give me a kiss on the cheek, and I breathe in his scent, which is heavy with bergamot today.

'Nice aftershave, but I prefer the sandalwood,' I tell him. I don't have a preference, actually, as all his aftershaves are nice, but I feel I need to score a point to get him back for calling Samson 'Fleabag', even though he does it every morning.

'Robbie says it's a bergamot week, and who am I to argue with him?' he replies matter-of-factly. Jono's partner, Robbie, is an aromatherapist-cum-massage therapist with a salon a couple of streets away from the shop, and one of his quirks is to give every week a particular base scent that theoretically stimulates various neural pathways to improve your mood. I reckon it's nonsense, but I do enjoy smelling Jono's different aftershaves.

'How was your weekend?' he asks after he's plugged in the barista coffee machine and switched it on to heat up. When we first opened the shop, we worked six days a week, only taking Sundays off, but we quickly agreed that was too punishing a schedule and, as Mondays tended to be quiet, we decided to shut the shop and start our working week on a Tuesday instead.

'Same old,' I tell him. 'I finished the new Amrit Kumar novel.'

'*Love and Loss Under an Indian Sun*? How was it?'

'Good. I've done a "Ruby's Recommendation" card for it.'

'Great. And Sam? Still no sign of love on the horizon?'

'It's only been two weeks, Jono.'

'Yes, but a woman like that needs to be adored. If I were straight—'

'You'd worship her like a goddess, I know. You've told me more times than I care to remember.'

'A flame-haired goddess.'

'Are you sure you're not in love with her? Does Robbie know?'

'Just because I'm gay doesn't mean I can't appreciate beauty in a woman, and my admiration for her is purely based on aesthetics, like a fine artist appreciating his subject. In fact, a lot of the great artists were obsessed with redheads, so I'm in good company. Look at Botticelli's *The Birth of Venus*, for starters.'

'OK, OK. You win!' I tell him exasperatedly. 'Redheads rule the world and the rest of us are flat and monochrome in their presence. Is that better?'

He sighs. 'I'm not saying you're flat and monochrome, Ruby. You're beautiful too, but in a different way. You're more pre-Raphaelite, with your wavy dark locks, your piercing blue eyes and your sumptuous curves.'

'Are you saying I'm fat now?' This is a new one from him, and I'm not going to let him get away with it.

'Of course I'm not! Bloody hell, you're prickly this morning. I'm paying you a compliment. Would you rather look like one of those depressing undernourished androgenous types who pound the pavement for hour after hour in revolting spandex, only to go home and feast on two sticks of celery and a carrot? Who invented spandex, anyway? They should be ashamed of themselves.'

I smile at him. As attempts to dig himself out of a hole go, that wasn't too shabby. I'm not quite ready to let him off the hook completely though.

'Curves,' I repeat mock-disapprovingly.

'Sumptuous curves. It's a good thing.'

'Hmm. I guess I do prefer my carrots in the form of a cake, but I'm not sure I want to be described as sumptuous. Definitely sounds fat in all but name.'

'Sit with it,' he advises. 'It might grow on you.'

'I doubt it. Remind me never to ask you if my backside looks big in anything.'

'You're a girl, you're meant to have—'

'Stop!' I order him. 'If you value your life, stop now.'

He grins and winks. 'If you don't want to hear the answer, don't ask the question. Coffee?'

'Yes, thank you.'

'I'll bring it over when the machine's warmed up.'

* * *

It's a typically busy trading day; the coffee bar is humming with conversation and a fair number of people are browsing the shelves. A teenaged girl is taking a selfie with Samson. I don't know what he thinks is going on when this happens, but he's a bit of a social media star locally, so he's completely used to people shoving their phones in his face. We've had a steady stream of enquiries and book orders too, as well as people collecting books that we've ordered in and put aside for them.

'Excuse me?' I look up to see a woman approximately my age, maybe a couple of years younger.

'Yes, how can I help?' I ask.

'I was looking for a book I saw on TikTok. Something about someone's beaver needing a trim? Do you know anything about it?'

The double-entendre isn't lost on me, and I study her for a moment, trying to work out if she's winding me up.

'I don't know that one, I'm afraid,' I tell her, being careful to keep my voice completely neutral. 'Do you have any more information?'

'Hang on,' she says before turning and yelling at a man facing away from me at the back of the shop. 'Hey, Jace! What was the name of that book?'

The man turns, and I instantly recognise Sam's most recent ex-boyfriend, Jason. He was obviously trying to lurk undetected, and he looks decidedly shifty as he approaches the counter.

'Hello, Jason,' I say coolly.

'Ruby.'

'Oh, do you two know each other?' the woman asks.

'We've met a couple of times,' I tell her.

'That's nice. Babe, what was the name of that book we were laughing at on TikTok? The one about the beaver?'

'Dunno,' he says. 'Brenda's beaver something or other.'

'That's it. Does that help?' she asks.

With a sigh, I enter 'Brenda's beaver' into the search box and I'm slightly surprised to see that it returns a title.

'*Brenda's Beaver Needs a Barber*, by Bimisi Tanayita?' I ask.

'That's the one! It's just the funniest thing ever. I was going to get it for Jace as a surprise for our anniversary, only I guess I've kind of spoilt that now.' She turns to him, giving him the full puppy-dog eyes. 'Sorry, babe.'

I'm no longer interested in her, or her bizarre-sounding book, as her revelation is tumbling around in my head and not making any sense.

'Sorry,' I say to her carefully, fixing my eyes on Jason, who suddenly looks like he's been caught with his fingers in the sweetie jar. 'Did you say your *anniversary*?'

'That's right,' she replies, obviously picking up that something strange is passing between me and Jason as her eyes flick between us. 'Two years. Why?'

I know the professional thing to do in this situation is to say nothing, but I can't let Jason get away with this. His eyes are wide, silently pleading with me, but I can feel the heat of righteous anger building inside me.

'It's nothing, really,' I say sweetly to the woman. 'I've heard of open relationships before, but I've never actually met someone who's in one.'

Her eyes narrow. 'What makes you think we're in an open relationship? What's Jason said to you?'

'Nothing. I just assumed you must be because he was dating my best friend Sam as well for a couple of months. They only split up a couple of weeks ago, so...' I leave the rest unsaid for her to fill in the blanks herself. I can practically hear the cogs whirring in her head as, beside her, Jason visibly deflates.

'*Sam?*' she hisses at him after what feels like an age. 'Who the fuck is Sam?'

'No one,' he stammers. 'She was just someone I saw a couple of times in the pub after work. I was friendly, like I always am, but she read more into it and started telling people we were together. She's a bit of a psycho, if I'm honest, you know the type. Clingy. Nothing happened though, I swear.'

The woman is switching her gaze between Jason and me, like she's watching some kind of tennis match. I can see the doubt in her eyes and, for a moment, I'm tempted to let this go for her sake, but there's no way I can let Jason talk about my best friend like that.

'If anyone's psychotic here, Jason, it's you,' I counter smoothly. 'You saw her more than a couple of times, and it was serious enough for her to be able to describe your woeful sexual technique in surprising detail.' Jason's looking at me furiously, but I'm on a roll now and I just can't stop myself. 'You might want to invest in some numbing cream or something. You know, to help you last a bit longer?'

This intimate revelation is obviously the final straw for the woman, who slaps Jason so hard that complete silence falls in the shop as everyone turns to witness the scene unfolding by the counter.

'You dirty, lying, cheating *fucker!*' the woman I suspect has just become Jason's latest ex yells.

'Babe, I can explain,' he begins lamely.

'Don't "babe" me,' she retorts, cutting him off. 'I'm not your "babe" and I'll be taking to my socials to make sure you don't get anyone to call "babe" again. You can fuck right off, wanker.'

With that, she sticks the middle fingers of both hands up at him and stalks out of the shop, slamming the door behind her and leaving Jason open mouthed. I've enjoyed the confrontation much more than I have any right to, and I'm making sure I can remember every sentence to give Sam a blow-by-blow account later. I have just one more piece of wisdom to drop to make this piece of schadenfreude perfect.

'Jason?' I ask mildly. 'Have you ever heard the phrase "Hell hath no fury like a woman scorned?"'

'Oh, fuck off, Ruby,' he says forcefully, before turning on his heel and walking out of the door. Just before it closes behind him, I hear him shout, 'Babe, wait!' but, from the stream of invective that comes back his way, it doesn't sound like she's very receptive to that idea.

'That'll teach you to cheat on my best friend,' I murmur as I turn to the next customer and plaster a smile on my face. 'How can I help you today?'

3

My plan to fill Sam in on the drama at the shop is derailed the moment I walk into our living room and find that we have a guest. A man is sitting on the sofa, looking very much at home with his legs crossed and his arms spread wide, resting on the seat back. He looks vaguely familiar but it takes me a minute to place him. When I do, my mood plummets. I may not have seen him for ten years, but he's every bit as unwelcome now as he would have been then.

'Peter Stockley?' I ask, just to make sure I'm not seeing things.

'The one and only, although my friends call me Pete now,' he replies with a smile, making no effort to get up. 'Nice to see you, Ruby.'

'This is a surprise. What brings you here?'

'Yeah, it's a funny story, as it happens. I've recently moved back in with Mum and Dad after the taxman, well, I don't need to go into the details of that. The point is that I bumped into Sam in the supermarket after work and we got chatting about this and that, reminiscing about the old days, you know how it is. Anyway, one thing led to another and I ended up asking her out for a drink. She's just getting ready.'

This doesn't make any sense to me and I'm struggling to digest it.

'So you just bumped into her quite by chance and, even though you haven't seen her in, what, ten years, you instantly recognised each other and struck up a conversation?'

'That's pretty much the size of it, yeah.'

'But Peter, Pete, whatever you're calling yourself now, you barely spoke to her when we were at school. What you did say wasn't very complimentary, from what I remember. Didn't you used to call her "Ginger minge"?'

'It was a term of affection,' he counters smoothly.

'I'm not sure Sam saw it that way.'

'Well, it's all water under the bridge, isn't it? It was ten years ago, Rubes.'

'It's Ruby,' I tell him firmly.

'Didn't I have a nickname for you too?' he asks. 'Hang on, it'll come to me.'

He's totally oblivious to my death stare as he tries to remember.

'Got it!' he exclaims. 'Here comes Rubes, with her monster pubes. God, those days were funny, weren't they? So much banter.'

'That's certainly one way of looking at it,' I tell him coolly. 'I'll just go and check on Sam for you, see how she's getting on.'

'No worries,' he says with a grin. 'I know how you ladies like to look your best for the fellas.'

* * *

Sam is standing in front of her wardrobe in her knickers and bra, obviously trying to choose an outfit, when I burst into her room without knocking.

'What the bloody hell is Peter "hands on" Stockley, the biggest pervert in our year, doing in our living room?' I ask her incredulously. 'Have you lost your mind?'

'It is a bit weird, isn't it,' she agrees calmly. 'But he gave off a very different vibe when I bumped into him. Much more grown up, I thought. His previous relationship ended badly, and I think it's forced him to look at himself a bit. Anyway, he seemed nice, so when he asked me out for a drink, I decided to say yes. It's not like I've had any luck with the apps, is it? Maybe meeting someone in real life is the way to go.' She holds up two summer dresses. 'Which do you think? The yellow or the blue?'

'Blue. But Peter Stockley, Sam? Have you forgotten the crude nicknames he gave to pretty much every female in our year, or the way he'd position himself to try and see up our skirts when we were playing hockey? The way he'd "accidentally" rub up against us in the lunch queue, or stare down our tops when we were sitting down and he walked past? In fact, didn't he drop a pencil into Verity Smythe's cleavage once and try to retrieve it?'

'Yeah, but all the boys were a bit like that, weren't they? He was just a bit more "out there". Anyway, he's ten years older now, so it seems fair to give him a second chance. I'm only going for a drink with him, Ruby. I'm not marrying him.'

'I know,' I tell her, trying to sound more conciliatory. 'But I also know you. You'll be happily ignoring the fact that he appears to talk almost exclusively in clichés because you'll be too busy looking for every positive, even the faintest spark. And then, when he starts groping you under the table—'

'He won't grope me under the table. I told you, he's changed.'

'I bet he hasn't,' I murmur.

Her eyes narrow. 'OK then, since you're so sure, you're on. What's the stake?'

'Dinner at The Mermaid,' I say after thinking for a moment. The Mermaid is a beautiful four-star art deco hotel that's recently been completely renovated, and the food there is to die for.

'Oh, you're confident. Fine. How do we determine who's won?'

'I'm relying on you to be honest. Any funny business or pervy remarks and I win. He has to be a perfect gentleman, all right?'

'Deal.'

I'm feeling pensive as I rejoin Peter Stockley in the living room. He hasn't moved and looks every bit as relaxed as when I left him. I'm convinced he won't have changed, but how to get him to reveal his true colours to Sam before it's too late and she inevitably falls for him? As it turns out, I don't need to do anything, as I've barely sat down in the armchair furthest away from him when he starts to speak.

'Before Sam comes out, I wonder if I could ask you a "delicate" question?' he begins, making air quotes with his fingers as he says the word 'delicate'.

Frankly, I'd rather not have any conversation with him at all, let alone let him ask me any questions, but I realise I might learn something useful.

'Of course,' I tell him. 'Ask away.'

'Is it true that when women live together, their monthlies sync up?'

What the hell?

'I have no idea,' I say curtly. 'Why on earth would you want to know something like that anyway?' I happen to know that Sam's and my cycles are aligned, but there's no way I'm sharing that fact.

'I thought you might be able to help me out, that's all.'

This conversation is becoming increasingly bizarre. 'How did you figure that out?'

'Well, Sam and I are going for a drink, right?'

'Yes.'

'But it might be just a drink, or it might be a drink and more.'

'More?'

'Come on, Rubes, we're both adults and you know what I mean. The point is that it would be really handy to know what stage of her monthly Sam's at. If she's got the painters in, I won't get my hopes up, but if she's, you know…'

I'm stunned.

'Let me just check if I've got this straight,' I say slowly. 'You want me to tell you what stage of my menstrual cycle I'm at, in case Sam is aligned with me, so you can work out whether you've got a chance of having sex with her tonight. Is that right?'

He looks absolutely delighted. 'You've hit the nail on the head.'

Shit, I should be recording this. Just that on its own would have been enough to get me a free meal at The Mermaid, I reckon, but it doesn't count because Sam wasn't here to witness it. I need to up the ante and hope she comes out soon.

'I'm happy to inform you, Pete, that I'm not currently menstruating,' I tell him. 'Can I ask you a question now?'

'Of course, I'm an open book. No secrets, that's my motto.'

'What is it that attracts you to Sam?'

'What do you mean? She's a good-looking bird, I mean, woman. Sorry, slip of the tongue. Ha, that's a good one. Slip of the tongue, right? I might slip her a bit of tongue later, know what I mean? I've never had a redhead before. I wonder if the collar and cuffs match.'

He winks. He actually winks. Dear God, how much worse can this get?

'Have you got a fella in tow?' he asks while I'm still digesting his last set of bombshells.

'I haven't, as it happens. I'm not in the market.'

'Really?' His gaze rakes appraisingly over me, making me feel mildly nauseous. 'I'm surprised to hear that, Rubes, I really am. You've grown into yourself since I saw you last, and I don't mind telling you that you're a bit of a stunner yourself these days. Tell you what, if things don't work out with Sam, maybe you and I—'

'No, thank you,' I say firmly, cutting him off.

'Oh, I get it,' he says after a brief pause, his mouth curving into a lascivious smile. 'You're a vagitarian.'

'A what?'

'You don't like the male meat, you're a rug muncher, a bean flicker. Tell me, have you and Sam ever... you know?'

Before I have an opportunity to tell him exactly what I think of him, his misogynistic terminology and his general demeanour, Sam appears. She's made a real effort, and my heart goes out to her because it's clear to me that the only way Peter Stockley has changed is that he's become even more brazen.

'Wow,' Peter says when he sees her, smoothly changing tack from pervert to charmer. 'You look stunning, Sam. Any guy would be proud to be seen out with you, so I feel very lucky.'

She shoots me a triumphant 'told you so' look, before turning to address him.

'I've had this dress for ages, it's nothing special,' she tells him modestly.

'It really suits you, brings out the colour of your eyes,' he replies, and I'm horrified to see that she's actually buying his bullshit, as she smiles at him. I need to warn her about the person he really is, and fast.

'Sam, can I borrow you for a minute before you disappear?' I ask her, taking her hand and leading her into the kitchen.

'I'm really sorry, Sam, and this has nothing to do with our bet,' I tell her quietly when I'm sure we're out of earshot. 'He hasn't changed at all; in fact, I think he's worse.'

I fill her in quickly on the details of my conversation, finishing with his unanswered question about whether the two of us ever got it on.

'You're kidding,' she says in horror when I finish. 'But he was so nice earlier.'

I need to draw him out with Sam in the room, I realise, beginning to wrack my brain for a plan. But Sam is quicker than me.

'Do you mind if we do a role play so I can double-check your story?' she asks. 'It's not that I don't trust you, it's just that The Mermaid is expensive, so I'd like a bit of corroborating evidence before I kick him into touch.'

'What did you have in mind?'

'Just go with it. We're going to set Pete a little test.'

I follow her out into the sitting room, where Pete is still looking completely relaxed.

'Sorry about that,' Sam says smoothly to him. 'Ruby was just in a bit of a fluster because you'd cottoned on to our little sapphic secret. You don't mind, do you?'

He looks like Christmas has come.

'Mind?' he says. 'Of course not. Actually, I think it's hot.'

'Do you? So many boys are threatened by it, but it's just a bit of fun, isn't it, Ruby?'

'Absolutely,' I concur. 'I'm sure you know what it's like, Pete, when two women share a flat and hit the peak of their cycle together with no man around. And, as I've often said to Sam, who knows how to please a woman better than another woman? In fact, if you like, I can teach you a few tricks that I know drive Sam absolutely wild. You know, in case you get lucky later.'

'Would you?' He's leaning forwards and practically salivating. 'I'm not very good at following verbal instructions, so you might have to, ah, show me.'

'Are you saying you'd like to watch us?' Sam asks, widening her eyes.

'Fuck yeah,' Pete practically bellows, all pretence now out of the window.

'Wouldn't you find that difficult though?' she persists. 'Watching and not joining in?'

'As long as I could, you know, touch myself.'

I'm slightly sick in the back of my throat, but force myself to keep smiling.

'He could join in, I suppose,' Sam says thoughtfully, as if she's really considering it. 'What do you think, Ruby?'

'It might liven things up,' I say, trying desperately not to let any images form in my head. I'll throw up if they do.

'Oh, fuck, this is better than my wildest dreams,' Pete exclaims enthusiastically, grabbing his trousers. 'I'm hard already.'

'I see,' Sam says, her voice suddenly dripping with disapproval. 'Well, I'm sorry to disappoint you, Pete, but neither Ruby nor I are lesbians, we've never got it on, we won't be getting it on tonight and you most certainly won't be joining in. In fact, I think it's time for you to leave.'

'What?'

'You heard me,' she tells him, her tone now icy. 'I'd like you to leave, please.'

'That's not fair. You led me on!'

'No. I stupidly allowed myself to believe that you'd grown up and changed. I wanted to believe that, even when Ruby filled me in on your frankly disgusting conversation with her. Our little charade just now was a test, and you failed it spectacularly. Goodbye, Pete.'

'But I can't go out with this.' He stands and indicates the bulge in his trousers.

'Not my problem,' she tells him as she stalks out into the hallway and opens the front door. 'Off you go, and don't come back.'

'Fine. Have it your way,' he says furiously as he heads for the door. 'Your loss.'

I smile as a quote from Jane Austen comes to me. 'I dare say we will be able to bear the deprivation,' I tell his retreating form.

'Fucking cock-busting lesbians!' he yells furiously as he storms off down the pavement.

'Have a nice life!' Sam calls after him before shutting the door and turning to me. 'I'm so sorry,' she says.

'I'm the one who's sorry,' I tell her. 'I know how much you wanted him to have changed.'

'Yeah, well. Aren't I the fool. I've literally scraped the bottom of the barrel now. Maybe it's time to give up.'

'Your Prince Charming is out there, I'm sure of it. He's just not called Peter Stockley.'

She giggles. 'We'll have to call him Threesome Pete from now on. What an expensive disaster.'

'I don't know, you got off lightly compared to what might have been.'

'I wasn't thinking about him, I'm thinking about the bet.'

'You're right,' I tell her with a laugh. 'You'd better give The Mermaid a call, hadn't you.'

In light of tonight's events, I've decided maybe it's better not to tell her about my run-in with Jason. I don't think that will do her self-esteem any good at all.

Somewhere out there, there has to be a man who deserves her, doesn't there? I'm quite happy being single, but Sam isn't cut out for it. Please, God, if you're there, find her her person.

4

'I have a plan,' Sam announces as she comes through the door. Samson and I are curled up together on the sofa. He's fast asleep and I'm nearly halfway through a thriller that I was hoping to give a 'Ruby's Recommendation' for in the shop. So far, it's pretty turgid, so I'm glad of the distraction.

'For what?' I ask, inserting a bookmark and putting the book on the coffee table. Samson's reaction to her arrival is a luxuriant stretch, but I'm not sure he even opened his eyes.

'For meeting a man who isn't a total dickhead. It's so obvious, I'm frankly amazed it's taken me this long to come up with it.'

Given that it's only been a few days since the Threesome Pete debacle, this is a quick bounce back, even for her.

'Go on,' I tell her.

'Church.'

'What?'

'I'm going to go to church.'

'You think you can just rock up on a Sunday morning, ask God for a nice man and he's going to drop one in your lap? I'm not sure I'd rate that in the top ten of master dating plans, Sam.'

'No, silly. I'm thinking about the other people who go to church, specifically single men. They're not allowed to be dickheads, are they. It's practically in their constitution.'

'Aren't they all octogenarians though?'

'No. Sasha at work was telling me about this church her cousin is part of. It's a super-church or somesuch. Apparently, it's full to bursting with people our age, and a lot of them are single. It'll be like shooting fish in a barrel, according to her. Anyway, I thought I'd go along on Sunday and see. You could come with me.'

'Uh-uh,' I tell her firmly. 'Sunday mornings are sacrosanct for me, as you well know. Plus, in case you've forgotten, we're going to my parents' for lunch.'

'Come on. I'm not sure I could walk in there on my own, and the service starts at ten, so we should be done in plenty of time to get to your mum and dad's.'

'Sorry, Sam. Sacrificing my Sunday lie in and lengthy bath to sit in a hard pew and listen to someone bang on about hell and judgement is not my idea of a good time.'

'I think they have chairs.'

'Still not coming. You're on your own for this one.'

'Please?' she wheedles. 'I'll make it worth your while.'

'How?' I laugh. 'You already owe me dinner.'

'You might meet someone yourself, you never know.'

'I don't want to meet anyone. I'm happy as I am.'

'When did you get so jaded?'

'I'm not jaded, I'm just perfectly happy with my life as it is.'

'It was Olly, at uni, wasn't it? He broke your heart, and you've never got over it.'

I'm momentarily floored. Neither of us has mentioned Olly for years and she's far too close to the truth for comfort. After what happened with him, I made a promise to myself that I'd never allow myself to be that vulnerable with a man again. The break-up with Olly and the events that followed are the only secrets I've ever kept from Sam.

'First, he didn't break my heart,' I tell her firmly, trying to throw her off the scent. 'I think you'll find it was the other way around. And second, I was already over him, which is why I finished with him, as you well know.'

'So you say, but there has to be more to the story. Otherwise why would you be single for so long afterwards?'

'There really isn't,' I tell her, keen to shut this down. 'I got bored with him. The male ego is so fragile, isn't it? I'm frankly amazed that most of them manage to function as adults at all.'

'For someone who has had so little to do with them, you're very down on men as a sex, you know that?'

'For someone who has had so much to do with them, all of it disappointing, I'm frankly amazed that you manage to be so optimistic about them.'

'Ouch.'

'Sorry, I didn't mean to be harsh. I just don't want to be match made.'

'Fair enough. Come to church with me though?'

I sigh. 'You're not going to let this go, are you?'

'I wasn't planning to, no.'

'Let me just recap your plan. You march in there, dragging me along as your emotional support buddy, and what? You think the single men will form a queue?'

'No, but I looked at their website. The service runs from ten until half past eleven, and then they have a social time with coffee.'

'Can't we just go for the social time then?'

'No, because what if my future husband asks about something that happened in the service? I need all the facts.'

'Oh, for God's sake!'

'Well, for my sake really,' she quips. 'But I assume God will be there too.'

'Fine. I'll come. But this is a one-time deal, OK? If you decide you need repeat visits, you're strictly on your own.'

She kisses me lightly on the cheek. 'You're the best friend a person could wish for, you know that?'

'Yeah, yeah,' I grumble.

* * *

Sam's friend Sasha was not wrong. When we pull into the car park on Sunday morning, we find ourselves outside a building that looks more like a warehouse than a church. No sooner are we out of the car than a middle-aged woman in a polo shirt bearing the church logo approaches us.

'Hi,' she says brightly. 'I'm Maddie, one of the welcome team. Forgive me, as I have a terrible memory for faces, but I don't think I've seen you before. Is this your first time here?'

'That's right,' Sam tells her. 'I'm Sam and this is my best friend Ruby.'

'Wonderful to meet you both!' Maddie says in a tone that implies that our arrival has made her day. 'Come along inside and I'll introduce you to some people.'

It takes a moment for my eyes to adjust to the comparative gloom indoors after the bright sunshine outside, but when they do, I can see the place is packed. Sam is right too; although there are a number of older people, I would estimate that at least half the people in here are our age or younger.

'I'll take you over to say hi to Geoff,' Maddie yells over the din of conversation. 'He's our adult and young families coordinator.' We follow her round the side of the auditorium until she spots her target, which isn't hard, to be fair. Geoff must be well over six feet tall, with sandy-coloured hair and glasses. He's wearing another branded polo shirt but, where Maddie's is black, his is bright green.

'Geoff,' Maddie says brightly. 'This is Sam and Ruth. It's their first time, so I thought you might like to look after them and show them the ropes.'

'Absolutely,' Geoff beams as Maddie hurries off, presumably to welcome other people. 'Welcome, Sam. Welcome, Ruth.'

'It's Ruby,' I correct him.

'Ruby, I do apologise. Maddie does get a little muddled up with names sometimes. Did she tell you I'm the coordinator for the adults and young families? We tend to sit together, unless there's a baptism or something. I'll show you where the others are.'

As we follow him into the thick of the crowd, I can't help wondering whether having Maddie as a welcomer, with her self-confessed poor memory for faces and inability to remember names, is a good idea. I'm just about to say as much to Sam when Geoff speaks again.

'This area here is where we all sit. I know it looks a bit bare now, but the service is going to start in a few minutes, so it'll fill up pretty quickly. Do you mind me asking what brings you here today?'

As Sam tells him some cock-and-bull story about searching for meaning in her life, a large countdown timer appears on screen and a voice comes over the PA system asking people to take their seats. Sure enough, barely a minute later, all the seats around us have filled up. Geoff is obviously popular, as many of them greet him enthusiastically. The seats next to me are taken by a young, earnest-looking couple.

'Ruby, this is Taylor and Ben,' Geoff tells me, leaning over Sam. 'This is Ruby, guys, and her friend Sam. They're new.'

'Lovely to meet you both,' Taylor says, extending her hand to shake ours.

'Taylor and Ben met each other right here at church,' Geoff tells us enthusiastically, causing Sam to raise her eyebrows at me in an 'I told you so' way. 'They were married last year and had their first baby three months ago. How is Reuben?'

'He's just a blessing every day,' Taylor tells him. 'We're so looking forward to his welcome service next month.'

'Is that like a christening?' I ask her, curious in spite of myself.

'No. In our church, we practise adult baptism. Have you dedicated your life to the Lord?'

'Umm, not exactly, no.'

'That's fine. There are people here at all stages of their spiritual journey. We run a number of courses that you might find interesting. I'm sure Geoff will give you all the information. Anyway, once someone has reached the stage where they're ready to say "Yes" to Jesus, we prepare them for baptism. For babies, we have a welcome ceremony, where we welcome them into the church and pray for them. It's really moving.'

Thankfully, before Taylor can probe any further into my Christian faith, or lack of it, the countdown clock reaches zero and the band walk out onto the stage. A couple of loud guitar chords sound and the audience whoops delightedly. For the next twenty minutes, it feels almost like I'm at a rock concert. The atmosphere is very similar; the audience are on their feet, waving their hands and swaying in time to the music. Only the song lyrics and bursts of prayer between songs remind me that I'm in a church. I have to admit, as productions go, it's pretty slick. The band leader gives the appearance that he's deciding which lyrics to repeat purely on the spur of the moment, but the way the band are effortlessly going along with it makes me think that this surface spontaneity is in fact strictly choreographed and rehearsed. Just as I'm starting to feel sensory overload coming on from the loud music, the lights and the images projected onto the huge screens, the band leader wraps things up in a final thundering crescendo and the audience erupts with cheers and shouts. Someone on the other side of the hall yells, 'Yeah, thank you, Jesus,' at the top of his voice, and a chorus of 'Amens' rattle around him like machinegun fire. It's exhausting.

Once everyone has finally taken their seats, someone else comes onto the stage to read a passage from the Bible. I recognise it from school as the story of the battle of Jericho and, as soon as the reading is done, a glass lectern is positioned and a man in his mid-forties, wearing chinos and a light blue shirt, strides out, holding an open copy of the Bible in his hand.

'That's Martin, our pastor,' Geoff whispers. 'Such a gifted preacher.'

He may be gifted, but I still have no trouble tuning him out as he talks about how the battle of Jericho illustrates how we need to be persistent as Christians. What I do notice is that the people around us, including Ben and Taylor, all have notebooks open on their laps and are scribbling copious notes. I am briefly impressed that Martin appears to be speaking without notes of his own, until I turn my head and spot something that looks suspiciously like a teleprompter at the back of the room. After half an hour or so, during which I try hard not to doze off – these chairs are surprisingly comfortable – the band starts playing softly and, in another carefully choreographed set piece, the pastor draws his talk to a close. I'm surreptitiously checking my watch. Only another twenty minutes to go, then Sam can do her social bit and we can get out of here. I wonder what Mum's making for lunch?

At the end of the service, Taylor and Ben rush off to collect baby Reuben from the crèche, along with some of the other members of the group who also must have small children. Geoff shepherds the rest of us into another massive room, where multiple coffee stations have been set up. Everyone seems very friendly, but I'm definitely feeling overwhelmed now, as the service finished with another full-on session from the band, and the noise of conversation in here is deafening.

'Have you come far?' a woman that Geoff introduced as Bernice yells in my ear. Sam and I have been separated, much to my consternation, although

I can see her talking to someone in a red polo shirt bearing the church logo a little way away. I guess the colours all mean something, but I have no idea what.

'Not really, I live in Margate,' I bellow back at her.

'By the sea, how lovely. Richard and I often head out there to enjoy the sea air when the weather's nice. Oh, you should meet him. Hang on.' She turns and beckons a man to join us.

'This is Richard,' she says by way of introduction. 'We're covenanted at the moment, but we're hoping Pastor Martin will give his blessing so we can get engaged soon.'

'Is Pastor Martin your father?' I ask.

'No. Why?'

'I was just curious why you'd need his permission to get engaged.'

'It's how things work in our church,' Richard explains. 'Pastor Martin is very worried about the divorce rate, so we take relationships and marriage very seriously.'

Sensing that this might be useful information for Sam, I decide to press him.

'So what does that mean in practice?' I ask. 'I guess casual hook-ups are a no-no?'

'Completely,' Richard says seriously. 'We strongly discourage any one-on-one socialising with members of the opposite sex unless you're covenanted.'

'What does it mean to be covenanted?'

'If you want to spend one-on-one time with someone, you both have to sign a covenant. It's like an agreement that sets out the boundaries of what is acceptable.'

'I see,' I tell him. 'What kinds of things are covered by this covenant?'

'We're allowed to hold hands when we're in public,' Bernice explains. 'We're allowed to kiss on the cheek, but not the mouth. Hugging is also permitted as long as it's A frame and doesn't last more than five seconds.'

'Seems a bit severe,' I remark.

'It's to prevent temptation. Kissing on the mouth, bringing the genitals into close proximity, these could very quickly lead to things getting out of hand. We believe any form of sexual contact is strictly prohibited outside marriage.'

Oh, Sam isn't going to like that at all.

'But isn't there a risk that people will rush into marriage so they can have sex?' I ask. 'I'd have thought that would drive the divorce rate up, not down.'

'That's why we have the process we do,' Bernice tells me. 'You have to be covenanted for at least a year before you can submit an engagement request to Pastor Martin, and he'll only allow you to marry once you've completed the relevant courses and workshops successfully. The whole process can take up to five years, but it obviously works because our divorce rate is practically non-existent.'

Poor Sam. She'll be climbing the walls in frustration if she has to go through this. A thought comes to me.

'So, once you're covenanted, you're allowed to see each other one-on-one, right?' I say to Bernice.

'That's right, yes.'

'But who polices it? You could be bonking each other's brains out and nobody would know.'

Bernice smiles wryly. This obviously isn't the first time she's been asked this question. 'Part of the covenanting agreement is that you both attend an accountability group every week.'

'A what?'

'An accountability group. It's like a self-help thing, to keep you focused on what's important and not be distracted by temptation.'

Bloody hell. If Sam decides this is her route to true love, she's going to need a whole drawer of vibrators to keep her from going mad. Except, knowing this lot, vibrators are probably banned as well.

5

'So, tell me about this sudden decision to go to church,' my younger sister Em asks with a grin as we sit down for lunch. 'Have you two become God-botherers now?'

'Mind your language, Emerald,' my father warns her. 'We didn't raise you to be disparaging about people who see the world differently from you.' Mum and Dad's decision to name us both after gemstones, because we're apparently the jewels in their crown, has been a lot easier for me than Em, who was bullied a bit at school for having a 'posho's' name. Unsurprisingly, the only people to use her full name are Mum and Dad; to everyone else she's firmly Em.

Em rolls her eyes theatrically but otherwise ignores Dad. 'Did Jesus come to you in a vision, like St Paul on the road to Damascus?' she asks me. 'Are you going to become a nun?'

'You'd make a good nun,' Mum observes. 'You could read all day and it's not as if it would have a detrimental effect on your love life because you don't have one. They'd probably even let you keep Samson.'

I'm just about to tell her what I think of that idea when I notice that Dad is looking at me quizzically. 'What?' I ask him.

'Nothing,' he replies. 'Just trying to picture you in a habit. I reckon it would suit you. Plus, it would give me something to brag about at the golf club. My daughter, the nun.'

'I'm not becoming a nun, OK?' I say crossly. 'I went because Sam asked me.'

'Are you becoming a nun then, Sam?' Em asks her.

'I might as well, at this rate,' Sam replies gloomily. 'Although, if the people at convents are anything like the crowd this morning, they'd probably burn me at the stake rather than let me in.'

'Why? What happened?'

'It was like stepping back into the Victorian age, but with better music,' Sam says despondently. 'My plan was simple. Go to a church where there are lots of nice single men and meet Mr Right. Not exactly hard.'

'Seems straightforward enough,' Em agrees. 'Were there lots of nice single men?'

'Loads, but they're kept strictly under lock and key. Get this: you're not allowed to spend time alone with any of them unless you're covenanted. Isn't that the term, Ruby?'

'Yup. You have to sign an agreement saying you're not going to get up to any funny business and then attend a weekly group to make sure you're not falling off the wagon.'

'You can't be serious.' Em's eyes are wide.

'Deadly,' Sam tells her. 'Everyone I spoke to was totally on message, but then I talked to this one guy, in the education team, and it got a whole load worse.'

'They all have branded polo shirts,' I chip in. 'We worked out in the car on the way here that the colour denotes your role. Black is welcome team, green is group coordinator or something like that, red is education and training, and blue is still a mystery. Sorry, go on, Sam.'

'Yeah, so I was talking to Bryan, with a "y", as he kept informing me. Before you even get to the covenanting stuff, or applying to get engaged, there are all these hoops you have to jump through. It's even more complicated if, as he put it, you have a "sexual past".'

'A what?'

'Exactly. I wanted to ask him how many twenty-eight-year-olds he knew that didn't have a sexual past, but then I looked around the room and thought he probably knew quite a few. So, anyway, if you have this so-called "sexual past", you have to attend and graduate from a course called *The Mary Magdalene Institute*.'

'What the bloody hell is that? I hope that's just for the girls, and the boys have their own course called *The Serpent between my legs beguiled me, and I did enter her*.'

'Don't be crude, Emerald,' Mum scolds.

'Nice Biblical reference though,' I tell her.

'Certainly better than theirs,' Dad agrees. 'It's lazy theology to assume Mary Magdalene was a prostitute, which is what I suspect they're getting at. There's no evidence in the Bible that she was.'

'Wasn't she the woman caught in adultery?' Mum asks.

'Nope. Again, people make the association, but there's no evidence.'

'When did you become such a Biblical scholar?' Em is obviously as surprised by this sudden outpouring of theology from Dad as I am.

'One of the people your father plays golf with is a vicar,' Mum explains with a slight sigh. 'We've been getting a lot of this lately.'

'Anyway, we're getting off the point,' Em states firmly, having cleared that little mystery up. 'Let me get this straight then. If you're not a virgin, regardless of your gender, you have to go to this *Mary Magdalene* thing.'

'Yup,' Sam agrees.

'Fucking typical.'

'Emerald!'

'Sorry, Mum, but it is. Blame the women, just like everyone has forever.' This is a well-worn theme of Em's, and I mentally prepare myself for the diatribe. It's not that I don't agree with her; I do, but her constant campaigning can get a little wearing. 'Why didn't they name their sex shame clinic after a man, hmm? Because it's always the woman's fault. She's a *fallen* woman. Where are the *fallen* men?'

'It gets worse,' Sam tells her. 'Even once you've graduated, it's on your record that you attended, and anyone interested in covenanting with you will be informed of that fact as part of the process. Bryan with a "y" made it clear that basically means graduates will only covenant with each other, because the pure ones won't want you. So, if I wanted to marry someone from there, not only would I have to basically shout my sexual history from the rooftops, but I'd probably be in my fifties before I'd be allowed to covenant the one man honest enough to reveal that he wasn't as pure as the driven snow.'

'Or you could lie,' Em offers. 'Tell them you've never even looked at a boy.'

'Why should I? I'm not ashamed. I'm not some nymphomaniac who whips off her knickers at the drop of a hat – sorry, Mrs Johnson. I've had a number of committed, loving relationships and a few disasters. No, they can keep their holier-than-thou attitude, thank you very much.'

'It's all nonsense anyway,' Em observes. 'Even the so-called pure ones are probably wanking themselves into a coma to deal with the frustration.'

'Emerald!' my parents shout together.

'What about you?' I ask Em a little while later, once Mum and Dad have stopped scowling at her. I know sisters often fight like cat and dog but, despite the six-year age gap, Em and I have always got on well. 'How are things with Charlie?'

She sighs. 'Tricky, at the moment. It was easy when we were both at uni, but now I'm stuck down here and he's up in Manchester. We're both looking for jobs in London, and we see each other as often as we can, but the train fares are mental.'

'You're not going to split up though, are you?' Em and Charlie have been together since their first year of uni, and I've never seen them anything other than totally loved up.

'I hope not, but it's hard to keep the spark alive.' She lowers her voice so Mum and Dad can't hear. 'We did try sexy video calls, but they just made me feel really grubby.'

I smile. 'Talking of grubby, you'll never guess who Sam brought home the other night. Do you remember me talking about Peter Stockley, back in the day?'

'Wasn't he the frotteur?' She turns and stares at Sam, who rolls her eyes.

'I thought he'd changed. We all make mistakes.'

'He was a nasty boy,' Mum observes. She's either given up on scolding Em for her language, or has no idea what frottage is. 'I blame his father. Do you remember him, Derek?'

'Nope,' Dad replies.

'I suppose you wouldn't,' Mum says with a sigh. 'He wouldn't have been interested in you, but I don't think there was a woman at the school he didn't try to feel up. He was so blatant about it too. No wonder Peter turned out the way he did. Disgusting, the pair of them. You'd probably get a better class of man on one of those boozy holidays to Spain that the younger generation seem so keen on. Maybe you should do one of those, Sam.'

'No offence, but I think Sam and Ruby are probably ten years too old for the thumping nightlife of Shagaluf,' Em says with a laugh.

'I'm really not sure university has been good for you, Emerald,' Mum tells her sternly. 'Your language has taken a real nosedive.'

Em turns to me and winks. Her second favourite hobby, after campaigning for women's rights, is winding up Mum and Dad. I really hope she finds a job and moves out soon, because I can't see her living at home being a success at this rate.

* * *

'I've been thinking,' Sam says to me after we've given our order to the waiter. She's been as good as her word, and we're currently sitting in the plush dining room of The Mermaid, sipping Chablis and enjoying the view of the sea through the large windows.

'Always worrying,' I quip.

'I need a break. You could probably use one too. When was the last time you went on holiday?'

'I went to Venice with Jono.'

'That doesn't count. He was buying books so it was a work trip.'

'Then it would be when you and I went to Cornwall last year.'

'Exactly. I've been getting it in the neck from my boss at work, because apparently travel agents are supposed to travel more than I have been, so I think we should go on holiday. Give me a break from trying to find Mr Right, and you a break from listening to me moan about the latest Mr Wrong.'

I study her for a moment, trying to work out if this is Sam floating a vague idea, or whether she's already decided on the itinerary and is just going to sell it to me so she can book it.

'What did you have in mind?' I ask carefully.

Before she has a chance to answer, the waiter delivers our amuse bouches, two small teacups filled with a pale orange liquid.

'From the chef,' he tells us. 'Essence of Tomato.'

I take a sip, and it's heavenly. The flavour is like tomato on speed, but it's also delicate.

'Oh, wow,' Sam breathes as she sets down her cup. 'Maybe I'll cancel the rest of my order and just have a couple of gallons of this.'

'Perhaps you should invite Threesome Pete round more often,' I suggest. 'If I get dinner here every time he comes, I might just about be able to put up with him.'

'No,' she says firmly. 'No more Threesome Pete and no more preachy church people. Actually, how do you think they'd react to him?'

'I think they'd implode,' I laugh. 'Can you imagine if they had the ability to do a mental X-ray to check your sexual health? His would be a living porno movie.'

'I must have been out of my mind. Anyway, holiday. How do you feel about a cruise?'

'Umm, aren't they really expensive and for old people?' I ask.

'Not any more. There are all sorts of cruises now, for every age group and price bracket. I mean, none of them are particularly cheap, but I reckon I can get us a deal through work.'

'I don't know,' I tell her. 'It sounds like a faff. Don't you have to dress up in the evenings, and hobnob with the captain and stuff like that? Can't we just go somewhere and lie on a beach?'

'Oh yeah, that would work really well with my skin tone,' she says sarcastically. 'Cruises are a really good way of seeing a variety of places in a comparatively short time, without having to pack and unpack all the time. There's a ten-day one on the Mediterranean I thought would suit us. I'll show you some pictures of the ship if you like. It looks lovely.'

OK, this is a fully fledged idea then. She pulls her phone out of her bag and fiddles with it for a while, before handing it over.

'According to Janet, our cruise expert, Scandia Cruises are one of the top companies, and the ship I'm showing you is their newest one. It only launched last year.'

I scroll through the pictures and I have to admit that I'm impressed. The

Spirit of Malmö is basically a floating hotel, with a variety of places to eat and drink, a large sun deck with a pool, and spacious-looking cabins done out in a very Scandinavian style, with lots of light wood. When I get to the prices, however, my heart stops.

'*How* much?' I ask incredulously.

'It won't be as much as that,' Sam says quickly. 'That's the top-tier cabin, which we don't need. And the price includes flights and all the food, so it's not as expensive as it looks. We embark in Rome, then visit Naples, Sicily, Malta, Sardinia, Majorca, Barcelona, Cannes and Florence before returning to Rome. Where else would you be able to see all of that in ten days? What do you think?'

I look at the pictures again. It does look nice, and the idea of exploring all the places she mentioned is appealing.

'Go on then,' I tell her. 'As long as the cost doesn't break the bank and we can find someone to babysit for Samson, you're on.'

'Oh, I've sorted that,' she says breezily. 'I texted Em about it yesterday, and she jumped at the chance. She's even offered to cover for you in the bookshop so Jono isn't on his own. I think ten days away from your mum and dad was too tempting for her to resist.'

'You are unbelievable!' I exclaim. 'What if I'd have said no?'

She grins. 'Why on earth would you do that? I'm handing you a dream holiday on a plate. No faffing about with research or organisation because I've done it for you. All you have to do is cough up the money and have a great time.'

I smile. She's right, so why do I still have the niggling feeling that I've been played?

6

'A cruise?' Jono asks dubiously when I tell him about it the next morning. 'I don't want to rain on your parade, Ruby, but that sounds like ten days cooped up with generation zimmer. Wouldn't you rather spend the time lying on a beach somewhere, with a delicious barman serving you exotic cocktails?'

'That sounds more like your fantasy,' I reply. 'Although I'm prepared to admit it's not a bad one.'

'I'd love it, you're right, but Robbie isn't really one for lying around in the sun, as you know. He prefers those retreat places where you go to drink kale smoothies and realign your chakras. I love him to bits, but I don't think we'll ever agree on holidays. Anyway, this isn't about me, it's about you. Explain the cruise idea to me, because I'm not getting it.'

'Neither did I to begin with,' I admit. 'But I'm being open minded. Hopefully it won't be "generation zimmer" as you put it because, according to Sam, who got it from her cruise expert colleague at work, Scandia Cruises attract a younger demographic than the traditional cruise market.'

He laughs. 'Just one foot in the grave instead of both then. I've never heard of Scandia. Who are they?'

'I'll show you. Hang on.' I launch the browser on the shop computer and bring up the Scandia Cruises website, scrolling down until I reach the promotional text. 'Look,' I tell him.

He positions himself in front of the screen and twiddles his moustache thoughtfully as he begins to read aloud.

'*Leave the world behind you with Scandia Cruises. Our state-of-the-art fleet is among the youngest currently in service, and our ships have been specifically designed to make life on board as comfortable for our guests as possible.* So far, so sales flannelly. Where's the nitty gritty? I want to see the cabins. Ah, here we go. *Our inboard Club Class cabins may be our entry-level accommodation, but there's nothing basic about them. Boasting a generous and class-leading 250 square feet, they include ample storage space, a luxurious bathroom and full set of amenities. You won't even miss that outside view, as it's available on your wall-mounted TV screen. Upgrade to Captain Class, and you'll have all this plus a choice of porthole or oceanview window (supplement applies).*' He studies the pictures. 'They both look pretty poky, if you ask me. What are you?'

'Commodore Class.'

He looks back at the screen, scrolls down a little and continues to read. '*In our luxurious Commodore Class cabins you will not only enjoy unparalleled views from your own private veranda, but you will also have exclusive access to the Commodore Class dining room (supplement applies). If you're travelling with a family, our Commodore Class suites give you even more space, with a separate sitting area and a PlayStation with a selection of games (supplement applies).* I'll admit that these cabins look nice, but is there anything that doesn't come with a supplement?'

'From the way Sam explained it, the basics are all included but you pay for the luxuries. So there's an all-day buffet restaurant, where you can eat as much as you like and not pay a penny, but if you want a massage or to go to one of the à la carte restaurants, for example, all of that is extra.'

'Could get pricey. What about booze?'

'Extra, but Sam says we get some credit thrown in because of our cabin class, so hopefully we won't have to pay any more if we're careful.'

'Sod that! If I'm going on holiday, the last thing I want is to have my drinks rationed.'

'They aren't rationed, and you could buy a drinks package which gives you a certain amount included every day, but Sam says that's not very good value for money and, as neither of us are heavy drinkers, we're going to see how far our credit will stretch. According to her colleague, you can land up with a bill of thousands if you overdo it.'

'You're really not selling it, Ruby,' Jono tells me.

'That's because we've already established that your idea of a good time is lying by the beach with a funnel in your mouth for them to pour the free booze into.'

'What's wrong with that?'

'Nothing, but this is a different type of holiday, don't you see? Yes, a week on the beach is nice, but this is more about culture. Look at all the places we're going to stop, and we've got the whole day to explore each one. Then, once we're all cultured out, we can relax by the pool or on our private verandas until dinner. The ship sails to the next port while we're asleep, and we wake up ready to explore a new place. I'll admit that I wasn't that impressed when Sam first told me about it, but the idea has definitely grown on me.'

'Hm. That does sound a bit more promising. I still worry you're going to be surrounded by old people though. Did you know, there are people who live on cruise ships because they're actually cheaper than care homes?'

'Scandia Cruises is aimed at the thirty-to-fifty age bracket. I read that somewhere on the website.'

'They say that because it makes them seem young and cool, but you're still two years below the bottom of the target demographic, and I reckon most of the passengers will be at least ten years older than the top.'

'Does it matter?' I ask a little crossly. 'They could all be a hundred and three, and I'm sure Sam and I would still manage to have a good time. You know, rather than picking holes in it, you could just say, "Have a lovely holiday."'

'Sorry.' He does look genuinely contrite and I can feel my irritation melting away.

'Look. I know it's unusual, but Sam can't really do your type of holiday because she'd burn to a crisp in the first five minutes, and lots of people rave about cruises. It'll be an experience, if nothing else.'

'I guess so. What about Fleabag over there, who's going to look after him?'

'If you mean Samson, the handsomest cat in Margate, the answer is my sister, Em. She's also offered to help in the shop if you want so you're not on your own.'

'Absolutely. I love your sister. She's like you only, you know, funnier.'

'Thanks a lot!'

'Relax, I'm winding you up.'

'You haven't done anything else so far today. Be nice to her, though, OK? I'm not sure she's having a great time at the moment.'

'Oh, why?'

'Living with Mum and Dad, long-distance relationship, not sure what she's going to do for a job, all the usual graduate angst.'

'Don't you worry. I'll take good care of her.'

* * *

'What on earth possessed you to book a cruise?' Dad looks concerned. 'I only hope you have better luck than us.' He turns to Mum. 'Do you remember that time we went to Santander, Margot? The whole ship reeked of diesel and chip fat, and I spent the entire night throwing up because it was so rough in the Bay of Biscay.'

'That was a ferry, Dad, and you had an inside cabin. Cruise ships are very different,' I explain. I'm starting to get a bit fed up with this. Can't anyone just be happy for me?

'Hmm. If you say so, love.' Dad's face is still dubious.

'I think it sounds rather nice,' Mum says, studying the itinerary I've printed off to show them. 'I'd love to go to Barcelona and see the Sagrada Família, but your father's always refused to take me.'

'That's because we'd be robbed blind before we even got within sight of it,' Dad counters. 'That whole area is notorious for pickpockets. I'd stay on the ship for that one, Ruby, if I were you. Same for Sicily. Everyone knows that's a Mafia stronghold. I haven't raised you to be fish food.'

'You're being a bit overdramatic, Dad,' I tell him. 'I think you have to have royally pissed off the Mafiosi before they come after you.'

'Yes, but you never know what they might take offence at, do you? You could be in a coffee shop sipping on an espresso and remark innocently that it's a bit weak. Unknown to you, the coffee shop is owned by Don Gangsteroni's grandmother, and before you know it, you're in his cellar having bits of you chopped off.'

Our conversation is interrupted by the arrival of Em.

'What have I missed?' she asks.

'Dad was just telling me how I'm going to be chopped up and fed to the fish if I get off the cruise ship in Sicily.'

Em says nothing, but her eyes light up with mischief.

'What?' I ask her.

'I was just wondering if that would necessarily be a bad thing,' she says with a grin. 'I mean, I'd miss you, but doesn't everything of yours, including your flat, come to me if you die? Plus, I wouldn't have to share my inheritance from Mum and Dad with you, so I'd be quids in.'

'Don't be inappropriate, Emerald,' Mum scolds her. 'You'd be devastated if anything happened to your sister and you know it.'

Em rolls her eyes. 'I was joking, Mum. Who's going to chop you up, Ruby?'

'The Mafia, according to Dad. I'm going to upset them by being rude about the coffee.'

'I'd ignore him,' she confides. 'He's been watching another one of those crime syndicate series on Netflix, and he's convinced it's all real. You know what he's like. This is why we don't let him watch *Snow White*. Can you imagine the trouble we'd have unravelling that? He'd be on to the police to report the Queen for attempted murder.'

'I am here, Emerald,' Dad says crossly. 'And I don't think you'll find that I have any difficulty separating fact from fiction, thank you. And, while I'm thinking about it, don't be so sure there's going to be an inheritance. Your mother and I might spend all our money on cruises, like Ruby.'

'I'm going on *one* cruise!'

'So you say,' Em says. She's evidently realised she's pushed Dad as far as she can so now she's turning her attention to me. 'Maybe cruising is addictive, like gambling. You'll do one, and before you know what's happened, you'll be cruising every year, with a different leathery lothario hanging off your arm each time.'

'Where did the leathery lothario come from?' I ask with a laugh. Unlike Mum and Dad, I can take Em's humour without getting upset.

'Every cruise has them. Predatory older men zoning in on vulnerable single women, flattering them and making them feel special, before disappearing over the horizon with their life savings.'

'Never mind Dad and his Netflix, you've been reading too many gossip magazines,' I tell her. 'And they're going to have slim pickings where I'm concerned. I don't exactly have a huge pot of life savings.'

'Watch out for them all the same,' Mum cautions solemnly. 'I'd hate for you to be a victim of some unscrupulous older man. I think you sometimes forget what an attractive woman you are, Ruby, and they'll be circling like vultures. You and Sam need to stick close together. Are you sharing a cabin?'

'No. We're not teenagers, Mum. Everyone gets their own cabin.'

'Shame. I'd feel better knowing that she was there with you.'

'What exactly do you think is going to happen? The way you're going on, it sounds like we're going to be plunged into some sort of zombie apocalypse, where the men take one look at Sam and me, go into a trance, and we'll be hiding under our beds while they try to break the door down to get to us. I think that's unlikely, don't you?'

'Just be careful, that's all.'

'Have you thought about disease?' Dad pipes up.

'I'm sorry, what?'

'Cruise ships are always on the news for an outbreak of something nasty. Salmonella, or Legionnaires' disease. They were one of the first Covid strongholds, don't you remember?'

'He's got a point, Ruby,' Mum adds. 'Stay away from fresh fruit and salads, and only drink bottled water.'

'We're cruising the Med, not the Nile!' I'm exasperated now. It would be nice if someone, apart from Sam, would show even a modicum of enthusiasm for this holiday. I'm going to prove them all wrong, I decide. We're going to go on this cruise, Sam and I are going to have a fabulous time, and they're all going to be sorry they were so negative.

7

'How would you describe yourself, socially?' Sam asks.

The cruise is just over a week away, and Sam and I are at home. She's staring at her laptop while I'm poring over the guidebooks I've bought for the various destinations we're going to visit and making notes on places I definitely want to see. Samson, typically, is taking no interest and is fast asleep on the sofa next to me.

'What do you mean?'

'If you had to describe yourself, what words would you use?'

'It would depend on the context. Why?'

'I'm wondering whether the reason I attract arseholes is because of the way I've described myself on the apps. I thought it might be helpful to hear the kinds of words you would use, to see if there's anything I could be doing differently.'

Something about this isn't ringing quite true, but I can't work out what. I stare at Sam, but her face is a picture of innocence.

'I thought you'd deleted all the apps,' I say eventually.

'I did, but you know me. Always the optimist, hoping the next guy won't turn out to be a jerk. So, come on. Give me some words.'

'I don't know. How would you describe me?'

'That's not going to help, is it? I want to hear a completely different perspective, not the same perspective on a different person.'

'Why don't I describe you then? After all, it's you on the app.'

She thinks for a minute. 'No, that won't work.'

'Why not?'

'Because it has to be my authentic voice. Come on, help me out here.'

I sigh and put down the book. 'Fine. I'd say I was kind, trustworthy and loyal.'

She stares at me in disbelief. 'That's it?'

'Are you saying I'm not those things?'

'No, you are. It's just...'

'What?'

'Those aren't very good marketing words. Someone reading that isn't going to think, "Cor, I'd love to meet her."'

'I'm not trying to market myself though. You asked me how I'd describe myself and I did.'

'What about "Gorgeous dark-haired beauty with blue eyes you can lose yourself in and a rack to die for"?'

'You're overstating my looks, and it's a bit shallow, isn't it? It doesn't say anything about me as a person.'

'Gets your attention though, doesn't it? If I was a man, I'd read that and immediately want to find out more.'

'If Threesome Pete read that, he'd go straight to sending a dick pic. How did you describe yourself before?'

'Auburn-haired stunner,' she admits with a giggle.

'Hmm. A bit tabloid, if you ask me. Did you include topless photos?'

'Of course not. What kind of person do you think I am?'

'An auburn-haired stunner,' I say, laughing. 'At least tell me you put in your measurements.' I put on a lecherous tone. 'Auburn-haired stunner Sam, 36, 28, 36, is waiting for your call on 0800 DIAL-A-DATE.'

'Stop it,' she says. 'It's not that bad.'

'It really is. Surely if all you describe are your visual assets, you're going to attract the kind of man who's only interested in the superficial. A proper man would be much more interested in you as a person.'

'What would Ryan Gosling do?'

'Oh, he'd read that I was kind, trustworthy and loyal and contact me immediately.'

'What if you looked like the back end of a bus though?'

'Ryan would see beyond mere looks.'

'I don't think he would. Can you imagine? There he is, all glamorous and amazing on the red carpet, with some moose next to him?'

'Thanks a lot!'

'I don't mean you, obviously. You're a gorgeous dark-haired beauty, as I've already said. Ryan would read your profile, but he'd also look at the pictures, and *then* he'd be straight in touch.'

'Sadly, I don't think Ryan Gosling is in need of dating apps. If he were, I might consider signing up.'

'We're in danger of getting off topic. What other words would you use to describe yourself?'

I think for a minute. 'Independent and intelligent.'

She smacks her forehead. 'No wonder you're single. Those aren't attributes any man wants in a partner!'

'Why not? This is the twenty-first century; surely we've moved beyond the days where I'm expected to be completely dependent on some emotional neanderthal who only says five words per day but is miraculously always there to catch me in his strong arms when I faint.'

'Tell that to the guys.'

'OK. Serious question. Are you ready?'

'Yes.'

'Why do you put yourself through it? What's in it for you?'

'Love, obviously.'

'But, not to put too fine a point on it, I'm not seeing love happen for you. What I see is a series of hopeless chancers who promise you the world and spectacularly fail to deliver.'

'You've got to kiss a lot of toads before you find your prince. What's your plan then? Surely you don't intend to stay single forever.'

'I haven't ruled out the possibility.'

'What about children, though? I know you want them.'

'I could adopt.'

'Hard work on your own.'

'Look,' I tell her firmly, a little irritated now. 'We've had this conversation thousands of times. I get that you feel you need a man to complete you, but I really don't. If, and it's a big if, I were to fall in love with someone, they'd need to bring something to my life that I couldn't get any other way. Currently, I can't see what that might be. I'm financially stable, I've got good friends and I'm sorted for sex. If I want cuddles, I've got Samson.'

Hearing his name, Samson opens his eyes, purrs loudly and stretches out his paw, digging his claws into my thigh and making me wince.

'I can see how much you're enjoying that,' Sam says with a smile. 'And I know you think you're some poster girl for the single life, with your "There's nothing a man can give me that a decent vibrator can't" anthem, but that's not sex. It's like waving a chicken nugget around and trying to convince everyone it's a banquet fit for a king.'

'What?'

'It's true. If you look on the side of a packet of chicken nuggets, there's usually something in the ingredients list about "mechanically recovered meat". Do you know what that is?'

'Do I need to? Is it relevant here?'

'As a matter of fact, I think it's a perfect illustration. So, after they've chopped all the good meat off the chicken, they're left with a carcass and all the gristly bits that you wouldn't normally eat. They lob all of that into a big machine, which crushes it and extrudes it and basically spits out this revolting chicken paste – the euphemistically labelled mechanically recovered meat – which then goes into your nugget. That's what you've got, mechanically recovered sex. It looks like sex, it might even feel a bit like sex, but it's not a patch on the real thing.'

'OK, I don't think it is a good illustration but, if we're going to use it, I'd argue that chicken nuggets are still food. They fill you up in the same way that a meal in a Michelin-starred restaurant would, but with a lot less faff and at a fraction of the price. Actually, I like this analogy.'

'But you can't live on chicken nuggets. They're all right as a stop gap, when you just need fuel, but you'd get ill if that was all you ate.'

'I wouldn't get food poisoning though,' I counter, pleased with myself. 'Have you ever met Jono's friend Laurent?'

'Is he the IT guy?'

'That's him. I think Jono was quite interested in him for a while before Robbie came on the scene. Anyway, we were talking about food, because he travels a lot with his work and, being French, I thought he'd be into trying all the local cuisines. Do you know what he said?'

'No.'

'He said that he almost exclusively eats in McDonald's when he's travelling, because he knows it will be consistent and not make him ill. So, you might look down on my chicken nugget sex, as you put it, but at least I'm not going to get sexual food poisoning from some dodgy bloke like Jason or Threesome Pete.'

'Are you seriously equating my sex life to eating dodgy street food?'

'If the cap fits.'

I can see the concentration on her face as she frantically tries to think of a comeback, but in the end she sighs.

'It's a fair cop,' she agrees. 'Jason was definitely not Michelin starred in the sex department.'

'What did you see in him?'

'He's not bad looking, and he could be quite funny.'

'How do you define "not bad looking"?' I ask with a laugh.

'He's got a nice smile, with decent teeth behind it. His personal hygiene was good too.'

'Hey, guys,' I mock-call. 'Meet my friend Sam. If you've got all your own teeth and don't smell like a bin, she's probably interested.'

'Sassy,' she says suddenly.

'What?'

'That's the word I'd use to describe you. Dark haired, beautiful, great rack, sassy as shit.'

'Hmm. I think I prefer "kind and loyal".'

'I'm not sure the way you've just come for me is particularly kind or loyal.'

'I didn't start this,' I tell her firmly. 'I was just defending myself against you and your mechanically recovered whatever.'

'OK, OK. Truce?'

'Truce.'

We both get up and hug fiercely. 'I love you; you know that?' Sam says into my hair.

'I know. I love you too, which is why I want to see you happy.'

'Don't worry about me. I've got irons in the fire.'

I pull back and look at her. 'Of course you have,' I tell her with a smile.

* * *

'I know I was rude about the whole cruise thing,' Em tells me as I'm packing my bag a week later. 'But I'll admit that seeing you put all those sun dresses and hats and things in your case is making me a little jealous. What time is the taxi coming?'

'Six. We've booked a room at the airport hotel, so we're going to have dinner and then crash out for as long as we can before we have to get up for the flight to Rome. Are you sure you're going to be OK here?'

'Oh, I'll be just fine. Ten days without Mum and Dad constantly in my earhole is my idea of paradise right now. And I'll have this handsome fellow to look out for me until Charlie arrives.' She reaches down to where Samson is contentedly curled up on the bed and strokes him, causing him to purr loudly.

'What's Charlie going to do while you're in the shop?' I ask.

'He's got some job applications to work on, plus I've appointed him head chef while he's here, so he'll have to be out and about getting ingredients and stuff for all the fantastic meals he's going to cook me. I'll be too tired, having been slaving away in the bookshop all day.'

'Please don't let him wreck my kitchen,' I implore her. Not long after Em started going out with Charlie, he tried to impress my parents by cooking dinner for them. I'm not entirely sure what went wrong, but I know it involved the smoke alarm going off, an emergency takeaway and Mum's favourite frying pan having to be consigned to the bin.

'He won't,' she assures me. 'He's much better now, honest.'

I reach down to stroke Samson, who stretches luxuriantly and increases his purring to the level of a small road drill.

'I'm relying on you to keep order,' I tell him. 'Any nonsense from Em or Charlie, and I want to know about it, you understand?'

'Hey, Samson's no grass,' Em says with a smile. 'He knows the code. Snitches get stitches, am I right?'

'Just look after the place, promise?'

'It'll be fine, stop stressing. Go and have an amazing time. Everything will be just as you left it when you get back. Assuming the police don't find our stash of drugs and arrest us, of course.'

'Em—'

'I'm joking!'

'Are you all set?' Sam asks, sticking her head around the door. 'The taxi will be here any minute.'

I take a final look around my room, checking if there's anything still there that should be in a case. I also consult the packing list I wrote, making sure that every item is checked off. Finally, I double-check that my passport is safely stashed in my handbag with the other travel documents.

'Yup,' I tell her. 'Ready as I'll ever be.'

As the taxi pulls away, I turn in my seat and look out of the back window to see Em standing on the pavement, holding Samson in one arm and waving with the other. Despite my warnings, I do trust her to take care of the flat, and I hope she and Charlie will be able to enjoy their time together.

Meanwhile, I've got a holiday to look forward to. Sam's right; we've both been working too hard, and this is hopefully going to be just the break we need.

8

'Ruby, wake up! It's time to go.'

I open my eyes groggily to see Sam's face looming over mine. She looks wide awake, but I've never been brilliant at really early mornings, a fact not helped by the large dinner and bottle of wine we shared last night.

'What time is it?' I ask.

'Quarter to four, but we've got to check in two hours before the flight leaves.'

'OK, OK. Give me a moment.' I push myself up into a sitting position and stare blearily around the room, before carefully levering myself out of bed and opening the curtains a crack to look outside.

'Bloody hell, it's still dark,' I complain. 'And it's pouring with rain.'

'Perfect going-on-holiday weather,' Sam enthuses. 'Get on the plane in rainy Britain; get off a few hours later in sunny Rome. You've probably got time for a quick shower if you hurry.'

I glance at her again, taking her in properly this time. She's already fully dressed and her make-up is flawless.

'How long have you been awake?' I ask.

'A while. I never sleep that well in a strange bed, and you were snoring a bit.'

'I do not snore!'

'Fine. You were breathing a little more audibly than usual, then. Better?'

'Not really. How long have I got?'

'Twenty minutes, max. The shower's not very enthusiastic, so probably just do the basics.'

I hurry into the bathroom and peel off the T-shirt and knickers I was sleeping in, before stepping under the shower and turning it on. Sam's description of it being unenthusiastic is spot on. It would probably take all day to get enough water out of it to wash my hair, so I do as instructed and focus on the basics before drying myself with a towel, brushing my teeth and applying the bare minimum of make-up. When I come out, she's not quite pacing as our room isn't big enough for that, but she's definitely fidgeting.

'Five minutes, Ruby,' she almost barks.

'It's fine. I've just got to throw some clothes on and put my overnight stuff in my case.'

When we hurry across to the terminal, I'm expecting to find a busy throng of people queueing to check in, but it's actually fairly quiet. It takes just a few minutes to deposit our bags and we pass pretty much straight through security.

'I could have had another hour in bed,' I mutter as we head towards the café that Sam looked up online to check it would be open at this time of the morning. 'We still would have had plenty of time.'

'Better to be safe than sorry. The ship won't wait for us if we miss our flight.'

'Where is everyone?'

'Early morning during termtime, so not exactly family holiday friendly. I expect most of these people are travelling for work.'

'What kind of job forces you to be in an airport at silly o'clock in the morning? It's inhumane.' As I look around me, I realise she's right. There's a distinct lack of holiday vibe here; the duty-free shops are quiet and most of the other passengers are sitting quietly, engrossed in their laptops and glancing periodically at the departure screens to check whether their flights are boarding.

'It probably works for them,' Sam explains as a server leads us to a booth and gives us menus. 'Get up early, fly to wherever for a day of meetings, home in time to see the kids before they go to bed.'

'Sounds like hell.'

'You're just grumpy because you need coffee. Come on, what do you fancy to eat?'

* * *

By the time we board the plane an hour or so later, I'm feeling a lot happier. The two espressos I drank with my breakfast of eggs royale have definitely kicked in, because I'm feeling wide awake at last and actually looking forward to the holiday again. According to Sam, we will hand over our luggage to the cruise line as soon as we've cleared security at the other end, and it will magically be waiting for us in our cabins when we board the ship this afternoon. In the meantime, we'll have around four hours to explore Rome before we have to get back to the meeting point so the bus can take us to the port.

'Did you buy Sistine Chapel tickets?' Sam asks once we're above the clouds and the fasten seat belt sign has been switched off. Although I don't mind flying generally, I'm not great at the take-offs and landings, and turbulence makes me very uneasy. Our climb through the rainclouds was very bumpy, so Sam wisely left me to my thoughts until things smoothed out.

'No,' I reply. 'On reflection, I decided it would be too tight time-wise. If the flight had been delayed, or the queues were longer than normal, we would have missed it. I'll get some for the day we leave.'

'Probably a good plan. So what's on the list then?'

'All the greats. The Colosseum, the Trevi Fountain, the Forum and the Pantheon.'

'Wow. Are we going to have time to fit all of that in?'

'Yup. I've booked us on one of those hop-on, hop-off bus tours. If we get there on time, we'll be able to get off and explore a bit, but even if the flight had been delayed, we'd have been able to see everything. I thought it was the safest option.'

She smiles. 'Have you ever considered a career in the travel industry? You've got a nose for organisation.'

'I'm quite happy with my bookshop, thanks.'

'One more question. Have you got itineraries as detailed as this for every place we're stopping?'

Now it's my turn to smile. 'What do you think?'

'You know the cruise line organises tours, don't you? We could just sign up for those once we're on board.'

'Yes, and if they're better than mine, that's what we'll do. But I've been doing a bit of thinking about what Jono and my family said. What if we are the youngest people by a country mile? I don't want to miss out on seeing things because we've got to go at a geriatric pace. You know what it's like in a large group – you can only go as fast as the slowest person.'

She thinks for a moment. 'Fair point. I did put you in charge of this because I knew you'd be the best at it, so I'll leave it to you.'

I settle back into my seat. What Sam doesn't know is that, somewhere beneath us in the hold, my suitcase contains a notebook with pages dedicated to every port. I've listed the attractions, the various options for getting to them, along with prices where they were available. I've also photographed each page with my phone, so I have a backup if my suitcase goes astray. I've even written down the names of cafés and restaurants that are off the beaten track but were recommended by the guidebooks, so we can hopefully leave the other tourists behind and have a more authentic experience. I've loved every minute of my research, and I'm confident that the reality will be even better. I close my eyes and, despite the strong coffee still sloshing around inside me, I'm soon fast asleep.

* * *

'Bloody hell, it's massive!' I exclaim as the bus pulls into the port at Civitavecchia that afternoon and we get our first glimpse of the ship.

'Said no one to Jason, ever,' Sam quips beside me, causing us both to giggle and earning us a sharp look from the couple on the other side of the aisle. Although the other passengers on our bus could hardly be described as geriatric, we must be the only people on here under the age of fifty.

I've seen plenty of pictures of cruise ships online and on TV, but this is the first time I've ever been up close to one, and it's genuinely huge. The hull is painted dark blue, with *Spirit of Malmö* in large white letters at the front.

Above that is a row of bright orange lifeboats, topped by countless storeys of balconies, like a massive hotel. At the very top of the ship, a large purple funnel with the Scandia Cruises logo on it is smoking gently.

'Actually, this isn't that big, by cruise ship standards,' Sam informs me. 'Some of the really big ones take over six thousand passengers, whereas this one only takes three.'

'That's still a hell of a lot. Are there enough lifeboats, do you think? It doesn't look like you'd get three thousand people in those.'

'I'm sure there are. Relax.'

'Sorry, I'm just a bit overwhelmed by it, I guess.'

The bus pulls up with a hiss of brakes outside the terminal building and we grab our hand baggage and climb down. When we get inside, we're confronted with several long queues, and it takes us a moment to find the Commodore Class one. As we inch forwards, I take the opportunity to scan the other passengers, and it's fair to say we are a diverse bunch. Although most of them are of a similar age to the people we were on the bus with, I'm relieved to see some faces closer to our age group, as well as a few families with children. There are even a couple of teenagers, scrolling boredly on their phones as they nudge their hand luggage forwards with their toes.

'Good afternoon, and welcome to Scandia Cruises,' the check-in assistant says warmly when we eventually reach the front of the queue. 'Can I see your passports and boarding passes, please?'

We hand them over and she taps rapidly on her computer keyboard.

'Ms Johnson, you're in cabin 7.064,' she tells me as she hands me a wristband. 'And you're right next door in 7.062, Ms Thorncroft. Once you get on board, a steward will direct you, so all you need to know now is that you're on deck seven. Your cabin number is on your wristband, which you just need to hold against the pad on your door to unlock it. You'll also use your wristband to pay for any onboard purchases. We've loaded on your initial credit, but we'd advise you to register a credit card with us to pre-authorise any purchases beyond that. Would you like to do that now?'

'Yes, thank you,' Sam tells her as we hand over our credit cards.

'That's all done for you,' she tells us happily once we've entered our PIN numbers. 'The ship's currency is the US dollar, so that's what you'll see on your bill. I notice you're also in the Friends of Marco Polo group, so you'll

want to head over to the Marco Polo desk once you've cleared security to pick up your information packs. Have a great cruise and we're delighted to have you on board with us.'

'What's the Friends of Marco Polo group?' I ask Sam as we join the queue for the airport-style security scanners.

'Nothing. It's just a way of keeping the single supplements down for the cabins, that's all,' she replies hastily, but I notice a shiftiness in her look that makes me suspect she's not telling the complete truth. 'Different groups go by different names on a cruise ship. It's nothing to worry about.'

I'd like to press her, as I'm sure there's something she's not telling me, but we're quickly embroiled in the business of clearing security. Although Sam and I make it through without any issues, we're distracted by a bit of a fracas in one of the other queues. One of the security guards is holding aloft what appears to be a set of metal teeth, and the man in front of him is puce in the face.

'I told you,' the man exclaims loudly. 'I wear them at night when I'm sleeping. *Dormire, comprende?* They stop me snoring. I'm not going to bite anyone with them.'

The security guard seems unimpressed, beckoning over a stout woman, who I'm guessing is his superior. After a bit of a debate in Italian, she shrugs her shoulders and the security guard hands the irate passenger back his teeth.

'I hope he's not on our deck,' Sam remarks quietly. 'I don't think I'd sleep well at night knowing Jaws was on our corridor.'

'Sorry?'

'You know, the baddie from that old Bond film. He had metal teeth and could bite through almost anything. Ah, there's the desk we need.'

We make our way over to a large counter with *Marco Polo* emblazoned across its front. Behind the counter is an enthusiastic-looking man who's definitely gone a bit mad with the spray tan.

'Sticking with the film connections, we had Jaws and now a real live Oompa-Loompa,' I murmur to Sam. 'I don't think I've ever seen anyone so orange.'

'Welcome, welcome,' he cries as we approach the desk. 'Are you part of our happy Marco Polo gang?'

'That's right,' Sam tells him. 'I'm Sam Thorncroft and this is my friend, Ruby Johnson.'

'Delighted to meet you both. My name's Barry and I'll be your group coordinator for the time we're together on board. We've got a really fun group this time. You're going to have a blast, and who knows what might happen, eh? Let me just find your packs.'

'Umm, Sam?' I ask nervously as he rifles through a box of envelopes. 'What exactly have you signed us up for?'

She doesn't get a chance to reply as Barry slaps two envelopes down on the counter with a flourish.

'Here you go,' he says, sounding like he's going to explode with delight as he opens Sam's envelope and slides out the contents. 'So, the details of everyone in the group are in this booklet. There are pictures and traffic lights so you can do a bit of research before you meet everyone. This is your traffic light badge, which you should wear at all our events. Oh, you're a green, how brilliant. If you need to change colour at any point, just come and see me and I'll sort you a new badge, OK? Now, our first event is this evening just after we depart. The other passengers will be going to the sail away party, which happens on the pool deck every time we leave a port, but we've taken over the Nautilus lounge for our Singles Mingle event, where you can meet all the other singles for the first time and start getting to know each other.'

I stare dumbfounded at Sam as the penny drops. She's signed us up to a singles cruise. I am going to kill her.

9

'I can explain,' Sam says earnestly as we join our final queue to board the ship.

'Save it. I'm so angry with you right now that I don't trust myself not to say something we'll both regret. A singles cruise? What the actual fuck, Sam?'

'Look. I meant what I said about the single supplement. On popular cruises, the supplement can be as much as it would cost to bring another person with you. By signing up for the Marco Polo group, the supplement dropped to 30 per cent.'

'I don't care about the bloody money,' I snarl. 'I care that you've dragged me onto this holiday under false pretences. If we weren't in sodding Italy, I'd be walking straight off and going home.'

'Why?' She seems genuinely surprised.

'Because I don't want to go on a fucking singles cruise, Sam! I have no idea what a Singles Mingle event is, but I know I really don't want to do it. Why didn't you tell me?'

She does have the decency to look a little shamefaced now. 'Because I knew how you'd react. Nobody's going to force you to come to the singles things if you don't want to. I'm sure you can go to the sail away party if you prefer.'

'What are you going to do?'

She smiles. 'What do you think?'

'Great. So my choices are either go to the sail away party on my own, like some sad loner, or come with you to Barry's mingling thing and be goggled at like a piece of meat.'

'You don't have to do either. You could stay in your cabin and enjoy the view.'

'That's even sadder.'

Our tense discussion is interrupted as we finally cross the threshold and board the ship.

'Oh, wow!' I breathe as I take in the view. We're in a room that's not unlike a hotel lobby in some ways, except it's on a truly massive scale. It looks like it spans the entire width of the ship; there are tables and chairs dotted about and, in front of us, the concierge desks are already busy. There's a huge staircase at one end, dominated by an abstract artwork that stretches towards the ceiling, three storeys up. Around the edge of the lobby are balconies, with open staircases running up and down between the levels. People are already strolling up them, looking completely at home, as if they've been here for months rather than a couple of hours. The centrepiece of the room is a massive crystal chandelier that hangs like a kind of inverted Christmas tree, with the top just above our heads. It sparkles as the crystals reflect the other light sources in the room, giving a kind of classy disco ball effect. I find myself wondering briefly how often they have to clean it before I'm distracted by a voice.

'Welcome on board,' a uniformed bellhop says to us. 'Can I help you find your cabin?'

'Yes, please,' Sam replies. 'We're on deck seven, that's all we know.'

'Can I see your bracelet?' the bellhop asks, and Sam turns her wrist so he can read it.

'OK,' he says. 'Can you see the panel behind the concierge desks? The nearest lifts are behind that. Just choose level seven. Once you get there, you'll find yourself in a lobby with a corridor on either side. Even-numbered cabins are on the port side of the ship, and odd numbers on the starboard. The numbering runs from the bow to the stern, but there are signs to direct you and I can tell you that yours is about halfway along on the port side.' He turns to me. 'Would you like to show me your bracelet so I can direct you?'

'Umm, no. I'm fine, thanks. I'm next to her, so if we can find her cabin we'll have found mine.'

'Very good. Enjoy your stay, and please don't hesitate to let a member of the crew know if there's anything you need.' He turns to deal with the next guest and Sam and I set off towards the concierge desks.

'I hate to admit it,' I tell her, our fight temporarily forgotten, 'but I didn't understand most of what he said. I know the bow is the front and the stern is the back, but I've never worked out which is port and which is starboard.'

'This I do know,' she says. 'Port is the left-hand side of the ship, marked by a red light on the side of the bridge, and starboard is the right, marked by a green light. I even know where the terms come from.'

'How?'

'My dad went through a sailing thing a few years ago. So, it comes from pre-history, when people steered boats with a board sticking out of the side. The steer board, as it was imaginatively called, was always on the right, which gives you starboard. The next problem is that you obviously couldn't pull alongside a jetty on the right because the steer board would get in the way, so you always put the left-hand side of the boat against the jetty, so that's the port side. See?'

'You've made that up.'

'Nope. Absolutely true. In fact, I might use it as a conversation starter at the Singles Mingle later. Are you quite sure you don't want to come?'

'Perfectly, thank you. And our conversation about the trick you pulled to get me on here isn't over,' I tell her frostily. I may have been momentarily distracted by the lobby and her knowledge of sailing jargon, but now she's mentioned the Marco Polo thing again, I can feel my anger resurfacing.

'OK, fine,' she says as we press the button to summon the lift. 'I'm sorry I wasn't honest with you about the singles thing, but I did it for the right reasons.'

'When is there ever a "right reason" to trick someone into a singles holiday against their will?' I ask incredulously. 'You know, I was stupidly looking forward to all the things we were going to see and do together.'

'And we're still going to do those things,' she assures me.

'We aren't, because you'll go along to the Singles Mingle thing, your head will be turned by the first reasonable-looking bloke in there, and I won't see you for the rest of the cruise.'

'That's unfair!'

'Is it? Admit it, the reason you chose this cruise is nothing to do with the supplement. This is all just a blatant attempt to meet more single men in your eternal quest for happiness. If it had been about the money, you'd have told me up front.'

'I'm not going to abandon you, I promise.'

'Hmm. We'll see.'

There are a number of other passengers in the lift, so we do the British thing and lapse into silence until we reach deck seven. When we get out, we're momentarily disorientated. There are two corridors, as the bellhop explained, but no way of telling which side of the ship is which.

'This one has the even numbers,' Sam says, pointing at a sign. I follow her down what feels like the longest corridor in the world as she calls out the cabin numbers.

'Here we are,' she says at last, holding out her bracelet to a door pad and receiving a beep and click in return. 'That one must be you. Shall we meet up in an hour or so, once we've unpacked?'

I follow her lead and push open the door of my cabin once the green light informs me it's unlocked. Thankfully, unlike the holiday, this is exactly what I was expecting. Although the carpet is the same dark blue as the hull, the ambience is lifted by the pale wood used for the wardrobes, bed surround and other furniture. It's not exactly large, but it feels bigger than the hotel room Sam and I shared last night. To my relief, my cases are stacked neatly by the bed. I'll unpack in a minute, but there's something I have to do first. It takes me a moment to figure out the lock, but then I slide open the door and step out onto the balcony. The bus, terminal building and ship are all air-conditioned, so the contrast in temperature is the first thing I notice. There's a refreshing breeze, but it's still warm out here as I close my eyes and tilt my face towards the sun, gripping the balcony rail and leaning out over the side.

'Never mind Sam and all her Marco Polo nonsense, this will do very nicely,' I sigh happily as I open my eyes and watch a gull fly past, its piercing cry ringing out across the port. Below me, the terminal building looks small, and

I can see the last buses dropping passengers off outside. I breathe deeply, trying to shake off the vestiges of our quarrel. I am annoyed with her, but she's got a point. I'm still going to see everything I wanted to, even if Sam gets embroiled with someone, as she undoubtedly will. It's just not the holiday I thought I was signing up for, and I'm definitely pissed off that she wasn't up front with me. Yes, I probably would have refused to come, but at least it would have been an informed choice. With a sigh, I turn and head back inside to start unpacking.

I quickly discover that, although my cabin is fairly small, there are lots of clever little storage spaces, including the narrowest full-length wardrobe I've ever come across. The bathroom is similarly compact, but again there are cubbies for me to store my make-up bag and other toiletries. Out of curiosity, I try the shower, and I'm relieved to note that the water pressure is considerably better than the dribble I endured at the airport hotel. London already feels like a world away as I grab the folder beside the bed with 'Scandia Cruises *Spirit of Malmö*, Essential Information' written on the front and settle in the armchair by the window. I'd like to test out the bed, but I know I'll fall asleep instantly if I try that, so I'm steering well clear of it for now.

The first page of the folder is full of safety information, the most important piece of which appears to be the requirement to watch the emergency procedures film on my TV, if the large bold type is anything to go by. Grabbing the remote control, I turn on the TV to find the film loaded and ready to go. I watch as it explains what to do in the different types of emergencies, how to put on my lifejacket and find the correct muster station, as well as the different alarms including the one to abandon ship. Not exactly encouraging viewing, especially as I have to tick a box on screen at the end to confirm I've watched and understood it. Thankfully, the rest of the folder is full of information about how to book the various onboard restaurants, spas and hair and beauty salons, along with the numbers to dial from my bedside phone. Having read that from end to end, I turn my attention to the envelope that Orange Barry pressed into my hand at the Marco Polo desk. I slit it open and slide out the contents, which are identical to Sam's apart from my badge, which is orange.

I remember Barry saying something about the traffic light system but, although I went to some traffic light parties at uni, I'm not sure how it's going to work in this context, so I open the booklet to see if it explains and, sure enough, the information I'm looking for is at the very beginning.

Traffic light system

In order to prevent confusion, we ask the Friends of Marco Polo to wear their badges at all our events and adhere to the traffic light system as follows:

Green – Go. People with green badges are looking for a match, so don't be shy. Go and say hello! Remember, however, to be respectful. Inappropriate comments or remarks may cause offence and, if serious, may result in you being expelled from the group.

Amber – Pause. Some of our group are unsure at this stage and want to sit on the sidelines for a while to see how things unfold. Don't avoid them, just be aware that they're not necessarily looking for a match right now.

Red – Stop. If you see someone with a red badge, that means they're not available. By all means be friendly and polite, but respect their boundaries.

Note: Guests are free to change their traffic light colours at any point. Just ask your helpful Marco Polo group leader for a new badge.

That's job number one then. Find Barry and swap my orange badge for a red one. If I do that, this might actually be bearable. I turn the page and find myself staring at the profile of a man with dark hair and dark brown eyes behind glasses. The page title tells me that this is Robin Andrews. As well as the picture, there's a short bio. A niggle of doubt starts to form in my mind again as I flip to the end to find Sam Thorncroft and read her bio, which is much as she described it a week ago. My heart is in my mouth as I continue to turn the pages. Sure enough, I come across an entry for Ruby Johnson. The picture is one Sam took of me when we had dinner at The Mermaid, but my eyes fall instantly to the text.

Raven-haired Ruby would describe herself as kind, trustworthy and loyal, but there's a whole lot more to this curvy beauty from the seaside town of

Margate in Kent. As you'd expect from a bookshop owner, she's good with words. A sharp, sassy chick who will swiftly cut you down to size if you don't measure up, Ruby is no fool when it comes to matters of the heart. You'll need to be someone truly special to steal the heart of this fiercely independent woman. Take the time to get to know her, however, and you'll have made a friend, or even more, for life.

Suddenly, Sam's questions a week ago about how I'd describe myself make complete sense. Killing her would be too easy. I'm going to chop her up and turn her into shark bait.

10

'Are you ready to explore our new home?' Sam practically sings as I open the door to her a little while later.

'You might not live that long,' I growl, shoving the open booklet with my bio at her. 'What the bloody hell is this?'

To my amazement, she's totally unrepentant as she takes the booklet and studies the bio. 'I'm rather pleased with that, actually.'

'*Pleased?* Apart from the fact that it's without a doubt the most cringeworthy description of me I've ever seen, it has no business whatsoever being there. *Fiercely independent? Raven-haired curvy beauty?* You make me sound like a cross between an ogre and a stripper!'

'It was a condition of being in the group, so I had to do it. Did you like the way I took your words and spiced them up? It's basically everything you told me only, you know, better.'

'I don't think I've ever felt so objectified.'

'Why? I might have mentioned your physical attributes, but most of it was about your personality.'

I take the booklet back. 'Yeah, about that. *A sharp, sassy chick who will swiftly cut you down to size?* Still making me sound like a monster.'

'You are sassy though, and you don't take any nonsense. I played up that it was worth spending time to get to know you; didn't you like that bit at least?'

I soften a little. 'Yeah, I guess that bit wasn't too bad.'

'Anyway,' she tells me, sensing a chink in my armour, 'it doesn't matter, because I put you down for an amber badge, so people know you're not immediately in the market.'

'Let's be very clear on one thing, Sam,' I tell her firmly. 'I'm not in the market *at all*. In fact, as soon as I see Orange Barry, I'm going to swap my badge for a red one.'

'He'll be at the Singles Mingle. You can swap it then.'

'Nice try, but wild horses wouldn't drag me to that. I've decided to go to the sail away party instead.'

'Really? I was hoping you'd be my wing woman and general jerk filter.'

'Uh-uh. You don't deserve a wing woman. You've brought this completely on yourself.'

I can sense her trying to decide whether to push me any further, before she wisely decides that it's probably a bad idea.

'Shall we explore then?' she says. 'We've got an hour before departure.'

Despite my irritation with her, I'm still excited about the holiday, so I plaster on a smile. 'Why not?' I reply.

* * *

It's fair to say that, even with the maps provided and all the signs, Sam and I struggled to find our way around to begin with. However, after a few wrong turns and dead ends, we started to get the hang of it and, by the time we made it back to our cabins, we were getting fairly confident. The high point of the tour, for me, was our visit to the concierge desks. Although they were still busy, an idea had struck me as we'd arrived in the grand lobby, and I'd dragged Sam over with me.

'What are you doing?' she'd asked.

'I'm going to find out which is the most expensive restaurant on this ship, and then you're going to book a table and buy me dinner as an apology for setting me up like this.'

She'd smiled. 'Actually, that seems perfectly reasonable. Lead on.'

In the end, the most expensive restaurant was not only ludicrously beyond our budget, but we'd both agreed, from studying the menu, that it wasn't our kind of thing anyway. Instead, Sam had booked us into the Italian one, which we both liked the look of very much. We've also booked onto a tour of Pompeii tomorrow, as it seemed easier than organising it ourselves. Finally, we picked up a booklet with the details of all the other shore excursions so we can compare them to my own plans and decide which is better. I'm still convinced that Sam is going to drop me like a hot brick as soon as she spots someone that takes her fancy, but she's adamant that we'll do all the port excursions together. We're now leaning over my balcony, watching the flurry of activity below as the ship gets ready to depart. When the last ropes are released, the ship gently starts to ease away from the quay and we enthusiastically join in with the cheering we can hear coming from the other balconies. As it noses out into the channel leading to the open sea, there's a deafening blast from the horn, which makes both of us jump.

'Right,' Sam says as Civitavecchia recedes slowly from sight. 'I've got a party to get to. Are you sure you'll be OK on your own until dinner?'

I'm too excited to be cross with her any more. 'I'll be fine,' I tell her with a smile. 'Go and have fun. What time do you want to meet?'

'Eight o'clock at the main dining room?' she suggests.

'I'll be there.'

'Thank you, Ruby.' Her tone is suddenly serious.

'For what?'

'For not totally losing your shit with me.'

I grin. 'There are ten days of this cruise. Plenty of time.'

'Nah,' she replies. 'The worst is over. It's going to be a blast from here.'

'Actually, that reminds me. I have a question before you go.'

'Of course. What's up?'

'Do I know everything now?'

'Absolutely. No more surprises. Or if there are, they'll only be nice ones.'

Having studied the Scandia Cruises dress code, which requests gentlemen wear smart casual clothing after 6 p.m. but doesn't actually tell you what that means for women, I've changed into one of my dresses so, having given Sam a quick hug, I head towards the pool deck where the sail away party is being held. Although the sun has dropped, it's still warm up here and there's a convivial atmosphere. A band is playing and people are standing around, chatting and drinking. The bar is well staffed so, even though there's a bit of a queue, it doesn't take me long to get a drink and I wander over to the railing with it. The ship is starting to pick up speed now, and the seagulls are diving into the foaming wake, evidently hoping the disturbance of the water will bring some fishy treats to the surface.

It's truly idyllic up here, but I'm very conscious of being alone. Everyone else is either in couples or groups of some kind. A burst of laughter from my left catches my ear and I turn to see where it came from. A man who appears to be in his late sixties is regaling his companions with a story. His face is flushed and they're all listening attentively, laughing uproariously when he evidently reaches the punchline. My focus shifts to a couple behind them; she's wearing an elegant, full-length dark blue dress and he's in pale chinos with a dark blue shirt open at the neck. They're holding champagne glasses and chatting quietly. As I watch, he slips his arm around her lower back and bends to kiss her. It's a lingering kiss, not showy or vulgar, but enough to signal to anyone watching that they are a couple very much in love. As they break apart, she smiles widely and chinks her glass against his. I find myself studying their hands, trying to work out if they're newlyweds or maybe recently engaged. He's definitely not wearing a ring, and her left hand is obscured by her body so, after a while, I give up and return my gaze to the sea.

'È una bella vista, vero?' a voice says next to me. I turn to see a man who I'd guess is in his late forties. His tanned face sits beneath dark shiny hair that's slicked back and, despite the fading light, his eyes are invisible behind his dark glasses. He must have bathed in his floral aftershave, because the scent is almost overpowering.

'I'm sorry, were you talking to me?' I ask.

'Oh, you are English,' he replies, switching languages. 'My apologies, you looked Italian. I couldn't help noticing that you seemed to be alone, and I asked myself, "Guido, why is such a beautiful woman on her own?" I was curious, so I had to come and find out. Tell me, what is your name?'

'Ruby, and I'm not alone,' I stammer quickly. 'I'm, aah, with a group.'

'A group?' He seems amused. 'Where is this group? I have been watching you since you arrived and I did not see any group.'

'They're in a room downstairs, having a party,' I explain while desperately trying to give off 'please leave me alone' vibes. I know I was feeling a bit isolated before, but I'd prefer that to being chatted up by Guido.

'It must be a very boring party if you would rather be up here on your own,' he observes, moving his hand along the rail so it's resting against mine.

'It's not a boring party, actually,' I tell him firmly, moving my hand away. 'I just came up here because I wanted a breath of fresh air. I'm going back to join them in a minute.'

'Ah, the movement of the boat, it is making you ill, yes? You will get used to it. You just need something to, how do you say, make you think of something else.'

'A distraction,' I say automatically, unable to resist offering the correct word.

'A distraction,' he repeats. 'Exactly. Guido will help to *distract* you, yes?' He smiles to reveal teeth so white and even that they must be veneers. Once again, he moves his hand along the rail, this time covering mine completely and leaving me in little doubt about what kind of distraction he has in mind. I think not.

'I'm not seasick, and I don't need distracting, thank you,' I tell him in my frostiest voice as I yank my hand out from underneath his. 'In fact, I think I'm going to go and rejoin my friends now. Goodnight, Guido.'

If he's picked up on my tone, he chooses to ignore it as he seizes my hand again, this time lifting it to his lips and kissing it before letting it drop.

'*Buonanotte, bellissima,*' he murmurs. 'I look forward to seeing you again very soon, Ruby.'

As I hurry away, my first priority is to find somewhere to wash my hands. Some of Guido's aftershave must have transferred onto them as I can still smell him as I go indoors. The barely perceptible movement of the boat might not be a problem, but his scent is definitely making me feel queasy. Having scrubbed my hands furiously in the nearest ladies', I'm now presented with a dilemma. There's still three quarters of an hour before I'm due to meet Sam for dinner and, although this ship has no shortage of other bars, my experience with Guido has made me wary. I pull out the map from my handbag and locate the Nautilus lounge. I know I said wild horses wouldn't drag me to the Singles Mingle, but at least Sam will be there.

'It's our missing traveller!' Orange Barry cries in delight when I arrive. 'Although you haven't got your badge with you, tut tut.'

'I forgot it, sorry. Actually, I wanted to talk to you about that. Can I swap it for a red one, please?'

His eyes widen. 'Really? You've found someone already? Who is it?'

'No, I haven't found anyone. I'm just not in the market.'

He tilts his head quizzically. 'But you signed up for the Friends of Marco Polo.'

'Technically, I didn't,' I explain. 'My friend Sam signed me up without my knowledge.'

'But you're single, yes?'

'Yes.'

'Phew. That really would have been an awkward conversation. We take a dim view of infiltrators.' He smiles conspiratorially as he says it, but I can't help thinking he's actually being serious.

'So what would have happened if I'd actually been in a relationship?' I ask, my curiosity getting the better of me.

'That would make you ineligible for our group, and you'd be charged the full single occupancy of a double cabin supplement,' he says, this time leaving me in no doubt that he means it.

'Just as well I'm single then, isn't it. But I'm really not looking for a relationship, Barry, so can I just have a red badge please?'

He changes to a sorrowful expression that doesn't quite reach his eyes. 'Sorry, sweetie,' he says. 'My group, my rules. You only get a red badge if you've coupled up exclusively with someone else in the group. Here's an amber one. Try to remember to bring it in future. I have got lots, but it's not an inexhaustible supply. Now, go and meet people. I've reserved some tables in the main restaurant for us all, so you've got plenty of time to get to know someone.'

I may have already had a glass of wine at the sail away party, but something tells me this is going to be a long evening, so I make my way over to the bar to get a drink. On the way, I spot Sam deep in conversation with a man, although his attention seems to be focused more on her chest than her face, from what I can see. No sooner have I secured a glass of wine than I'm approached by another member of the group, who I notice is wearing a green badge.

'Hi, I'm Brad,' he says in a broad American accent, holding out his hand. 'Don't worry, I'm not coming on to you. What's your name?'

'Ruby,' I say politely.

'And whereabouts are you from, Ruby?'

'The UK. Kent.'

'I know Kent. I'm from California, but I live in London at the moment. I'm an expert in distribution centres, so my work takes me all over. Before London, I was in Australia for six months. Have you ever been?'

'No, sorry.'

Brad doesn't appear daunted by my lack of travel experience, and I gently tune him out as he begins to tell me about all the places he's visited. After a while, I notice Sam detaching herself from the chest-staring guy and start scanning the room. When she notices me, she beams and comes straight over.

'Ruby!' she exclaims, cutting Brad off mid-flow. 'I wasn't expecting to see you until dinner, but I'm so glad you're here.' She takes my arm and turns to Brad. 'I hope you'll excuse us for a moment, Brad.'

If Brad is disappointed, he's doing a good job of hiding it. 'Of course. I'll see you around, Ruby.'

I can safely say that I've never been more delighted to see Sam, and I happily link my arm with hers as we stroll over to an unoccupied table in the corner of the room.

11

'What made you change your mind?' Sam asks. 'I thought you said wild horses wouldn't drag you here.'

'Yeah, but then I met Guido.' I tell her about feeling a bit out of place at the sail away party, and Guido's come-on. She's reassuringly horrified.

'He sounds like a total loser,' she asserts when I've finished telling the story.

'Yeah, I was a bit creeped out, so I decided to come and hang out here for safety. How have you been getting on?'

She lowers her voice. 'What did you make of Brad?'

'Not much. He seems very pleased with himself.'

'Ugh.' She wrinkles her nose. 'I must have been talking to him for nearly quarter of an hour. Actually, scrap that. *He* was talking to *me* for quarter of an hour. How many questions do you think he asked me, besides my name?'

I smile. 'Brad seems like the kind of guy who could happily monologue about himself for hours, so I'm going to guess none.'

'Yup. God, he was dull. Anyway, then I moved on to Chris.'

'Was he the one you were talking to just now?'

'Yes. He did have the decency to ask a couple of questions, at least.'

'He seemed very taken with your chest, from what I was able to see. Every time he thought you weren't looking, he was staring at your cleavage.'

'Yeah, I spotted that. I wanted to grab his chin, lift it up and say, "Oi, mate. My eyes are up here, on my face." He's not the first person to do it though, so I'm not going to hold it against him.'

'He might like that.'

'What?'

'You "holding" it against him.'

'Eeuw. Anyway, slim pickings so far, but there are plenty of other fish in this pond, so I'm still optimistic.' She glances at my chest. 'I thought you were going to get Barry to give you a red badge?'

I sigh. 'I tried. Turns out red badges are only for people who've coupled up with someone else in the group.'

'Really? It didn't mention that in the handbook.'

'Barry's rules, apparently.'

'Hmm. Well, I'm glad you came. Shall we go and get something to eat?'

Before we have a chance to make our escape, Barry claps his hands to try to get everyone's attention. It takes a few goes before everyone is silent and he can make his announcement.

'Right, lovely singles,' he yells. 'Hopefully you've started to get to know each other a little, because we're going to up the ante tomorrow. When you're back from your shore excursions, we're all going to assemble in here for a game of Blind Date.'

'Uh-oh,' I murmur to Sam.

'It will take the same format as the famous TV show, hosted by the peerless Dame Cilla Black,' Barry continues. 'How many of you know it?'

Only a couple of hands go up.

'Dear Lord, talk about a blast from the past. Do you remember it?' Sam says to me.

'Yes. My parents were avid watchers back in the day.'

'The format is simple,' Barry explains. 'I will be choosing one woman and one man at random from those of you with green badges. You will need to bring along three searching questions to ask your potential matches. I'll also be picking three ladies and three gentlemen to be the potential blind dates. You'll be behind a screen so you can't be seen, and you'll need to answer the questions in as romantic a fashion as you can. At the end, the person asking the questions will get to choose one of you to go on a blind date. I've organised for the two lucky couples to do a *Godfather* movie tour from Messina. You'll be collected from the port and taken to Savoca to see the filming location for the wedding, as well as a number of other iconic locations used in the movie. I've even thrown in a sumptuous lunch, so it's a prize worth winning. Before I let you go, do any of you amber badges want to change colour so you've got a chance of being included?'

Sam grabs my hand and tries feverishly to shove it in the air, but I'm too strong for her, thankfully. A couple of hands do go up though, and Barry delightedly hands over green badges.

'OK, lovely people,' he chants. 'Enjoy your dinner, have a fabulous time in Naples tomorrow, and I'll see you back here for our fun and games at 6 p.m. sharp. Contestants, I'll let you know if I've selected you by leaving a note in the holder outside your cabin before ten tonight. Good luck, everyone!'

'Do you think Barry is like a clown?' Sam asks me as we start to make our way towards the main dining room. We deliberately held back until Brad had left so we could keep an eye on him and make sure we didn't end up sitting with him.

'How do you mean?'

'He's so relentlessly cheerful, like he's on happy pills or something. Do you think he's secretly crying inside?'

'Maybe he just loves his job. I wonder how many couples actually come out of these things?'

'There must be some. I mean, how many of us are there? Thirty?'

'I'd say nearer fifty.'

'Statistically, I'd think you'd get at least one couple out of that lot, wouldn't you?'

* * *

By the time I woke this morning, the ship was already docked, but I'd felt beautifully refreshed after one of the best nights' sleep I think I've had in ages. Sadly, the same couldn't be said for Sam, who'd sounded distinctly groggy when I'd called her to check she was awake. Thankfully, after a shower and breakfast from the buffet, washed down with copious amounts of coffee, plus the discovery of a note from Barry informing her she'd been picked for Blind Date, she'd perked up and we'd been just in time to join the Pompeii tour. My heart had sunk a little when I'd spotted Brad on the bus, but thankfully he'd already collared some other poor victim and I'd smiled as I passed his seat and overheard him telling her that he'd lived in Rome for a year and was pretty much fluent in Italian. I don't know whether she's a part of our group or not, but she already looked desperate to escape him.

'So, my questions,' Sam says to me as we stand in the Forum gazing towards the temple of Jupiter. 'According to the information from Barry, each one has to tell them something about my life, and then I have to ask them how they feel about it. For example, "I'm very close to my parents. What would you do to impress my mum and dad if I took you home to meet them?"'

I giggle as a memory comes to me. 'Probably not be groping you when they walked into the sitting room.'

She claps her hand to her mouth. 'I'd forgotten about that. That was Micky in sixth form. I don't know who was the most embarrassed out of the four of us.'

'I wish I'd been there.'

'It was mortifying, especially the way he stood up and said, "Nice to meet you, Mr and Mrs Thorncroft," with his erection clearly visible through his trousers. Dad just looked at his outstretched hand and said, "Son, if that's been where I suspect it's been, I have no intention of shaking it." He never came near my house again and we broke up shortly after that.'

'Did your parents ever say anything?'

'Nope. What could they have said? "That boy we found with his hand in your knickers seemed absolutely charming, when are you going to invite him round properly?" I think we all just wanted to pretend it had never happened. Anyway, we're getting off topic. What questions am I going to ask?'

We ponder the matter in silence as we pass the temple and head for the Forum baths.

'It must have been an amazing place,' Sam murmurs. 'I just can't get my head around the fact that all these people woke up, expecting a normal day, and then boom. All over. It makes you realise how precious life is, don't you think?'

'Perhaps you should put that in one of your questions,' I offer. 'I spent today in Pompeii and it made me realise how precious life is. Where do you feel most alive and why?'

She stops and stares at me. 'That's brilliant! I knew you'd be good at this. Hang on, let me write that down.' She pulls out her phone and launches an app, typing in the question. 'Two more to go.'

'One of them ought to focus on the handsomest cat in Margate, don't you think? So instead of asking what they'd do to impress your mum and dad, you could ask what they'd do to impress Samson.'

'You're on a roll,' she enthuses, typing the question into her app.

* * *

By the time we get back to the ship, late in the afternoon, Sam is decidedly pink from the sun despite her sunhat and liberal application of factor 50, which gives us our final question. I can't believe that I'm actually quite looking forward to watching her strut her stuff at tonight's singles event, but then these things are probably more fun as a spectator.

When we get to the Nautilus lounge, Barry is already a whirling dervish of excitement and organisation. A large screen has been erected at the rear of the room to prevent the interviewers from seeing the people they're going to be questioning, but we're amused to find that the other interviewer is Brad.

'Whoever he picks is in for the dullest date in the history of time,' Sam remarks when he's safely out of earshot. 'Still, at least I know that whoever I pick *won't* be him, so that's something to be thankful for.'

'I suspect the accent and voice would have given it away.'

'Sam, darling girl,' Barry coos as he bustles over. 'I need to take you and Brad to another room while we set up in here. Have you got a drink? Good. Come with me. You look stunning, by the way, so gorgeous.'

It may be a long time since I've seen the show, but I have to admit that Barry does an excellent job as host, channelling Cilla Black to perfection. Three men are carefully secreted behind the screen before Sam is brought in to wild applause.

'Your friend seems to be entering into the spirit of it,' a British voice says next to me. I turn to see a man who's probably a few years older than me, with light brown hair and hazel eyes set either side of what would have been a perfect Roman nose had it obviously not been broken at some point. His lips are surprisingly full for a man, but they suit him somehow. I would describe him as striking rather than just 'good looking' and, like me, he's wearing an amber badge.

'Cameron,' he says, offering me his large hand.

'Ruby,' I reply politely. 'And yes, this is Sam's idea of heaven. She's a hopeless romantic, so this will play to all her strengths.'

'OK, quiet, please, ladies and gentlemen,' Barry calls, waving his arms to try to quell the din. 'We're ready to start. Sam, would you read your first question.'

'Certainly, Barry,' Sam simpers coquettishly, drawing a muted cheer of approval from the audience. 'My first question is this. I spent today in Pompeii with my best friend, and the tragedy that unfolded there made me realise how precious life is and how we should seize every moment and live it to the full. Where do you feel most alive, and why?'

'Great question, Sam,' Barry enthuses. 'Who would you like to answer it first?'

'Number one, I think.'

'OK. Gentleman number one, please answer Sam's question.'

'Hi, Sam,' a deep voice with a strong Welsh accent says from behind the screen. 'You sound like a lady who knows how to enjoy herself. Pick me tonight, and I'll show you such a good time I promise you'll die with a smile on your lips when your turn comes.'

There's a mixture of groaning and applause from the audience at the cheesiness of the response.

'Number two, please?' Sam calls.

'Hi, Sam. I love the sound of your voice, so I know that I'd feel most alive wherever you were.'

'Oo, bit needy,' Cameron murmurs as the audience applauds.

'And number three,' Sam announces.

'Hi, Sam. I was also in Pompeii today, and I know exactly what you mean.

Life is as fragile today as it was when Vesuvius erupted. That's why I've taken the plunge and come on this cruise and, if you pick me, I promise I won't waste any of your precious time.'

'Oh, good answer,' I say to Cameron.

'Question two,' Sam announces. 'I share a flat with my best friend and the handsomest cat in Kent. If I brought you home to meet them, what would you do to create a good impression? I'd like number two to answer this one first.'

'Well, Sam,' the voice says. 'I'm more of a dog person myself but it's a well-known fact that cats and dogs can live in perfect harmony as long as the cat is in charge. So, if you're happy to take control, I'll be right at your heel.'

'Eeuww,' I say to Cameron. 'She won't like that. Not only did he not answer the question, but she's really not into submissive men.'

'I'll take your word for it,' he replies with a smile.

'Number one. What's your answer?' Sam asks.

'I love cats, Sam, and I'd be happy to stroke your pussy all night if it made you happy.'

The audience groans at the double-entendre, and I can see Sam rolling her eyes theatrically at Barry.

'Moving on swiftly, number three,' Sam calls.

'I've got a cat myself, so I know they need time and space to warm up to you. To begin with, I'd focus on getting to know your friend, until the cat felt ready to come and talk to me.'

'Oh, he's good,' Cameron says. 'I'm not sure he's got the humour part, but they're nice answers.'

'Final question,' Sam calls. 'I'm a redhead, so I burn easily in the sun. What would you do to protect me? Number one.' I can see her bracing herself for the answer and, when it comes, she's proved absolutely right.

'That's easy,' the voice says. 'Firstly, if you pick me, we won't be leaving your cabin so you won't need to worry about the sun. However, we'll have such a sizzling time that I can't guarantee you won't get some carpet burns.'

'Dear God,' I murmur to Cameron. 'I didn't think that people like him still existed. Actually, scrap that. I have met a few of his type, mainly Sam's exes.'

'Hmm. Number two?' Sam asks.

'I also burn really easily, and I'd be happy to share my suncream, and anything else, with you.'

'Number three?'

'I think the trick is not to spend too much time in the sun. So I'd plan regular breaks for coffee, maybe a long lunch in the shade, ice creams, and a cocktail by the pool at the end of the day. Maybe even a dip to cool off if we're both feeling hot and bothered.'

'That brings us to the end of your questions,' Barry announces. 'You'll be spending a dream day with one of these men tomorrow. Which is it going to be?'

'Easy decision,' Sam tells him with a smile. 'I pick number three.'

'And that's our Robin, from Surrey. Come round, Robin, and meet your date.'

As Robin appears, I recognise him from the first bio I looked at in the booklet. Sam is evidently delighted as she practically throws herself into his arms.

'May I ask a presumptuous question?' Cameron says as the audience whoops and cheers.

'As long as I reserve the right not to answer it,' I reply.

'I couldn't help noticing your amber badge and, if I understand the traffic light system properly, that means that, like me, you're not looking for a relationship at the moment.'

'That's right.'

'Do you mind me asking what you're planning to do now that your friend is going to be off with Robin tomorrow?'

'I don't know. I confess I hadn't really thought about it.'

'Tell me to get lost if you like, but I don't have any concrete plans either, so if you'd like to buddy up to see Messina, I'd be more than happy to accompany you for the day. You'd be doing me a favour, actually. There's a lady over there called Ashleigh who I suspect has definite designs on me, despite my amber badge, so I could do with rescuing.'

My first reaction is to do what I would normally do and tell him that Ashleigh isn't my problem and I'll be just fine by myself, thank you very much, but I look into his face and I'm certain that, unlike slimy Guido, he's not trying it on. And, although we've only exchanged a few words this evening, he seems easy to talk to.

'Sure,' I say recklessly, giving him a smile. 'Why not?'

12

'So, I had a look at your bio last night,' I say to Cameron as we disembark into the Sicilian heat. Although the cruise line has lots of tours on offer, Cameron and I have decided to do our own thing. Sam was initially riddled with guilt that she was going to be abandoning me so early in the cruise, and I confess I did let her wallow for a little while during our delicious dinner in the Italian restaurant before telling her that I'd made alternative arrangements, although I didn't mention that they included Cameron.

'I would have expected nothing less,' he tells me with a smile. 'I studied yours as well. Tell me about your bookshop.'

Our conversation flows easily as we head towards Messina cathedral to have a look at the astronomical clock and hopefully climb the tower before the main tourist hordes arrive. I tell him about my life in Margate, and he listens carefully and asks questions.

'I think I've been past it a few times,' he says when I explain where the bookshop is. 'Margate is part of my patch, and I have a few customers in the town.'

'Customers?' I ask with a smile. 'I thought you were a police officer.'

'I'm with Kent Police, yes. I'm a firearms enquiry officer.'

'What does one of those do?'

'It's easiest to explain with an example. Let's say you decided you wanted to buy a shotgun.'

'Unlikely, but OK.'

'It's not that unlikely. You'd be amazed by some of the people who own shotguns. Anyway, you fill out the relevant application forms and get your doctor to certify that you haven't been treated for any mental health conditions that might bar you from owning a gun. That all lands on my desk. I'll come and visit you, have a chat about what you plan to use the gun for and generally make sure there aren't any red flags. I'll also check that you've got a safe place to keep it, all that kind of thing. If I'm satisfied, I'll issue you with a shotgun licence and you're good to go.'

'Really? And there are enough people in Kent packing weaponry to make this a full-time job?'

'There are enough people in Kent packing weaponry to keep three of us busy.'

'Bloody hell. I thought it was illegal to possess a gun.'

'No. The rules are very strict, especially with regards to firearms, which is things like rifles and pistols. If you wanted to own something like that, you'd need to provide a pretty compelling reason. But with shotguns, the onus is on us to prove you're not a proper person before we can deny you a licence.'

'Have you ever had to do that? Deny someone a licence?'

'Oh, lots of times. I've had people swear blind they're fit and healthy, only for the doctors' report to contradict them. The most tragic are the ones who've owned guns for years but their mental health deteriorates to the point we have to turn their renewals down. These guns are often family heirlooms, so it's like parting them from a favourite pet. I've had grown men in tears.'

'And what do people use these guns for? I'm still not wild about the idea that lots of my neighbours are armed to the teeth.'

'Clay pigeon shooting is the most popular thing by far. There are centres all over Kent and they're all well subscribed. There are a few who do game shooting, and the farmers, of course. Most of them have at least one shotgun, and often a couple of rifles as well.'

'What do they need rifles for?'

'Keeping deer under control. Deer play havoc with the crops, and it's illegal to shoot them with a shotgun. You must use a rifle.'

'It's a different world. Oh, look. We've arrived.'

We're standing in a piazza with what looks like an elaborate fountain to our left and the squat form of the cathedral in front of us.

'The cathedral isn't as old as it looks,' Cameron informs me, studying his guidebook. 'The original building was consecrated in 1197, but that one was pretty much destroyed in an earthquake in 1908. It then sustained more damage in the war, so the building we're looking at is basically a twentieth-century reconstruction.'

'What about the clock?' I ask.

'Same thing. It was built in 1933 to replace the original. It's pretty clever though. There are seven layers of figures facing the square, and all of them move at different times.'

'I remember reading that. Are any of them likely to move while we're here?'

'Not the bottom ones, as they only change once a day. We should get to see the next one up though, as that changes every quarter of an hour.'

'What is it?'

He consults the guidebook again. 'The carousel of the ages of life. So we have a child, a young man, a warrior and an old man. According to this, the figure of death waves his scythe at them when they change. Should be fun.'

I look at my watch. 'Ten minutes until the next change. What else have we got?'

'The layer above that is the sanctuary of the Madonna, and that changes at midday. We might see that later if we're still here. Then we've got Biblical scenes that change four times a year, and another Madonna who receives a letter from an angel at midday. It all happens at midday, according to this. So Dina and Clarenza, above the Madonna there, ring the bells every quarter hour but the rooster between them flaps its wings at midday, and the lion at the very top also waves its flag, moves its tail, turns its head and roars three times at midday.'

'Something tells me we need to be here then.'

'Absolutely.' He looks up at the tower and I'm struck by the way the sunlight catches his eyes, making them almost luminous. 'Did you want to go and see about climbing the tower?' he asks, oblivious to my staring. 'Apparently, the views from the top are quite something.'

Unfortunately for us, it turns out that the tower is closed today for cleaning and maintenance, so we retire to a coffee shop that was recommended by one of my guidebooks and order espressos and pastries instead.

'Do you mind me asking why you're an amber badge?' Cameron asks as I take a sip of my coffee, savouring the intense flavour.

'This whole cruise was Sam's idea,' I explain. 'She never mentioned anything about it being a singles thing.'

'Ah. From your tone of voice I'm guessing you weren't enthusiastic about it when you found out.'

'No.'

'But surely you must have smelled a rat when you had to write your bio and submit a picture? I'm no expert, but I don't think that's normal on a cruise holiday.'

'I didn't submit my bio, Sam did.'

He laughs. It's a rich, deep laugh that makes me smile. 'Tell me,' he asks. 'Does she always run rings around you like this? I mean, you seem a very smart woman, so I have to admit I'm surprised.'

'Thankfully, no. And I hope she's got the message that I might inflict serious injury on her if she ever pulls a stunt like this again. Would that make me ineligible for a shotgun licence?'

'Too right it would. Anyway, when did you twig?'

'Pretty much as soon as I met Orange Barry, but by then it was too late to escape.'

'Never mind Friends of Marco Polo, I think Barry would fit in better with the Friends of Dorothy.'

'What is cruising's obsession with this "Friends of" concept? I saw something for the "Friends of Bill" in the daily programme. Who on earth are they?'

'I think it all stemmed from the Friends of Dorothy thing. That was the code word for gay meetings on board ships back in the day.'

'What day?'

'No idea. Presumably when being gay was still frowned upon. Anyway, the Friends of Bill are the Alcoholics Anonymous members. Being on a cruise ship literally surrounded by booze is probably fairly triggering for them, so the Friends of Bill meetings are there to help keep them on track.'

'And who was Bill?'

'Bill Wilson, the founder of AA, I think.'

'You're a mine of information.'

He smiles. 'I try.'

'OK, your turn. Why are you an amber badge?' I ask.

'In my case, I have to confess to shamefully not reading the small print. I had some holiday to use up and booked this as a spur-of-the-moment thing. A mate of mine at work is always going on cruises and banging on about how brilliant they are, and being part of a group sounded more fun than just sitting around by myself on a beach somewhere. Unlike you, I knew it was a singles cruise, but I didn't realise it was a dating thing. I just thought we'd be a group of people hanging out together so we weren't on our own.'

'Ah. When did the penny drop for you?'

'As soon as I read the booklet and saw the traffic light information, I knew I was in trouble. The moment I got to the Singles Mingle, I found Barry and grabbed myself an orange badge. I'd have got a red one if I could, but—'

'Yeah, I know,' I interrupt. 'I tried that too. Didn't the bio thing make you suspicious?'

'Nope. Because I knew it was a singles thing, unlike you, I just thought it was a nice way of getting to know a bit about the other people in the group.'

'OK, so I understand why you didn't realise it was a dating thing either. But don't you want to meet someone?'

'I could ask you the same question.'

'We're not talking about me.'

He sighs. 'It's complicated. I was in a long-term relationship that finished a couple of months ago.'

'Ah, and you're not over him or her.'

'Her, and I am, or at least I think I am. It was toxic at the end, so I think we were both relieved when she called it. It's just that we'd known each other since we were small, and the idea of starting completely from scratch with someone new seems too daunting. What if I've got loads of bad habits that didn't annoy Ellie, but would drive every other woman in the world round the twist? What if we don't click like Ellie and I did? It all terrifies me.'

'Wouldn't you want to meet someone though? Or do you think that's it? Ellie was your person and now you're destined to be single forever.'

'I don't want to be single forever, but I'm still fairly bruised and not about to rush into anything.'

'Bad news for Ashleigh.'

'There's definitely something predatory about her,' he says with a frown. 'She makes me feel like a seal in one of those wildlife documentaries. I'm sitting on the ice floe hoping desperately she won't tip me into the sea and devour me.' He shudders.

'So we can rule her out then.'

'Definitely, but I have always hoped I'd meet the right person and start a family one day. It's the "how" that I'm struggling with.'

'I think the "how" of starting a family hasn't changed in millennia,' I tell him with a grin. 'I'm sure you'll figure it out.'

He smiles. I like his smile; it lights up his whole face. 'I meant the "how" of meeting someone new and knowing if they're right for me. Anyway, enough about me. What about you?'

'I'm happy as I am,' I tell him, trotting out my well-worn mantra. 'I've had relationships in the past, but nobody's ever lit that fire inside me that makes me want to be with them forever. Also, if the people that Sam has been dating recently are anything to go by, the quality of the men out there is pretty depressing.'

'Do you see yourself staying single forever?'

'I don't know. There's just enough Disney princess in me that the idea of falling in love appeals, but the reality has always fallen short. It would need to be someone very special, I think.'

'A Disney prince, perhaps.'

'God, no! They're so annoying, aren't they? All floppy hair, perfect noses and huge eyes. No, I'd settle for someone who was ordinary looking, as long as they had something special about them.'

'And what would that be?'

I laugh. 'If I knew that, I'd know what I was looking for, wouldn't I! Anyway, it's nearly midday, so we'd better get out there if we're going to see this clock strut its stuff.'

***

I'm tired but contented when I come back to my cabin at the end of the day. Cameron proved to be the perfect companion, helped in my opinion by the fact that we'd both been clear from the outset that we didn't have any expectations. Messina turned out to be quite hilly in places, and my calves are aching in protest as I step into the shower. When I'm done, I wrap a towel round myself and stretch out on the bed for a quick snooze. This bed really is incredibly comfortable.

I've barely nodded off before I'm awoken by a furious pounding on the door.

'Ruby, are you in there?' Sam's voice calls.

'Coming,' I reply reluctantly as I lever myself off the bed.

'I need to debrief,' she says, sweeping through the door before it's even fully open and forcing me to retreat down the narrow passage to the bedroom area. 'Why aren't you dressed?'

'I had a shower and fell asleep.'

'Oh. I was going to suggest going for a drink, but we've only got a little while before Barry's evening entertainment.'

'What's on tonight?'

'Speed dating.'

I groan. 'Sooner you than me. Still, you've done it before, so I'm sure you'll be able to pull out the necessary conversation.'

'That's what I need to talk to you about. I'm not sure I'm going to do it.'

'But I thought the whole point of this was for you to do this stuff.'

'Yes, but that was before I met Robin.'

'Ah.'

'He's different,' she enthuses. 'More mature than the other people I've dated recently. I actually felt like I was with a grown-up today. It was the little things, like him pulling my chair out for me when I was sitting down and opening doors for me. Why are you laughing?'

'You're right. We're at the funeral of feminism. I should be crying. Did he pay all the bills too?' I put on a deep voice. '"It's OK, darling. I'll pay for dinner and you can pay me back in kind later."'

'We split the bills, actually, and he's not like that. That's what's so extraordinary about him. He was genuinely interested in me as a person, rather than just a collection of female body parts.' She lowers her voice to a whisper. 'I'm thinking of going amber for him.'

'Whoa!' I hold up my hands. 'I get that you think he's a nice guy, but whatever happened to "plenty more fish in this pond"? Aren't you in danger of settling for the first guy you see? There might be an even better person for you here.'

'I want to spend more time with Robin. Apart from anything else, there's a mystery I need to solve.'

'Which is?'

'His job. He won't tell me what he does for a living and it's not in his bio. When I asked, he just said that he'd rather not say until he knew me better, as people had a habit of judging him because of what he does.'

'You could just Google it. I'm sure he'll have a LinkedIn profile or something.'

'Where's the fun in that? Anyway, if he's a spy, which is where my money is at the moment, there won't be anything, will there.'

'You think he's a spy?' I ask slowly.

'It's got to be something like that, hasn't it? Otherwise why the secrecy?'

'I'm pretty sure spies have cover stories. That's the whole spy schtick. He'd tell you he was a cultural attaché or something.'

'Hmm. Maybe you're right. Anyway, I'm determined to get it out of him. I'm going to find him at the singles thing and talk to him about going amber together.'

'Why stop at amber? You could go the whole hog and go red.'

'After one date? Even I'm not that impetuous. Anyway, I wondered how you'd feel if I spent the day with him again tomorrow. I know it's not what we agreed, but...' She tails off, her eyes full of hope.

'It's fine,' I tell her. 'Don't worry about me.'

'Thanks. You're the best.' She gives me a quick hug before making for the door. 'I'm just going to freshen up before we go to the singles thing. I'll bang on your door in ten, OK?'

It's only when she's gone that I realise she didn't ask anything about my day. Maybe that's for the best; I don't want her trying to matchmake Cameron and me. We're just friends.

13

'All right, lovely singles,' Barry yells over the hubbub of conversation in the Nautilus lounge. 'I'm sure we're all desperate to find out how our Blind Date couples got on before we get into tonight's event. Where are Brad and Gail? Come out, don't be shy.'

Brad steps forward confidently, dragging a somewhat reluctant-looking Gail by the hand.

'There you are,' Barry cries ecstatically as if he hasn't seen them for years. 'So, Brad, tell us about your date.'

'We've had the best day,' Brad says. 'I feel such a connection to Sicily, having spent a considerable amount of time in Rome before. We really enjoyed seeing some of the locations from the iconic *Godfather* movie, and I was able to impress Gail with my grasp of Italian over lunch.'

'She doesn't look that impressed to me,' a familiar voice says in my ear, and I smile as I turn to Cameron. On my other side, Sam is thankfully oblivious, as her attention is completely focused on Robin.

'She doesn't, does she,' I reply quietly. 'Look at the vice-like grip he's got on her hand. Probably the only way to stop her escaping.'

'And what about you, Gail? Did you have a good day?' Barry asks.

'Not really,' she says, flashing a contemptuous look at Brad and forcibly removing her hand from his.

'Oh dear. Have you got any advice for Brad in his next encounter?'

'Yes. Talk about yourself less, and maybe find out a bit about the other person. If you'd bothered to do that, you'd have learned that I'm actually fluent in Italian myself and there's more to the language than just sticking random vowels onto the ends of English words.'

'Ouch, that's got to hurt,' I murmur to Cameron. 'Calling out his linguistic ability in front of everyone.'

'Mmm. It seems our Brad may not be such a cunning linguist as he thinks.'

'I see what you did there, dirty boy.'

'Sorry. It was too good a joke to resist.'

'I'm really not sure it was.'

'So,' Barry asks, adopting a wistful expression. 'It seems like love didn't blossom on this occasion. Brad, is there anything you'd like to say to Gail?'

'Yeah. I'm sorry you didn't have a good time, Gail. I think you're an amazing lady, and I wish you all the best, genuinely.'

Her expression softens. 'You're not a bad man either, Brad. Just work on the feedback I've given, will you? You're enough as you are; you don't need the bullshit to make yourself look better.'

'OK. Let's hope you guys have better luck on the speed dating tonight. Ladies and gentlemen, let's give Brad and Gail a round of applause!'

As the clapping dies down, Barry starts scanning the room again. 'Where are you, Sam and Robin?' he calls. I nudge Sam and she and Robin step forward.

'And how about you?' Barry asks. 'Did things go well?'

'Superbly, thank you, Barry,' Sam enthuses. 'Robin and I had the best day. We really enjoyed the locations and the lunch, but most of all we enjoyed just getting to know each other, didn't we?'

'Sam's very easy to talk to,' Robin agrees. 'In fact, if neither of us meets another match at tonight's speed dating, I'd be happy to spend the day with her again tomorrow.'

If Sam's disappointed that Robin isn't showing the same commitment that she was expressing to me earlier, she hides it well.

'Which brings us neatly on to tonight's event,' Barry tells us all delightedly. 'The rules are simple. Ladies, you'll be sitting on the chairs I've laid out around the edge of the room. Gents, you'll be sitting in the chairs facing the ladies. You'll have three minutes to find out as much as you can about each other before I ring the bell and you have to move on. I'll give each of you a piece of paper on which you should write your own name at the top, and the names of anyone you'd like to spend the day getting to know better tomorrow underneath. If one of the people on your list has also written your name, I'll pair you up and let you know via a note outside your cabin before ten tonight. One lucky couple will also win Barry's Bonanza, which is a private guided tour of Malta with lunch thrown in, so it's all to play for. Before we start, do any of the amber badges want to join in?'

'You should totally do this one,' I say to Cameron.

'What on earth makes you think that?' he asks incredulously.

'I know you're not looking for a relationship, but it's good practice for talking to women.'

'Do I have a problem talking to women?'

'You know what I mean. Go on. You don't have to write anyone down.'

He looks at me for a moment before raising his hand. 'Barry, Ruby and I would like to take part, please.'

I stare at him. 'What? I never agreed to that.'

'If I'm doing it, you're doing it too,' he says with a mischievous grin as Barry happily thrusts name badges, pencils and pieces of paper into our hands. 'I'll see you on the other side.'

I must be losing my touch, I think, as I reluctantly allow myself to be guided to a chair. Not only did Sam hoodwink me onto this cruise, but Cameron just outmanoeuvred me as well. I meet Sam's eye across the room and have to stifle a laugh. Speed dating may be my idea of hell, but it's almost worth it to see the look on her face.

My first date is Euan, and his accent immediately identifies him as the phantom pussy stroker from the Blind Date evening.

'Oh, God. I'm *so* embarrassed,' he confesses when I call him out on it. 'I blame bloody Barry. He told us to be a bit suggestive in our replies, and I was so nervous I opened my mouth and went way too far. I'm not like that in real life, honestly.'

'I think it's only fair to tell you that Sam, whose pussy you offered to stroke, is my flatmate, so you were technically offering to stroke my pussy too,' I tell him, trying not to giggle as he goes absolutely puce. 'You'll forgive me if I don't take you up on it.'

'I'm never going to live this down, am I?' Although crimson with embarrassment, he does at least smile.

'Probably not while you're on the cruise, no. Anyway, what do you do for a living, Euan?'

He's palpably relieved at the change of subject. 'I'm the manager of a supermarket in my hometown of Aberystwyth. What about you?'

Ten points for asking me a question, Euan, I think to myself. 'It seems we share a love of the seaside and retail,' I tell him with a smile. 'I'm the co-owner of a bookshop in Margate.'

In fact, Euan turns out to be quite easy to chat to and not at all smutty, and it feels like we're just getting going when the bell rings. If I'm disappointed at his departure, that's nothing compared to the sinking feeling in my gut as his place is taken by Brad.

'How's it going, Brad?' I ask wearily.

'I've been better, Ruby,' he says honestly. 'Tell me. I know we didn't talk for long the other night, but was that stuff Gail said about me true?'

I study him for a moment. His cockiness is gone and he looks more like a little boy who's lost his favourite toy.

'I can't speak for your Italian, as I haven't heard it,' I tell him as gently as I can. 'But you did talk about yourself a lot and I don't think you asked me any questions.'

'I guess I do that when I'm trying to make a good impression,' he admits. 'I'm terrified of awkward silences, so I just talk to fill them.'

'There's nothing wrong with wanting to avoid awkward silences, Brad, but you can fill them by asking questions about the other person. Try it on me.'

'OK, umm, I know where you live so I can't ask you that again.'

'No, but you could ask about my work, or what I like to do with my spare time. Make me feel like I'm the most interesting person you've ever met. You could throw in relevant information while you're doing that, but the trick is to keep it short. If I'm interested in you, I'm going to ask you questions and that'll be your opportunity to talk about yourself. Do you see?'

He looks uncertain. 'I guess so.'

The bell rings before we have a chance to go any further. 'Try it out on the next person,' I encourage him. 'Let me know how you get on.'

'The next person is Gail, so I don't think it's going to go well.'

'Did you really like her?'

He sighs. 'I did.'

'Then think of it as an opportunity to redeem yourself.'

The next few speed dates pass in a bit of a blur and it quickly becomes clear that we're not going to get round everyone before dinner, but I'm very aware that Sam's Robin is getting closer. I wouldn't mind the opportunity to interrogate him for three minutes, so I'm relieved when he takes his place in front of me just as Barry calls that this is to be the last date this evening.

'You're Sam's flatmate,' he observes as he sits down and reads my name badge. 'Nice to meet you, I'm Robin.'

Across the room, I can feel Sam's eyes boring into me, but I ignore her.

'And what do you make of Sam?' I ask him.

He smiles. 'She's a fascinating woman. We had a really interesting day together and it felt like we didn't stop talking the whole time.'

'So why not snap her up and spare yourself the speed dating?'

'I didn't want to be pushy. I like her a lot but, if I'm honest, I think she's a bit out of my league.'

'What makes you say that?'

'She's a big personality, and I worry she might find me a bit boring after a while.'

'Look,' I tell him firmly. 'I love Sam to bits, of course I do, but I'll let you in to a little secret. Her recent dating history is fairly disastrous so you're not exactly up against strong competition.'

He smiles again. 'I know. She was pretty open about it.'

'If I may be so bold, I think you're asking the wrong question here. It's not about whether you're boring or not, although I don't think you can be that dull if the two of you were talking all day. It's more about whether you're a jerk and, based on what I've seen of you so far, you're not. She really likes you, although what's all the secrecy about your job? She's convinced herself you're a spy because you won't talk about it.'

He laughs. 'I can assure you I'm not a spy.'

'So why the secrecy?'

'It's complicated. I will tell her when the time is right, I promise. It's just that I want her to get to know me as Robin, and my job kind of gets in the way of that.'

'Fine. I'm not going to press you. All I will say is that Sam clearly thinks a lot of you, to the point that she was willing to change to an amber badge for you. Be gentle with her, OK?'

'I will,' he promises. 'And thank you.'

As soon as the speed dating is over, Sam and Robin come together as if drawn by an invisible magnet, and I realise that my dating advice probably means I'm on my own for dinner, as well as the whole day tomorrow. I could see what Cameron is up to, I suppose, but I don't want to give him the wrong impression by spending too much time with him. That decision is taken away from me, however, as he comes to find me before we make our way to the dining room.

'How was it for you?' he asks with a smile. 'Did Cupid's arrow find its mark?'

'Ha. If anything, I was more agony aunt than anything else, and I'm still not entirely sure I'm talking to you after you roped me into it.'

He grins. 'And you weren't setting me up at all, I suppose?'

'Fine, I suppose I deserved it. What about you, how did you get on?'

He groans. 'I got Ashleigh, naturally, who made it perfectly clear she'd already written my name on her list. She's terrifying, but all the other people seemed nice.'

'Have you written her on your list?'

'Of course not! She'd eat me alive.'

'Some people might like that. Anyone else catch your eye?'

'No.'

I only have a moment to register the strangeness of the relief that floods through me from knowing that Cameron hasn't been snapped up by one of the other singles before he speaks again.

'Oh, look over there!'

I follow his gaze and see Sam and Robin chatting to Barry briefly before they hand over their green badges and he replaces them with red ones.

'We have our first couple, ladies and gentlemen!' Barry yells. 'Congratulations to Sam and Robin, and all the best with your budding romance. Now, don't forget to hand in your papers before you go to dinner, everyone else. If you want to be the next golden couple and enjoy Barry's Bonanza, you have to be in it to win it.'

I glance down at my speed dating card, which unsurprisingly has no names on it, fold it carefully and slip it into my pocket. Although I probably deserved it, and I escaped unscathed this time, I'm going to have to watch both Sam and Cameron like a hawk if I'm to stop them signing me up for anything else. I'm also stupidly pleased that Cameron didn't write anyone down either. Is that wrong?

14

'Are you sure you don't mind?' Sam asks. We're finishing breakfast and I'm mentally kissing goodbye to the tour of Malta that I'd booked because Sam has not only dropped me like a hot brick to spend the day with Robin, which she did at least have the decency to warn me about last night, but she's also just revealed that she wants to take him on the tour that I'd meticulously researched and was looking forward to. To be honest, although I should be annoyed, I'm not that bothered as I have much bigger fish to fry, namely the note that was posted outside my cabin last night.

'It's fine. You lovebirds go and enjoy yourselves,' I tell her, plastering on a smile and trying to act normally. 'I can't believe you've gone all the way to red.'

'It was Robin's idea,' she confides. 'But I'd met enough of the other people at the speed dating to know that none of them appealed like he does, so it wasn't a difficult decision.'

'Any progress on finding out what he does for work?'

'None. I have found out where his cabin is though, and he's either keeping a low profile or he doesn't earn that much because it's on deck four, near the back.'

'What does that mean?'

'It's pretty simple. On a cruise ship, the higher your cabin is, the more you pay. Also, cabins in the middle of the ship are more expensive because there's less movement. So, a low-down cabin at the back near the engines is going to be one of the cheaper ones.'

'Is that a problem?'

'Of course not. I'm just gathering as much evidence as I can to see if I can work out what he does.'

'He promised me last night he'd tell you when the time is right. Maybe you should trust him instead of going full-on private investigator?'

'Hmm. Maybe you're right, but I can't resist a mystery, as you know. Anyway, what are you going to do today?'

'I don't know yet.' This isn't completely true; my first task is to track down Cameron so I can find out why he and I seem to have been selected for Barry's Bonanza. I don't want to embroil Sam in it though; she'll only get the wrong idea.

'I'm really sorry I'm not spending much time with you. I will make it up to you, I promise.'

She won't, but I smile nonetheless. 'I know you will. Now go and enjoy your day.'

I watch as she hurries off to get ready before meeting Robin. As soon as she's gone, I start urgently scanning the room for Cameron, finally locating him fiddling with the coffee machine.

'Good morning,' he says cheerfully as he settles himself opposite me.

'Never mind that. What the hell is going on, Cameron?'

'What do you mean?'

'You know what I mean,' I tell him, spreading out Barry's note. 'This.'

To give him his credit, he doesn't falter. 'OK, don't be cross with me, but it was pretty obvious last night that Sam was going to blow you out again today. She has blown you out, hasn't she?'

'Yes. What's that got to do with this though?'

'So, I, umm, may have staged a bit of an intervention.'

'Just spit it out, Cameron.'

'OK. Well, I couldn't help noticing that you didn't hand in your date card last night.'

'What?'

'Sorry. It's a police thing, I guess. I'm very observant, and I saw you folding it up and putting it in your pocket.'

'It's not a crime, is it? You're not going to arrest me for failing to hand in an empty form?'

'Of course not, but it got me thinking. We took part in the speed dating just as much as anyone else, so why shouldn't we be in with a chance of winning Barry's Bonanza? It's actually a good prize and I think you deserve it for being such a selfless friend to Sam. So I disguised my handwriting, filled in your name at the top of my form, wrote my name underneath as a match, and put it in the box.'

'But that's only half the equation. It only works if there's a matching paper with your name at the top.'

'Exactly. So I pretended to Barry that I'd lost mine and he happily gave me another one. I filled it in with your name underneath, put that in too, and we won! So unless you have other plans, which I sincerely hope you don't, an air-conditioned Mercedes is waiting on the dock to take us for a VIP tour of Malta at Barry's expense.'

'But...'

'What?'

'Surely Barry must know that we didn't spend any time together at the dating thing last night? He's going to smell a rat, isn't he?'

'I've learned two things about Barry. He's a hopeless romantic and he's not very observant.'

I study him for a moment. I know I ought to be cross about being outmanoeuvred again, but it's actually a lovely thing for him to have done, and I can't help but grin at him. 'For a police officer, you have some very shady practices.'

He smiles back. 'Sometimes you have to resort to unconventional methods for the greater good.'

'What if we hadn't won? Did you have a contingency for that?'

'I was fairly confident we would.'

'Why? Is there something else you need to confess?'

'Nothing shady this time. Just honest deduction, I promise. The way I saw it was this: on a speed dating event like that, you're probably not going to get that many matches. You might get one or two, but the odds are slim. That's part one. Part two is all about the box and Barry. I carefully made sure that ours were the last two slips to go into the box, meaning they'd be on top of the pile and therefore be the first two that Barry drew out. He's got his match for the big prize, job done. He probably didn't even look at the others.'

'Did they teach you that in police college?'

'Not exactly, but they did encourage us to look at problems from a variety of angles, not just the obvious ones.'

I think for a moment. 'There is a big flaw in your plan though.'

'Which is?'

'Barry's going to expect us to wax lyrical about our date and basically become a couple. Either that or we have to say it was a disaster and not speak to each other for the rest of the cruise.'

His expression falters for a moment. 'Good point, but I'm sure that's not an insurmountable problem. Let's figure something out while we're on the tour.' He swigs down the last of his coffee. 'Coming?'

* * *

I have to admit, as the day draws to a close, that Barry's Bonanza is actually rather better than the tour I'd booked for Sam and me. The car took us straight to Mdina, where we had a happy time exploring the silent city before it got too hot and, crucially, before the main tourist buses arrived. Once we'd seen everything we wanted to there, we were whisked across to St Julian's for lunch in a superb pizzeria before being given a guided walking tour of Valletta in the afternoon. When we started to flag, we were taken back to the ship and we're now sipping ice-cold drinks by the pool, which is pleasantly quiet as most people are still on their shore excursions. This is the first time I've been here since my unfortunate encounter with Guido, but I'm relieved to see no sign of him today.

'I have a suggestion, if you're open to it,' Cameron says as a gentle ocean breeze just takes the edge off the heat.

'OK.'

'It's about Sam, Barry and how we deal with all of it.'

'Go on.'

'The way I see it is this. From what you've told me about Sam, she's going to be pretty heavily invested in Robin until the end of the cruise, assuming they don't fall out first.'

'That's true,' I admit. 'He seems like a nice guy, from what I saw of him last night, so I'd say their chances of falling out are pretty slim. Sam's an all-or-nothing person when it comes to romance, so she'll definitely be putting the work in.'

'That leaves you kind of on your own. I know you don't mind that, and I don't want to presume anything, but it does potentially make things awkward because you're part of the Friends of Marco Polo group, so Barry's going to be on the lookout to matchmake you.'

'Especially after the stunt you pulled last night,' I remind him.

'Yes. Especially after that. Although we did have a great time today, didn't we?'

'Yes. Carry on.'

'I've also got a problem, because Ashleigh just doesn't seem to be getting the message, despite my best efforts. So the big question, to my mind, is how to get Barry and her off our backs so we can both enjoy the rest of the holiday without interference.'

'That would be good, I agree.'

'Here's where we get to the controversial bit. There's an easy way to do it, but I'm not sure you'll like it.'

'Just tell me what it is.'

'Before I do, can I just reiterate that I know you're not looking for a relationship, and neither am I. But I do enjoy doing the shore trips with you, and I hope you enjoy them too.'

'Cameron, you're starting to annoy me now.'

'Fine. You and I go red as a couple.'

'*What?*'

'Think about it. It solves all our problems. Barry gets off our back, Ashleigh stops harassing me and we can carry on doing the shore excursions, just as friends.'

'And what am I supposed to tell Sam?'

'That's up to you. You could tell her the truth or you could let her stew. I'm easy either way.'

'It seems a bit like a nuclear option. Isn't there anything less extreme?'

'If there is, I can't think of it. I'm always open to suggestions though. I don't think it's actually that extreme. Yes, Barry will be all over us like a rash tonight, but then his focus will shift to the rest of the group.'

'I need time to think about it.'

'OK. No pressure from me. One more question though.'

'What?'

'Am I dreaming, or is that Brad and Gail chatting at the bar?'

I follow his gaze and he's right. Unfortunately, Brad looks up at exactly the same time and waves, before saying something to Gail.

'Shit,' I murmur to Cameron while plastering a fake smile on my face. 'They're coming over. I can feel a sudden migraine coming on. I may have to escape to my cabin to lie down.'

'Hey, guys,' Brad calls as they approach. 'How was your day?'

'Good, thanks, Brad,' I reply politely. 'What about you?'

'Better, I think. I took your advice.'

'He was great company today,' Gail enthuses. 'Strip away the bullshit and it turns out there's a pretty decent guy under there.'

'Plus,' Brad admits with a rueful smile, 'I've no idea what Maltese sounds like, so I couldn't try to pretend I speak it.'

'Just as well,' Gail chides. 'I don't think I could stand that again. "Uno Biero", honestly.'

'What was wrong with that?' Brad asks. 'The guy understood me.'

'Nothing, except the correct phrase is *una birra*.'

'It turns out that Gail is something of a polyglot,' Brad explains. 'How many languages did you say you spoke?'

'Seven, although only five of them are fluent.' She pats his arm affectionately. 'He's a changed man. Not only has he been asking questions, but he's actually remembering most of the answers. Be still, my beating heart!'

'So what have you guys been up to today?' Brad asks, evidently showcasing his training. 'Just hanging around here or have you been out?'

I settle back and let Cameron tell them about Barry's Bonanza, which they admit they'd also been hoping to win. The body language between them is easy and familiar; they're totally unrecognisable from the tense couple we saw last night, and this makes me realise that we have another problem.

'Cameron,' I say to him once Brad and Gail have wandered off. 'We're not going to convince as a couple. Our body language will give us away as just friends. Sam will spot it, even if nobody else does.'

'Does that mean you're seriously considering my suggestion?' he asks with a smile.

'Yes, but that's a big hole.'

'You're overthinking. Maybe we're just not into public displays of affection. We are British, after all. We might need to hold hands, but no more than that. Like I said, I'm open to alternatives if you can think of a better plan.'

Our conversation is interrupted by the arrival of an excited-looking Ashleigh, who makes a beeline for us the moment she spots us.

'Hi, Cameron!' she says enthusiastically, plonking herself on his sun bed and completely ignoring me. 'I've been looking everywhere for you.'

'Hello, Ashleigh,' Cameron replies cautiously. 'Have you had a good day?'

'Terrible.' She sighs dramatically. 'I had to join a group tour, and spent the day sitting next to this old duffer who droned on and on about his tomato plants at home. Honestly, if you're that fussed about your plants, why come on holiday? Stay at home with the damned things.' She switches tone to flirtatious, flicking her long blonde hair and leaning forward to give him the best view of her cleavage as she does so. She's still completely ignoring me. 'Cheer me up. Tell me about your day.'

'Ruby and I won Barry's Bonanza. You know Ruby, don't you? Ruby, this is Ashleigh.'

Forced to acknowledge my presence at last, Ashleigh turns and, for a moment, her face is a mask of contempt.

'Barry's Bonanza?' she asks, looking confused. 'I don't understand. I wrote your name.'

'And it seems Ruby did too,' Cameron tells her. There's an uncomfortable pause while Ashleigh digests this information, looking between Cameron and me as she does.

'You wrote *her* name?' she says eventually. Her tone is now accusing and her mouth has curled in distaste. 'I see. I didn't realise you two were a thing. Well, forgive me for intruding. I'll leave you to it.'

I have to stifle a laugh as she gets to her feet and flounces off.

'You've definitely got an admirer there,' I tell him.

'She's terrifying, isn't she?'

'I don't think I'll be getting a Christmas card from her, somehow.'

He smiles. 'So, about going red then…'

I contemplate his proposal. I can see the advantage to him, but there is also one element that does appeal to me enormously, which is the opportunity to get one over on Sam. I'm not normally competitive, but maybe it's time for me to start paying her back for all the tricks she pulled to get me here, and for abandoning me when she specifically promised she wouldn't.

'Fine,' I say to Cameron suddenly. 'You're on.'

'Really?'

'Yes.'

'And Sam?'

'We have to convince her we're the real deal. She won't see it coming and it'll serve her right.'

His smile broadens. 'I have the feeling this is going to be a lot of fun.'

I relax back into my lounger and close my eyes. It's either going to be a lot of fun or it'll crash and burn spectacularly and, if I'm honest, I couldn't call which way it's going to go. Whatever happens though, it will liven up the holiday no end.

15

'Before we get into the second half of our speed dating, I'm very excited to announce that we have another brand-new couple, courtesy of last night's prize!' Barry yells once we're all assembled for our daily social in the Nautilus room. He's been positively overflowing with joy since Cameron and I quietly asked to swap our amber badges for red ones.

Since getting them, we've been carefully skulking at the back of the room, out of Sam's eyeline. To be fair, she's been so engrossed with Robin I think we could have set a bomb off in here and she wouldn't have noticed, but Barry's announcement has evidently piqued her interest, as I can see her scanning the room to see if she can spot the new couple.

'Ruby and Cameron, step forward, please,' Barry calls. Cameron takes my hand in his and, for a moment, I'm frozen in confusion. It's a long time since I've held a man's hand and this is the first physical contact we've had. It's not unpleasant at all; in fact, it's rather nice. It's just odd and it takes me a minute to adjust to the sensation. As we make our way over to join Barry, I meet Sam's gaze. To my delight, her eyes are wide in confusion, and I can't help flashing her a winning smile.

'I have to tell you, ladies and gentlemen,' Barry coos as we join him in the middle of the room, 'that this is a first for me. In all my years of running these groups, I've never had two amber badges get together like this. In fact, I'll go further and bet you that none of my fellow Marco Polo coordinators has had this happen either. It just goes to show that nothing is impossible where love is concerned. Guys, why don't you share your story with the group?'

I glance at Cameron, who grins mischievously at me and murmurs, 'Ladies first.'

'I'm not sure that was in the plan,' I whisper back.

'Wing it.'

I can feel Sam's eyes boring into me, and that's enough to give me the impetus I need.

'Well, Barry,' I begin. 'As you'll know, I made no secret of the fact that I wasn't looking for love when I joined the cruise. My best friend Sam over there made the bookings and curiously neglected to tell me that we were going to be part of this group. However, once I'd got over the initial shock, I decided to make the most of it, and that's when I met Cameron. We toured Messina together and I thought we'd become friends, but then we had last night's speed dating and I realised it could be more, so I wrote his name on my card and we were lucky enough to win Barry's Bonanza. The rest is history.'

Barry looks like he's going to explode with delight. 'And what about you, Cameron?'

'Oh, I spotted Ruby on the very first night, at the Singles Mingle event, but I was too shy to talk to her. However, when I saw her friend Sam get matched with Robin at the Blind Date evening, I realised it would leave Ruby on her own, and that gave me the courage to approach her. Like her, I didn't imagine that it would lead to anything more than friendship, someone to spend time with, but I think last night's speed dating and the time we spent together today was a revelation to both of us. We've had a brilliant time, thanks to your prize, and I'm very excited to see where this might lead.'

'Aww, you guys are totally made for each other. Have you had a chance to talk about the future and how that might work for you both?'

'It's a bit early to be talking too much about the future, Barry,' I admonish him. 'But Cameron and I are both based in Kent so distance isn't likely to be an issue, at least.'

I'm so good I'm almost convincing myself. As long as I keep my gaze away from Sam, I reckon I can pull this off. I give Cameron's hand an encouraging squeeze and, to my delight, he returns it.

'Well, I'm absolutely thrilled for you both,' Barry says so warmly that, for a second, I feel bad about the deception. I give myself a mental shake and remind myself that I didn't consent to this, so I'm perfectly within my rights to do whatever is necessary. 'Ladies and gentlemen,' Barry calls, 'let's give a huge round of applause to our newest couple, Ruby and Cameron! Why don't you give us a kiss?'

Before I know what's happening, Cameron has lowered his head to mine so our foreheads are touching. 'OK?' he whispers and, after a brief moment of hesitation, I nod. As our lips meet, my initial surprise at the sensation quickly gives way to something else. I know it's not a 'real' kiss, that we're merely putting on a show for Barry, Sam and Ashleigh, but it's still very intimate. As he pulls away, I can feel my mouth tingling slightly from his stubble as it turns up into a smile. Sam's eyes are out on stalks, I realise, which only increases my pleasure.

'I thought we weren't into PDA,' I murmur to Cameron.

'Just giving Barry what he wanted,' he replies, his mouth also curved into a smile.

As soon as Barry releases us back into the group, I sense Sam detaching herself from Robin and, sure enough, she makes a beeline for me, grabbing my free hand.

'Cameron,' she asks in a voice so saccharine it could give the sugar plum fairy diabetes, 'would you mind *very much* if I stole Ruby away, just for a second or two?'

I'm aware of Cameron tightening his grip and, for a moment, I wonder whether this is going to turn into some weird tug of war between them, with me as the rope.

'I won't be a minute, I promise,' I say to him as I gently extricate my hand from his. Realising just in time that I need to make this look authentic, I reach up and give him another quick kiss, catching a whiff of his citrussy aftershave as I do.

'What the actual fuck, Ruby?' Sam asks as soon as we're out of earshot of the rest of the group.

'Nice to see you too,' I reply sarcastically. Cameron and I may be faking it, but I'm still a little taken aback by her ferocity.

'Don't get me wrong,' she continues, oblivious to my reaction, 'I'm delighted for you both, but who are you and what have you done with my best friend? You know, the one who always says she doesn't want a relationship and she's fine as she is.'

'I changed my mind,' I say simply.

'No. Changing your mind is deciding to have strawberry ice cream instead of chocolate. This is seismic. You know how it always makes the news for days if a government makes a U-turn? This is even bigger than that. How come you never said anything to me? I'm a little pissed off that I had to find out from Barry.'

'This is the first I've seen of you since breakfast,' I remind her.

She sighs. 'That's a fair point. How did it happen though? Come on. Spill the beans.'

'There's not much to tell. We've spent some time together; I like him and he likes me. It's hardly rocket science, Sam.'

She narrows her eyes suspiciously. 'Bullshit. I know you, remember, and it would take a lot more than him just being a nice guy to persuade you to ditch your "there's nothing a man can give me that I can't get from Samson or my vibrator" mantra. What is it? Is he a secret millionaire? Does he have a degree from the university of how to give better sex than the XCite 3000 multispeed?'

'He's just a nice, genuine guy. And, unlike Robin, he's not secretive about what he does for a living.'

'Harsh, but again fair. What does he do?'

'He's in the police.' I decide not to elaborate on the firearms bit as I'm not sure I understand it well enough to explain.

'Oho!' She laughs. 'So that's what it is.'

'What?'

'You've had your head turned by the thought of him in uniform, wielding his impressive truncheon. Get Alexa to play "You Can Leave Your Hat On" by Tom Jones, and let the striptease commence.'

'You have a very dirty mind, has anyone ever told you that?'

'Why, thank you.' She curtseys playfully. 'I'm hoping the two of you are going to give me something to focus it on. So, come on. Give me all the details. I want to know *everything*.'

I sigh. This has gone as far as I can take it. Much as I've enjoyed winding Sam up and I want to get her back for abandoning me, I'm not cut out for extensive deception, I realise.

'Full disclosure?'

'Full disclosure. Leave nothing out.'

'Promise you won't tell Barry.'

'What's it got to do with him? His work is done. You've literally made his year.'

'Promise.'

'Fine.'

'We're not a real couple.'

'What?'

'It was Cameron's idea. Go red as a couple and get everyone off our backs.'

I watch as she digests this new information and, to my surprise, her expression changes to one of outrage.

'So you're saying that you and Cameron are faking this whole thing?'

'Yes.'

'But...' she splutters, temporarily lost for words.

'We aren't committing a crime, Sam. Everybody wins. We can gracefully drop out of the cringey dating games and Barry gets his happy ending.'

'Bollocks,' she spits. 'You fraudulently took a prize that was meant for a real couple, and that's a crime. I bet you've been having a right old laugh, haven't you. "Look at the stupid romantics trying to find love. Let's just cheat instead." I know you made me promise, but I've got a good mind to tell Barry exactly what you've done.'

'We haven't been having a laugh at anyone's expense, Sam,' I tell her firmly, feeling annoyed myself now. 'If anyone here's behaved fraudulently, it's you by signing me up for this without my consent, before promptly buggering off and leaving me to cope with it on my own.'

'That's not fair!'

'Isn't it? Look, I'm really pleased that you and Robin have found each other, and I hope he turns out to be Mr Right and you have football teams of rosy-cheeked children together, but don't you *dare* come for me when all I'm trying to do is make the best of the situation you've dumped me in.'

This is enough to take the wind out of her sails, and her defiant expression crumples. 'I've been a shit friend on this cruise, haven't I?'

'It's not been your finest hour,' I admit.

'I think I just over-reacted because I wanted it to be true,' she observes eventually. 'I'm sad now, because I was genuinely excited to think you might have met someone. It looked so natural when he kissed you.'

'Sorry to disappoint you.'

She wraps me in a big hug. 'You could never disappoint me,' she murmurs into my ear. 'I was just hopeful, for a moment.'

'You're such an incurable romantic.'

'It's a fair cop.' She laughs. 'Cop, geddit?'

We hug for a while longer before she releases me and looks me in the eye. 'What's the plan, Ruby?' she asks.

'How do you mean?'

'Now that you've come out in public, you're going to have to maintain the charade. Have you thought about that?'

'I'm sure we'll manage. It's not like we have our tongues permanently down each other's throats.'

'Why don't we spend the day together tomorrow as a four?' she suggests eagerly. 'You could get to know Robin and I can grill Cameron about his intentions for my best friend.'

'He doesn't have any intentions, and I don't think playing gooseberry to the two of you is on our sightseeing list. How's it going, anyway?'

As I hoped, she seizes on the opportunity to fill me in. 'Things have moved on a little,' she says with a smile.

'Which means?'

'Well, he's an amazing kisser, let's just say that.'

'That's good.'

'We're taking things slowly though. It's a little bit frustrating, because he got me all revved up with all this incredible kissing, but when I started to try to move things on, he slowed it right down.'

'Hm. What's that about, do you think?'

'I don't know. I did get a bit upset actually, because I thought maybe he didn't fancy me as much as I fancy him.'

'Did you ask him about it?'

'Yeah. He said he's totally into me but wants to get to know me more before we let a physical relationship get in the way.'

'Get in the way? Of what? Surely the whole point of getting naked together is that there's nothing in the way.'

She sighs. 'I'm not sure. He says he wants us to know each other fully as people before we know each other intimately. It's actually kind of hot, in a weird way.'

'Maybe he's got a point. Keep him on ice until he lets on what he does for work. It would be awful to go to bed with him and then find out he's a professional kitten strangler or something.'

'I don't think that's an actual job.'

'You know what I mean.'

Her expression lights up again. 'If you're not going to spend the day with us tomorrow, have dinner with us at least?'

'I'll have to ask Cameron. Thinking of which, we should go back in before he thinks I've been kidnapped and raises the alarm.'

As I follow her back into the hubbub of the Nautilus lounge, I reflect on our conversation, particularly on the need to keep up the pretence that Cameron and I are in a real relationship. Maybe I should have thought this through more carefully before saying yes to his suggestion. Oh well, it can't be changed now, and I do trust him. How hard can it be?

16

'Did you always want to be a policeman?' I ask Cameron. Since winning Barry's Bonanza, we've fallen into the habit of eating breakfast early and heading out to explore, before returning mid-afternoon to laze by the pool with a cold drink. Yesterday was Sardinia and we're in Mallorca today.

'God, no!' He laughs. 'I wanted to be a Formula One racing driver, obviously.'

'Really? Why?'

'Probably something to do with all the glamorous locations, the beautiful women and the money.'

'Interesting. I didn't have you down as that shallow.'

'Oh, come on. Relaxing on my mega yacht in Monte Carlo before driving to an incredible win and celebrating with a supermodel? What's shallow about that?'

'I can't think. Anyway, what stopped you?'

'Tiny, frustrating little details. It turns out you need to be able to drive really fast, and you also need a killer instinct.'

'And that's not you?'

'I'm not really the competitive type.'

'I can see that might hold you back. What about Premier League football? I admit that Manchester can't really compare with Monte Carlo, but there's still plenty of money there, and most of the players have glamorous girlfriends.'

'I do play football, actually.'

'There you go then.'

'I think it's probably too big a leap from the Emergency Services Football League to the Premier division, but thank you for the careers advice. I'll bear it in mind.'

'So how did the police come about?'

'Very boringly. They had a stand at a careers fair I went to, I got chatting to them and thought it sounded interesting. What about you? Did you always know you wanted to own a bookshop?'

'No. I knew I wanted to work with books, but my initial plan was to become a librarian.'

'What stopped you?'

'I realised I'd have no control. I would have been totally at the mercy of the local authority and whatever spending priorities they had. Unsurprisingly, libraries are fairly low on the list and don't get a lot of funding. Then I met Jono, my business partner. His big passion is rare and antique books, so we decided to combine the two things and open our business. I mean, it wasn't quite as simple as that as we had to raise capital and persuade the bank that our business proposal was viable, but you get the picture.'

'Aren't you at risk from the big players though, like Amazon?'

'There's just enough room for us both to co-exist. Yes, Amazon has the lion's share of the market, but there are still a surprising number of people who prefer to browse in a bricks-and-mortar bookshop. Do you know, I've got customers who come in just because they love the smell of the books? You can't get that online. Plus, I like to think we offer exceptional customer service and a mean cup of coffee, as well as the opportunity to meet the handsomest cat in all of Margate.'

'The famous Samson.'

'Exactly. You'd be surprised how many people drop by just to see him and end up buying a book or two while they're there. He's a master of upselling. Thank goodness he doesn't charge commission, or he'd cost us a fortune. Why guns?'

'Sorry?'

'Why become a firearms officer rather than, say, a detective?'

'That's easy.' He smiles. 'A lot of detective work is really, really dull. You've got to have a passion for the minutiae and get excited about forensics. Plus, most policing is irregular hours because criminals are selfish and don't work a nine-to-five schedule. One of the things I love about my role is that I generally get to work fairly regular hours and most of the people I deal with are law-abiding citizens. As long as they stay in the right hands and are properly secured, guns don't pose any risk to the public.'

'Really? Every time I see a news article about another school shooting, I can't help thinking they should be outlawed altogether.'

'I agree that there's no justification for members of the public to own assault rifles or weapons of that nature. But some of the shotguns, particularly the ones that have been handed down through the generations, they're literally works of art, with beautiful engraving and exquisite workmanship. Guns like that tend not to pose a risk unless the owners fail to lock them up properly and they get stolen. We're very strict with owners about how they store, transport and use their guns for that very reason.'

Our conversation is interrupted by a very flustered-looking Sam. I haven't seen that much of her since I told her about Cameron and me. We did have dinner together as a four but, although Robin was perfectly charming and polite, I found the way that Sam kept simpering at him a little off-putting. She's also not an early riser when she's on holiday, so we've only really met up at the Marco Polo socials. If I'm brutally honest, I'm still a little annoyed with her for being so high-and-mighty when I told her about Cameron and me, so her opening remark gets my hackles up a little.

'Ruby, I need you. Now,' she barks.

'Umm. I'm actually in the middle of talking to Cameron,' I reply mildly. 'Can it wait?'

'No. I'm in full-on crisis mode and I need my best friend this instant. It's an emergency, for God's sake.'

'Has someone died?'

'No.'

'Is anyone critically ill?'

'No. Why are you being so obtuse?'

'Because I'm trying to ascertain what on earth could be so important that it requires me to abandon my tour buddy and this rather delicious drink.'

'It's Robin.'

'Has he had an accident?'

'No, of course not.'

'You haven't fallen out with him, have you?'

'No. Well, not exactly. I've found out what his job is.'

'OK. Unless it's something highly illegal or Mafia related, I'm still not getting emergency vibes. Why don't you get yourself a drink from the bar, catch your breath and then fill us in.'

'It is a bloody emergency. You'll understand when I tell you.'

'Get a drink first. Go on. Shoo.'

Reluctantly, she turns and heads for the bar.

'Why wouldn't you just let her tell you?' Cameron enquires when she's safely out of earshot.

'Because this holiday has been all about her so far,' I tell him. 'Why should I drop everything and come running because she's found out what her boyfriend's job is? I mean, how bad can it be? He's probably an accountant or something completely harmless, and she's just got herself in a stew because it's not the swanky career she imagined. She's prone to drama, so hopefully giving her a simple task will calm her down a little.'

After a minute or so, Sam returns with a glass of white wine the size of a goldfish bowl and plonks herself on the end of my sun lounger.

'Right. Take a deep breath, have a mouthful of wine, and then tell us what the problem is,' I say to her.

To my surprise, she gulps down nearly half the liquid before she speaks. 'He's a vicar,' she says baldly.

'What?' I ask in surprise. None of the options playing around in my head had come close to that.

'You heard. He's a fucking vicar, Ruby. I mean, only I could pull off something like this, right? I swear off preachy church people and promptly start dating someone who's not only a church person, but preaching is literally his job. He should have been upfront with me, not drop it on me when I'm already falling for him. This is so fucking unfair.'

'I can understand why he didn't want to tell you,' Cameron observes mildly. 'I mean, he said that people tended to judge him because of what he does for a living and, I hope you don't mind me being direct, but that's kind of what you're doing, isn't it?'

Sam glares at him.

'Cameron's got a point,' I add hastily before she says anything regrettable. 'He wanted you to get to know him as a person, without the vicar stuff getting in the way. Is that so wrong? I mean, you're falling for him as a person, and the fact that he's a vicar doesn't actually change that, does it? He's still the same guy.'

'Yes, but it can't work, can it? I mean, I'm not religious. And there's the whole "no sex before marriage" thing that his sort are so hot on. No wonder he kept slowing me down. I should have realised why. God, I'm such a fool.' She takes another big swig of wine and lowers her forehead into her palm. 'I even told him about some of my past relationships. He must think I'm such a slut.'

'OK, stop,' I tell her firmly. 'Let's go back and unpick this properly before you turn it into a spiral of doom. When did he tell you?'

'Lunchtime. We were at this tiny restaurant sharing a delicious *paella*, and he said, "Sam, I think it's time you knew what my job is. I told you I lived in Dorking, and that's true. I'm actually the vicar of three small churches just outside the town."'

'And what did you say?'

'I didn't know what to say. For a moment, I wondered if he was joking, but I could tell from his expression that he wasn't. I just said, "Oh."'

'Hm. How did he react to that?'

'He asked if I had any questions. He told me about how he'd felt called during his final year at university, and a bit about the selection process and stuff. It was surreal. He made it sound so normal and banal, but all the time I was freaking out inside. Anyway, I tried to keep my poker face on until we got back to the ship, and then I came to find you.'

'I still don't get what's so wrong with being a vicar,' Cameron observes.

'Sam had a bad experience in a church recently. I'll tell you later,' I explain before turning back to her. 'OK. Let's put this in context, shall we? I think we can understand why he didn't tell you from the outset, but why do you think he decided to tell you now?'

'I don't know,' she says miserably. 'Because God hates me and wants to ruin my life at every turn?' She puts on a deep booming voice. 'Here you are, Sam. Here's the prize you could have won if you'd saved yourself for marriage.'

'Has he said anything about your past? I mean, you've admitted that you've told him.'

'No, nothing.'

'But if he'd had a problem with it, don't you think he would have found a way to distance himself from you, rather than sharing more?'

'Maybe he sees me as a project. He earns brownie points from God by helping me to find the Lord and turn my life around.'

'I don't think he'd be kissing you the way he has been if that was his plan. There would be all sorts of ethical problems with that. Has he placed any religious expectations on you? Now that he's told you, is he expecting you to pray with him, for example?'

'No. He was just the same as he's always been.'

'Right,' I tell her. 'So he's the same Robin who wasn't bothered by the fact that you've had boyfriends before and isn't expecting you to turn into some kind of nun overnight. You're clearly keen on each other, so what's the problem?'

'How do we take this into the real world, for starters? I mean, church is his whole life and I'm not churchy at all. And if we're not going to take this into the real world, what's the point of carrying on?'

'I'd suggest that's something you need to talk to him about. From what you've told me, it sounds like he's not that bothered about whether you're churchy or not. He just likes you for who you are. Maybe that's enough. Has he had girlfriends in the past?'

'Yes, but not since he started training for the priesthood.'

'So, for all you know, he might have an even more colourful past than yours.'

'I doubt his past has Threesome Pete in it.'

'Neither does yours, technically. Pete falls into the category of "lucky escape". I'll bet you Robin's got a few stories like that as well. Ferocious women with their eyes on being Mrs Robin and ruling the vicarage with a rod of iron.'

This does finally raise a glimmer of a smile. 'I doubt any of them would be sexual deviants though.'

'You never know what goes on behind closed doors. Now, go and talk to him. He's probably worried sick that he's spooked you and ruined everything.'

She drains the last of her wine and stands up. 'You're right. Thanks, Ruby. You're the best, has anyone ever told you that?'

I smile back at her. 'You may have mentioned it once or twice.'

'Can I make an observation?' Cameron says once she's gone. 'It seems to me that you're often a rather better friend to Sam than she is to you.'

'She's usually better than this,' I explain. 'But when she falls for someone, she falls hard. Controversially, I think Robin could be quite good for her. She's dated some real dickheads lately, and I don't think you're allowed to be a dickhead if you're a vicar, are you?'

As we finish our drinks and head inside to get changed for whatever Barry has lined up for us this evening, my mind is very much focused on the conversation I hope Sam and Robin are having. If he's opening up to her, that must be a good sign, mustn't it? I just hope she doesn't panic and ruin everything.

17

We haven't seen anything of Sam or Robin since her sudden appearance at the pool yesterday afternoon. They didn't come to the Marco Polo social, which was a shame as they missed Barry pretty much dissolving into a puddle of ecstasy when Brad and Gail went red. They also missed out on Barry's latest game, worryingly entitled Pass the Partner.

Our fears that it was going to prove to be some horrifying variation of strip poker, where the singles each had to remove a layer of clothing when the music stopped, thankfully proved to be unfounded. Instead, Barry had made up a number of parcels, in the centre of which were either names or an activity. The ladies had to pass round the blue parcels containing the names, while the gentlemen passed round the red ones, which had the activities. The logistics were impressive, as everyone ended up peeling off the final layer at the same time, thus revealing who they were to be paired with the next day, and an activity they had to complete.

'You've got to give the guy credit,' Cameron had observed as the couples had peeled off, with varying degrees of enthusiasm, to make plans. 'I don't know what they pay him, but he's earning every penny.'

'What have you two got planned for tomorrow?' I'd asked Brad and Gail as we'd made our way towards the main dining room for dinner.

'I'm giving Brad a Spanish lesson,' Gail had told me. 'He's got to order our lunch and ask directions without using any made-up words.'

'I don't know why she thinks it's necessary,' Brad had said to Cameron. 'I've already told her I'm fluent in Spanish.'

'And we both know that's total *mierda*,' Gail had countered with a laugh. 'That's bullshit to you, honey. Your first proper Spanish word.'

I did knock on the door of Sam's cabin before we left to get the bus up into Barcelona this morning, but there was no response. I've decided to take the optimistic view that she's somewhere with Robin, rather than worrying that she's thrown herself overboard. I know she goes all-in when she falls for someone, but I truly don't believe she'd ever resort to self-harm if a relationship didn't work out. At least, she's never shown any signs of it in the past.

'I know everywhere we've visited so far has been amazing,' I say to Cameron as the bus trundles towards the city centre, 'but Barcelona is one of the places I've been looking forward to the most.'

'Me too,' he agrees. 'Although I think we'll find a day is nowhere near long enough to see everything.'

'I've got tickets for Parc Güell and the Sagrada Família,' I tell him. 'I reckon those two should satisfy even the most ardent Gaudí fan. If we find we haven't had enough, we could probably just about get a peek at Casa Batlló, but I don't have tickets for that and we might be needing ice cream by then.'

Cameron smiles. 'I do like the way your mind works. Just the right blend of culture and snacking.'

'Absolutely. If I don't have a *churro* at some point today, Barcelona will be ruined forever.'

'I reckon we'll be able to cross that one off with our morning coffee.'

* * *

As the bus drops us closest to Casa Batlló, we decide to take a quick look at that before the half-hour journey on the public bus up to the park. The heat is already starting to build, and the city is busy, so watching the world go by from the relative comfort of an air conditioned seat proves to be a welcome oasis.

'Is there anything in this city that wasn't designed by Gaudí?' Cameron asks as we pass Casa Milà, another world heritage site.

'He does seem to have been given free rein,' I agree, consulting the guide-book. 'According to this, it all stems from the Modernisme movement at the end of the nineteenth century which, along with bringing back the Catalan language, was one of Catalonia's attempts to distance itself from Castillian Spain. It's based on the Art Nouveau school, although I think we can agree they went a bit mad with it.'

'Public transport is such a good way to see a city, don't you think?' he remarks a little while later as we pass through tightly packed shops and apartment blocks. 'I mean, we could have done the official tour, but this is giving us a real flavour of the place.'

'Yes. It's always a bit daunting to try to figure out how it works, but as long as you do your research in advance, it's usually manageable. I got the idea from this guy my business partner, Jono, was keen on for a while. He works in IT and travels a lot with his job.'

'Like Brad,' Cameron interjects with a smile.

'I'm not sure anyone travels quite like Brad,' I reply. 'Anyway, he was explaining how he always tried to use public transport when he went to new places, because you saw much more of the location and people than you did from taxis. I think a lot of his trips were basically airport to office to hotel to airport, and he found that frustrating because, although he'd technically been to Stockholm or wherever, he hadn't actually seen any of it. So using buses, trains and trams gave him that missing part of the jigsaw, and I thought it was a brilliant idea.'

'I'm certainly going to be copying it from now on,' Cameron agrees. 'Although I'll have to up my research game.'

'The internet is your friend,' I tell him smugly as the bus pulls into our destination. 'Shall we?'

* * *

By mid-afternoon, the heat is oppressive, but Cameron and I are doggedly plugging on. Having covered a good chunk of the park, we've ridden the bus back down into the city centre and, after the obligatory ice cream stop, we're now heading for the Sagrada Família, our final tourist attraction before we return to the ship and the promise of a long, cold drink by the pool. The pavements around the cathedral are packed, and Cameron takes my hand as we make our way through the crowds. Despite the heat, his hand is dry and his grip is firm, but I'm unable to enjoy the sensation as much as I'd like because we're jostled several times as we try to get to the entrance and I'm having to concentrate on not losing my footing. Once inside, although it's still busy, we savour the relative cool as we take in the extraordinary architecture. For the first time on this trip, I'm starting to wish I'd invested in a proper camera, as my elderly iPhone is struggling to do justice to it. Eventually, having seen pretty much all we can, we make our way back to the entrance and step out into the dazzling sunlight.

'I want to get one decent shot of the exterior,' I say to Cameron as I let go of his hand, shielding my eyes from the sun with one arm and raising my phone over my head with the other so it's above the crowds and hopefully has a clear view of the cathedral. I'm just about to press the button to take the picture when I'm almost knocked from my feet as someone cannons into me.

'Oof, sorry,' I say automatically as the iPhone slips from my grasp. I glance downwards, hoping it hasn't smashed as it hit the pavement but, to my surprise, there's no sign of it.

'Is everything all right?' Cameron asks.

'No. My phone's disappeared,' I tell him. 'I was taking the photo and then this guy bumped into me and I dropped it, but I can't see it anywhere.'

'Let me help you look,' he says, trying to clear some space so we can search, but I already know it's too late.

'I think I've been robbed,' I tell him. 'I bet that guy jostled me on purpose and stole it while I was distracted. Fuck.'

'OK, don't panic,' Cameron says, suddenly sounding every inch the policeman. 'Does it have tracking?'

'Yes, I've got "find my iPhone", but you need another device to log into and he's probably long gone already. I've read about these gangs that use scooters to get in and out before you even know what's happened. What a bloody idiot I am, waving my phone around like a ditzy tourist without thinking of the consequences. Everyone knows what it's like round here.'

'You are not to blame,' Cameron says firmly. 'Right, let's find a police station and report it.'

'What's the point? They won't get it back.'

'They may well not do, but you'll need a crime number to claim on your insurance for starters, and I hate to be all boring and procedural, but the police will only have accurate statistics for the crime rate around here if people report them. There's a tourist information kiosk over there. I bet they'll know where the nearest police station is. Come on.'

I'm feeling decidedly shaky as I start to follow Cameron towards the tourist information kiosk, and he obviously notices because he takes my hand in his again. 'It'll be all right,' he assures me. 'They didn't take anything else, did they?'

I do a quick inventory check and, although my bum bag is where it should be, I realise that my shoulder bag is also gone.

'What was in it?' Cameron asks when I tell him.

'Nothing of any value. Sun cream, lip balm, stuff like that. Bastards!'

The assistant at the tourist information centre is more than helpful but explains that the nearest police station is a subway ride away and my mood only darkens when we arrive to find a large queue of people waiting to be seen.

'Let's leave it,' I say to Cameron. 'It was an old iPhone anyway and we haven't got that long before we have to get back to the ship.'

'I'm tempted to agree,' he replies. 'Let me try one thing first though.' He pulls a small leather folder out of his pocket and approaches the desk, pulling me by the hand behind him.

'I'm sorry to bother you,' he says to the harassed-looking policewoman behind it and earning irritated looks from some of the people in the queue. 'I'm a policeman from the UK and I wondered whether there was a quick way to report a crime. I know you're probably swamped, but if there are some forms or something we need to fill in, I can just take them and do them for you now.'

She stares at him for a moment but, just when I'm convinced she's going to give him an earful, she smiles.

'¿Policía Ingles?' she asks.

'Yes, umm, *sí*.'

'*Un momento.*' To the obvious consternation of the person sitting in front of her, she pushes back her chair and disappears through a door behind her. Cameron turns to me with a quizzical expression, and I'm rather glad neither of us speaks Spanish as I suspect that whatever the poor guy the policewoman has just abandoned is muttering is not complimentary about us.

A few moments later, she reappears with a man in tow. She indicates Cameron and the man approaches him with a smile.

'Welcome to Barcelona, *Policía Ingles*,' he says, holding out his hand. 'I am Alejandro Martinez, the chief of police here. Let us go through to my office, where we will be more comfortable. Please.'

He opens the door and Cameron and I follow him through, down a wood-panelled corridor until we reach his office. He holds the door open for us and ushers us inside.

'Please sit down,' he says, indicating the chairs in front of his desk before walking round and sitting behind it. 'How can I be of help?'

'It's only a small thing,' Cameron tells him. 'My companion here has just had her phone and bag stolen outside the Sagrada Família, and we felt we ought to report it. Unfortunately, time is short because we have to rejoin our cruise ship. I hope you don't mind me cutting the line.'

'Of course not.' He turns to me. 'Your phone, it is an iPhone, I think?'

'That's right. How did you know?'

'They are the most popular for the thieves. Was it new?'

'No. About five years old.'

'Hm.'

'What?' Cameron asks him.

'There are two types of people who steal phones around that area. If your phone had been new, I would have told you that it had almost certainly been stolen by an organised gang, and there would be no chance of getting it back. I would give you a reference number and send you on your way with an apology. But the gangs have no interest in a phone as old as yours, which means it's probably been taken by an opportunist, and many of them are not very clever. Do you have the tracking feature?'

'I do.'

'Let us try it, shall we?' He beckons me round to his side of the desk and, between us, we launch the website and I enter the login details. After a moment, a map shows my iPhone in a suburb towards the north-east of the city. Alejandro sighs expressively.

'I think we can solve this for you,' he says before picking up his own phone, dialling a number, and barking a stream of Spanish into it.

'You know who has it?' I ask incredulously when he disconnects the call.

'I'm pretty certain, yes,' he replies. 'That address is where Jose lives. He is not a bad boy, but he is also not clever. He hangs around with a nasty crowd and tries to impress them with stupid things like this. I've told him many times, "Jose, this is not the direction you want to go in your life," but he doesn't listen. At the moment, he is too young for prison, but if he doesn't change soon, that is where he will go. His poor mother is, what is the English phrase?'

'At her wits' end?' I offer.

He smiles. 'Yes. She is a good woman, a devout Catholic who goes to mass every Sunday to pray for Jose. Sadly, I do not think God is listening to her.'

We're interrupted by Alejandro's phone ringing. '*Sí*,' he barks into the handset, and I can hear a babble of Spanish from the other end.

'Your phone, it is white, with a pink rubber case?' he asks me after a few moments.

'That's right.'

'My officers have it. They will be here in around forty minutes. Can I get you something while you wait? Coffee?'

'No, I'm fine, thank you. I'm sorry for causing you so much trouble.'

Alejandro laughs. 'It is nothing. If I come to your country and suffer misfortune, maybe you will extend the same courtesy, hmm?'

* * *

While we wait for the officers to return with my phone, Cameron and Alejandro have been swapping stories and are getting on so well I'm starting to wonder if they're going to become lifelong friends. I'm not able to track the passage of time as there isn't a clock in here, so I'm hoping that Cameron is keeping an eye; much as I want my phone back, I don't want to miss the boat.

Eventually, Alejandro's phone rings again and, after a brief conversation, he ducks out and returns holding my phone, handing it to me as if it's some kind of trophy.

'I am sorry about your bag,' he tells me. 'My officers asked, but Jose dumped it as soon as he realised there was nothing of value inside.'

'You've already done more than we could have asked for,' Cameron assures him. 'Thank you so much. If I could just ask one more favour, which is a taxi to take us back to our ship?'

'Your ship,' Alejandro repeats, staring at his watch in horror. '*Joder*, I completely forgot. Give me the name, maybe I can get the port authorities to delay departure for long enough so you can get there.'

'It's the *Spirit of Malmö*,' Cameron tells him as he grabs his phone once more and starts barking Spanish into it. However, the expression on his face tells me everything I need to know before he speaks.

'I am so sorry,' he tells us. 'Your ship has already departed.'

18

For a moment, time seems to stand still as Cameron and I digest Alejandro's bombshell. The ship has gone; we're stranded in Barcelona. Alejandro is still rattling away in Spanish to the person on the other end of the phone, but all I can do is stare at Cameron in horror.

'Sorry about that,' Alejandro says as he disconnects his call. 'I was trying to find out if the pilot was still aboard, because sometimes we can get passengers out to the ship on the boat that collects the pilot, but my colleague at the harbour tells me that it's already left as well.'

'What do we do?' I ask Cameron.

'We'll have to find our own way to the next port and meet the ship there,' he tells me. 'Have you got your passport?'

I fish it out of my bum bag and show it to him.

'Great. Now all we need to do is work out how to get to Cannes before the ship does.'

'The fastest way is to fly,' Alejandro tells us. 'There are regular flights to Nice from Barcelona. You're welcome to use my computer to book them.'

Twenty minutes later, we've established that the first flight we can get onto is at half past two the next afternoon but, as Alejandro stated, it's still a lot quicker than trying to get there by train; we checked just to be sure and found it would take over eight hours.

'It's a bit tighter than I'd want it to be,' Cameron observes as he books us in. 'But it does give us two hours to get to the ship once we land. Let's hope there aren't any delays. Right, let's have a look at hotels for tonight.'

'Hotels?' Alejandro sounds almost offended. 'You won't need a hotel. You will be staying with me and my family. It's the least we can do.'

'Oh, I don't think we could impose on you that much,' I tell him. 'You've already done more than enough.'

'Nonsense,' he says robustly. 'If I go home and say to my wife that some English friends had a misfortune in Barcelona and missed their ship, but I left them alone in a hotel, what do you think she will say to me? She will say, "Alejandro, I am ashamed of you." I am sure it is the same in your country, yes?'

I glance at Cameron, and I can see from his guilty expression that his thought process is exactly the same as mine. If our situations were reversed, I'm sure neither of us would have had any qualms about sticking Alejandro in a hotel. Spanish hospitality is obviously rather more impressive than British.

Alejandro has evidently taken our silence as consent, as he's engaged in another quickfire conversation on his phone. The voice on the other end is female and, to her credit, seems to be giving Alejandro as good as she gets.

'That's settled,' he says when he finishes the call. 'My wife is expecting you. Come, let's go.'

'I'm really not sure this is necessary, Alejandro,' Cameron says carefully as we follow him towards the back door of the police station. 'We've put you to enough trouble.'

Alejandro grins. 'It's nothing compared to the trouble I will have if I arrive home without you. If I left you in a hotel now, my wife would come and fetch you herself. We have been married very happily for eight years. Do you know why? Because I learned very early not to say no to her. She is expecting visitors. Let us give her what she wants, hmm?'

Even though it's early evening, it feels like we've been hit by a wall of heat as we step out of the air-conditioned building into the car park behind. Alejandro leads us over to his car, a dusty SEAT estate. I'll admit I was expecting Cameron to do the patriarchal thing and get into the front of the car next to Alejandro, but he surprises me by climbing in the back with me.

'Even by Barcelona standards, it is hot,' Alejandro observes as he starts the engine and turns the aircon up to max. 'It will be better when we get to my home. I live in the hills above the city, and it's cooler there.'

As the car noses out into the Barcelona traffic, Cameron takes my hand again and gives it a reassuring squeeze. 'Are you OK?' he murmurs into my ear.

'I don't know,' I whisper back. 'Alejandro's nice, but this all feels a bit intense.'

'Look at it this way,' he offers. 'We're going to experience proper Spanish-slash-Catalan culture, away from the tourist trail. And he's the chief of police, so we couldn't really be in safer hands. Let's enjoy this, and then tomorrow we'll catch our flight and rejoin the cruise. We'll have stories to tell that even Brad won't be able to equal.'

The thought makes me smile, and I squeeze Cameron's hand tightly as we start to leave the city behind and climb into the hills.

* * *

Alejandro is right. Although it's still warm when we step out of the car nearly an hour later, there's a pleasant breeze taking the edge off the heat, and I turn my face towards it, enjoying the sensation. Alejandro barely gets the front door of the house open before he's rugby tackled by two of the cutest children I think I've ever seen.

'Cameron, Ruby, this is my daughter Sofia,' he tells us as he gently disentangles himself from a raven-haired girl that I'd estimate to be around six. 'And this is my son Pedro.' Even without introductions, the family resemblance between the two children is strong enough to mark them out as brother and sister. Although he can't be more than four, Pedro is nearly as tall as his older sister already. As soon as the two children spot us, their eyes widen in curiosity.

'Sofia, Pedro, aquests són en Cameron i la Ruby. Són amics d'Anglaterra que es quedaran amb nosaltres aquesta nit,' Alejandro tells them.

'Sí, pare, ho sabem. La mare ja ens ho va explicar,' Sofia replies. I may not be able to understand what she's saying, but the tone is clearly recognisable as one that every little girl worldwide would use when explaining something to a particularly dim parent. It makes me smile. Pedro still says nothing, staring at us as if we were exotic creatures from another world.

'Are they speaking Catalan?' Cameron asks Alejandro.

'That's right. Most people in Barcelona speak both Spanish and Catalan. At work, I tend to speak Spanish, but we use Catalan at home.'

As we step into the cool hallway, the two children scamper ahead of us. The air is thick with the most delicious aromas and I breathe them in appreciatively. It seems ages ago that Cameron and I were enjoying lunch, and I realise that I'm ravenously hungry. Alejandro leads us straight through the house and out onto a terrace at the back, where a woman with a baby clamped to her hip is laying a table.

'*El meu amor*,' Alejandro says as he leans in to kiss her, before unexpectedly switching to English. 'This is Ruby and Cameron, who I told you about. Ruby, Cameron, this is my wife Gabriela.'

'I am very pleased to meet you,' Gabriela tells us, holding out her free hand. 'You are very welcome to our home.'

'Gabriela lived in the UK for a few years after finishing her studies,' Alejandro explains proudly, evidently clocking the look of surprise on our faces. 'She speaks better English than anyone I know.'

'That wouldn't be hard,' she retorts. 'Most of the people who come through your police station struggle to make themselves understood in our native tongues, let alone any other languages. Now, please relax. Dinner will be in an hour or so. Alejandro tells me you've had a difficult day, but I find this terrace is a good place just to sit and unwind.' She switches back to Catalan for what seems like a lively exchange with Alejandro, who is easing the cork out of a bottle of sparkling wine.

'Cava,' he says as he offers us each a glass. 'It's made locally and is among the best you'll taste anywhere.' He guides us to a couple of chairs that are positioned to take full advantage of the view over the valley beneath us.

'This place is incredible, Alejandro,' I tell him as I take a sip and enjoy the sensation of the bubbles dancing on my tongue.

'It is. Gabriela and I had a small flat in the city when we were first married, but our dream was always to move up here. When her grandfather died last year, he left us some money and we were able to buy this. It is so much better for the children; the air is clean up here and they have space to use their energy. Talking of children, I need to supervise their bath time. Are you OK here for a little while? If you need anything, just call.'

'We'll be more than OK, thank you, Alejandro,' I tell him.

'I love my flat in Margate, but this is next level,' I murmur to Cameron a while later as we sip our drinks. Every so often, Gabriela appears with a small plate of something and places it on the table between us. So far, we've had deliciously tender calamaris, patatas bravas, and spicy chorizo. Our protests that she doesn't need to spoil us have fallen on completely deaf ears. I have managed to prise the baby, who I've learned is called Felipe, off her, and he's currently sitting on my lap, staring at me in wonder with his enormous dark brown eyes.

'Mm,' he agrees. 'I know it's a pain to have missed the ship, but I kind of feel we've actually been lucky, in a funny way. Just think, we could be in the Nautilus lounge right now, watching Barry's latest crazy game. It doesn't really compare, does it.'

'Shit,' I say suddenly. 'I haven't told Sam what's happened. She'll be worried.'

'You can try sending her a message,' he offers. 'They might still be in range.'

'Doubtful, but there isn't really much else I can do.' I pull out my phone and start a WhatsApp.

> Hi Sam. Just to let you know Cameron and I missed the ship!! We're still in Barcelona, but we're going to catch a flight and meet up with you in Cannes tomorrow. Hope everything is OK your end. Rxx

I watch the ticks carefully, but there's only a single grey. The message hasn't got through.

'Is everything OK? Are you enjoying the view?' Alejandro asks as he joins us. Sofia and Pedro are with him, their wet hair slicked back.

'Yes. Ruby was just trying to send a message to her friend on the ship to let her know everything is OK, but I think they're out of range.'

Alejandro grins. 'Of cellphones, certainly. But they will have to work a lot harder to be out of range of Alejandro. What is your friend's name?'

'Sam. Sam Thorncroft,' I tell him. Once again he pulls out his phone to make a call. I don't understand any of it beyond the words *Spirit of Malmö*, *Sam Thorncroft* and *Ruby*, but he's evidently very pleased with himself by the time the call ends.

'My friend the harbourmaster has radioed your message to the ship's captain. They will leave a note outside your friend's cabin to let her know that all is well.'

'Thank you,' I tell him sincerely. 'You really have been our guardian angel today.'

'It is nothing,' he replies as he leans down to pick up Felipe, although his expression indicates that he's enjoying the compliment. 'Now, I think dinner is ready. Shall we sit at the table?'

Alejandro opens a bottle of red wine as Gabriela serves out the soup to start with. The children sit with us, Sofia and Pedro in chairs and little Felipe in a highchair, digging into their food as enthusiastically as we do.

'So what were you doing in the UK?' I ask Gabriela as Alejandro clears away the soup dishes and she starts to pass round plates of delicious-smelling stew.

'I worked as an au pair to begin with, but the hours were long and the pay not so good. So then I started doing translation work and tutoring, and that was much better. Eventually, however, I missed home. Your winters are so cold! So I came back to Barcelona, met Alejandro and…' She waves expressively.

'I was just starting out in the police,' Alejandro says, picking up the tale. 'We were called to a bar because some English tourists had had too much to drink and were being impolite. I walked in and saw Gabriela trying to talk them down in her perfect English. I knew straight away that I was in love, but she wasn't so easy to convince. I had to work very hard for a number of weeks before she would agree to go on a date with me.'

Gabriela smiles. 'I needed to know he was serious. A lot of boys, they only want one thing and I wasn't falling for that. What about you? How did the two of you meet?'

I freeze in panic; what to tell them? Thankfully, Cameron is ahead of me.

'We met on a cruise, actually,' he tells them. 'We were both part of a singles group, but we hit it off and here we are.'

'How lucky,' Gabriela observes. 'You seem like a good match, just like Alejandro and me.'

* * *

'That was very clever,' I say to Cameron a little later. We're sitting back out on the terrace sipping our coffees while Alejandro and Gabriela clear up and put the children to bed.

'I was pleased with it. Nothing there was a lie, but they obviously wanted us to be a couple, so I just shifted the timelines a bit to make it sound like we'd known each other longer than we have. You don't mind, do you?'

'Not at all. I couldn't work out what to tell them, so you came to my rescue.'

Despite the coffee, I can feel the events of the day creeping up on me as Alejandro and Gabriela rejoin us.

'Of course, you must be exhausted,' Gabriela remarks as I subtly try to stifle a yawn. 'Alejandro will show you where you are sleeping. I assume your toiletries are all still on the ship, so I've put out a few things, but if there's anything else you need, just tell me.'

'Thank you,' I reply gratefully as Cameron and I get up to follow Alejandro. 'Dinner was delicious, and I'm sorry for putting you to so much trouble.'

'Pah, it is nothing,' she says, laughing. 'It's always lovely to meet new people. Sleep well.'

I may be dog tired, but no sooner has Alejandro shown us to our room than my mind snaps back to full alert.

'Ah,' Cameron says as his eyes fall upon the bed.

'I'm not sure we thought this through,' I agree.

'I'll go and find Alejandro and ask whether there's somewhere else I can sleep,' he suggests.

'You can't do that. We've caused them enough hassle as it is.'

'I could sleep in the chair?'

'Yeah, and cripple yourself. No. I'm sure we can manage this. We're both grown-ups; let's just be mature about it.'

'It's not very big. I don't think there's room to put a pillow wall down the middle, even if there were enough pillows.'

'You'll just have to behave then, won't you?'

He yawns widely. 'I think you're quite safe. I'm so knackered I can barely keep upright, let alone try anything on.'

'Right then. I'm going in the bathroom to get changed. You can look away when I come out, and I'll do the same for you.'

Not only has Gabriela laid out toiletries, but there are two T-shirts on the bed, so I grab one and head into the bathroom. Cameron is sitting in the chair with his hands covering his eyes when I come out and slip under the duvet, and I make a point of facing the wall when he comes out. Nevertheless, I'm very conscious of him as he clambers into the bed behind me. It really isn't very big, so we end up sort of awkwardly spooned together and I'm surprised how much I enjoy the warm solidity of him pressing against my back once we've finished shifting around trying to get comfortable. However, despite the distraction of Cameron's body next to mine, it doesn't take long for the events of the day to catch up with me and I fall asleep quickly.

19

When I wake the following morning, I'm completely disorientated. Nothing makes sense, from the room I'm in, to the clothes I'm wearing and the fact that I'm not alone in the bed. It takes me a good few minutes to piece everything together. Cameron's arm is around my waist, but I can't really begrudge him that as this bed really is tight for a double. At least he isn't a snorer; his breathing is soft and even behind me. God, I hope I didn't snore. I surreptitiously raise my hand to my mouth to check whether I've drooled in my sleep, but there's no evidence.

I crane my neck so I can see the clock on the bedside table. Half past seven. Despite falling asleep quickly, it hasn't been the most successful night, and I stretch to try to get a little more comfortable. That's when I notice it and freeze. It may be a number of years since I've shared a bed with a man, but there's no doubt what the object pressing against my right buttock is. When I was going out with Olly, all those years ago, his idea of early-morning foreplay was often nothing more advanced than prodding me in the back with his erection, so I'm familiar with the sensation. I'm acutely embarrassed but also curious in equal measure. Does Cameron know he's doing it? Is it deliberate? What does it mean if it is? He doesn't seem the type to just shove his penis at you. I've read that men often have involuntary erections first thing. Is that it?

I hold my breath and listen, trying to work out if his deep breathing is because he's asleep or turned on. Of course, it's impossible to tell. What to do? If I move again, he might think I'm grinding into him and encouraging him, but I can't stay like this all morning. Although, maybe if I stay very, very still, it will go down. Just as that thought comes to me, Cameron groans and shifts, pressing his penis more firmly against my buttock. To give him his credit, it does feel like a fairly substantial penis from what I can sense, but I'm no closer to working out how to extricate myself from this situation. In the absence of anything else, I decide that humour is probably the best way to defuse this.

'Umm, Cameron?' I whisper.

No response.

'Cameron!' I hiss.

'Hmm?'

'Is that a gun in your pocket, or are you just pleased to see me?'

'What?'

So much for humour. 'There's something hard pressing against me, and I think it's you.'

'What do you— Oh, shit! I'm so sorry.' It may be a small bed, but Cameron has suddenly shot so far towards the other side of it that he's practically hanging over the side. 'It's, umm... I wasn't, umm...'

I roll over to face him. He's absolutely crimson with embarrassment and refusing to meet my eye.

'It's just a thing that sometimes happens to men,' he begins. 'I didn't mean anything by it, I promise.' He's actually managing to turn even redder, and I'm fighting the urge to laugh.

'Oh,' I tell him, trying to look stern. 'Well, now I don't know whether to be offended because you were assaulting me with your erection, or whether to be offended because it wasn't intentional.'

'Of course it wasn't intentional!' he moans. 'I mean, it's not that you're not attractive, it's just that... Oh, God. I'm making this worse, aren't I?'

'I tell you what. I'm going to get up and have a shower. Why don't you use the time to do whatever it is that you need to do with little Cameron there.'

'I can assure you I don't need to do anything,' he tells me strenuously.

'OK. I'll see you in a minute.'

As I head towards the bathroom, I glance back at him. His face is a picture of misery, and I suddenly feel sorry for him.

'Cameron,' I say.

'Mm-hm?'

'Look at me.'

He raises his eyes to meet mine and I'm suddenly aware that I'm standing in front of him wearing nothing but my knickers and a slightly too small T-shirt that my nipples are currently trying to break through. If little Cameron was reacting to me earlier, my current getup probably isn't going to help.

'It's fine,' I tell him, trying to style it out. 'In fact, I'm almost a little flattered. Don't sweat it, OK?'

Without waiting for an answer, I turn and flee into the bathroom.

* * *

'Did you sleep well?' Gabriela asks as she hands us cups of coffee a little while later. Alejandro has already left to drop Sofia at school on his way to work.

'Very well, thank you,' I lie politely. Cameron seems to be finding the contents of his coffee cup absolutely fascinating.

'Don't worry about him,' I assure Gabriela. 'He's always a bit moody in the mornings. I keep telling him he doesn't need to be *up* so early, especially on holiday, but he won't listen.'

I'm watching Cameron carefully and, to my amusement, he actually flinches when I say the word 'up'. Fun though it is to tease him, I am going to have to find a way to break through his embarrassment at some point, otherwise today is going to be a very difficult day.

'I have to drop Pedro at his preschool in a minute,' Gabriela informs us, totally oblivious to the atmosphere between Cameron and me. 'Feel free to relax here, and I'll take you to the airport when I get back. I know your flight isn't until this afternoon, but better to be early than late, yes?'

'Thank you. I'm sorry we're causing you so much trouble,' I tell her sincerely.

'Ah, it is nothing. It makes an otherwise ordinary day interesting,' she replies.

'Cameron, what do I have to do to cheer you up?' I ask when Gabriela has disappeared. 'You've got a face like a wet weekend.'

'I'm just so embarrassed,' he says. 'I feel like some kind of sex predator.'

'Listen,' I tell him robustly. 'I'm not going to lie, I was a little disconcerted when I woke up and found little Cameron prodding me in the back like that, but I'm sure you weren't trying anything on. I'm sorry. Maybe I shouldn't have said anything, but I was trying to make light of it. I know what it's like for you men. Sometimes little Cameron takes on a life of his own.'

'Can you please stop calling it that?'

'What?'

'Little Cameron.'

'What would you like me to call it then?'

'I'd prefer it if you never mentioned my penis ever again, if I'm honest, but the point is that I think giving your private parts names is weird.'

This is too good an opportunity to miss.

'Really?' I say, feigning surprise. 'I thought everybody did. My vagina is called Frou-Frou. Sam calls hers Tallulah.'

This, finally, seems to be the key to unlock him. 'You're kidding.'

'Why would I joke about something so personal?'

'Tallulah I kind of get, but Frou-Frou? You know that's the name of the horse in *The Aristocats*, don't you?'

'For a man, you seem to know your vintage Disney better than I'd expect.'

'I may have seen a few films in my time. I have an eight-year-old niece.'

I smile. 'That would explain it. Sometimes, when I watch Samson striding around as if he owns the place, it's almost like "Everybody Wants to Be a Cat" is playing in his head.'

'Best Disney song ever,' Cameron states firmly, and I'm glad to see that he's coming back out of himself. He's even smiling.

'I quite like "A Whole New World", from *Aladdin*,' I counter.

'Nah. Too patriarchal. Why does Jasmine need a man to show her the world? Call yourself a feminist?'

'Good point. There are a lot of good tunes in that film though.'

We're still happily arguing the merits of various Disney films and the songs in them when Gabriela reappears and, unsurprisingly, she has firm opinions of her own that carry us all the way to the airport. Cameron, I'm glad to see, is fully recovered and giving as good as he gets.

'Thank you so much, Gabriela. For everything.' I give her a massive hug as she drops us outside the terminal.

'Ah, it was a pleasure, and I got to use my English. Sometimes I worry that it will go rusty, like an old car. Come and see us again next time you're in Barcelona, won't you.'

I haven't got the heart to tell her that there's unlikely to be a next time, so I just squeeze her tighter and promise that we will.

* * *

Even though it's outside peak tourist season, the terminal building is heaving, and I'm very pleased that we don't have any baggage to check in, as the queues are enormous. We do cause a few eyebrows to be raised when we rock up at security without any hand luggage either but, after querying it, they seem to buy our story and let us through into the departure lounge. Although I scrubbed myself thoroughly in the shower this morning, and made liberal use of the deodorant that Gabriela had kindly put out, I feel very grimy in yesterday's clothes and underwear.

'I can't wait to get back to the ship,' I say to Cameron once we've settled ourselves at the gate.

'I know what you mean. With any luck, we'll have time for a shower and a change of clothes before whatever Barry has cooked up for this evening.'

'I'm also bursting to find out if Sam's ironed things out with Robin.'

'He seems like a really nice guy. What is her problem with him being a vicar, anyway?'

While we wait for the call to board the plane, I fill Cameron in on Sam's disastrous experience at the church we went to.

'Doesn't seem very Christian to me,' he observes. 'It's a long time since we did anything like that at school, but I'm sure there were warnings about not judging other people in case you were judged yourself, or something like that. Anyway, I'm sure Robin isn't like that. He doesn't come across as the judgemental type, does he?'

'No.'

We lapse into silence but, unlike this morning, it's comfortable. After a while, the plane begins to board for the short flight to Nice, and both Cameron and I breathe a sigh of relief when it takes off on time.

'I'm going to suggest we skip the sightseeing and get a taxi straight to the port when we arrive,' Cameron says a while later as the pilot switches on the fasten seat belt signs for our descent into Nice. 'I don't know about you, but I don't want to run the slightest risk of missing the ship again.'

'I agree. Do you know, I'm actually looking forward to seeing the Marco Polo group again.'

'Even Brad?'

'Oh, Brad's OK now that Gail's taming him.'

'Do you think they'll make it in the real world? I kind of want them to. Sam and Robin too.'

'You, my friend, are a hopeless romantic.'

'What's wrong with that?'

'Nothing, as long as you're prepared for endless disappointment.'

'Ouch. Are you sure nobody broke your heart?'

'Absolutely.'

'Something must have happened to make you so cynical.'

'I just watch what Sam's been through,' I tell him.

'Yes, but even you have to admit that Robin's probably a better calibre than the other guys you've told me about. Maybe this time…'

'Maybe,' I say, humouring him. 'It would be nice. I will admit that I struggle to picture her married to a vicar though. Even one as nice as Robin.'

* * *

If boarding the plane with no luggage was odd, disembarking is even stranger. While everyone else files off towards the baggage carousels, Cameron and I make straight for the exit and taxi rank. As we speed towards Cannes, I pull out my phone and disable flight mode, only to receive a message almost immediately from Sam.

> Hi, got your note via the captain. You must know some people in high places! Anyway, hope you've made it to Cannes OK. Just to let you know that they're not letting us go on shore yet because we're anchored outside the harbour and the sea is too rough for the tenders. They're going to try various different positions though, so hopefully it'll be sorted by the time you arrive. Looking forward to seeing you and hearing all about it. Sx

I've barely made it through that one when a second message pings in.

> Me again. Bad news I'm afraid. They can't find a way to position the ship so the tenders can get alongside. Captain has been on to say that they're going to weigh anchor as soon as they can get a pilot onboard and set off towards Livorno. Robin thinks you might be able to scrounge a lift with the pilot? Sx

My mood is plummeting as I show the messages to Cameron.

'Let's get to the harbour and see what's what before we lose hope,' he tells me, but I notice his smile has also disappeared and been replaced by a look of grim determination.

However, when we reach the harbour, we don't even need to speak to anyone to see that we're too late. The *Spirit of Malmö* is already a long way out to sea.

20

'*For fucking fuck's sake!*' I howl, unable to stop tears of frustration pouring down my cheeks as my lovely cabin, with its comfortable bed and hot shower, along with all my clothes and toiletries, heads for the horizon without me for the second day in a row.

'Hey, we've got this,' Cameron soothes as he wraps me in a hug. Although we've kissed, held hands and shared a bed, this is the first time he's hugged me and I press my face against his chest, breathing him in. Like me, he smells a little bit jaded and sweaty, but it's comforting nonetheless. I allow him to hold me until the tears subside.

'I think we know the drill by now, don't we,' he tells me when I eventually disengage from his embrace. 'Book hotel rooms, book transport, hope we catch the bloody ship tomorrow.'

'I'm also going to need a change of clothes,' I tell him. 'I think these ones could practically stand up by themselves.'

'Agreed. One thing at a time though.' He pulls out his phone and launches a hotel booking website. He takes his time scrolling through the options and fiddling with the filters before looking up at me with a frown.

'Bloody hell, Cannes is expensive,' he remarks. 'Most of the hotels are fully booked for tonight, and from the meagre pickings that are left, I can't find anything for less than two hundred euros, and that's room only. On top of that, there's only one hotel that has two rooms available and they're two-fifty each.'

He hands me the phone so I can look for myself, but he's right. I know we got lucky by staying with Alejandro and Gabriela for free last night, but this is starting to look like a very expensive diversion, given that we still need to eat, get clothes and toiletries, and find our way to meet the ship tomorrow. I hand the phone back.

'What do you want to do?' I ask. 'I'm not sure I want to sleep on the beach.'

'We'd probably get moved on anyway. I'm sure a place like Cannes has strict rules on stuff like that. I do have one suggestion, but you might not like it.'

'Go on.'

'We could share a room again. Not ideal, I know, but it halves the cost.'

'I don't know. I didn't get much sleep last night, and I'm not sure I fancy another early-morning wake-up call from little Cameron.'

'Please stop calling it that. To be fair, I think hotel beds are generally larger than the one we were in last night, so we shouldn't be, umm, pressed together in quite the same way.'

'Let me have another look.' I take the phone from him again and look through the rooms listed. All of them are doubles, but one has a super-king-sized bed. It's well over two hundred euros, but it does include breakfast, which is a plus.

'What about this one?' I ask him. 'Plenty of room for you to build a pillow wall to keep little Cameron in check.'

'You're enjoying winding me up, aren't you?'

'It passes the time.'

He sighs expressively. 'Right. I'm going to book this, OK?'

'Yup.'

Having done that, he turns his attention to the transport. Again, there's lots of scrolling and fiddling before he speaks again.

'This isn't much cop either,' he remarks. 'There aren't any direct flights to Pisa from Nice. We have to go via Paris.'

'Paris? That's miles in the wrong direction. Can't we go by train?'

'Nope. Apparently there's a big strike tomorrow, so nothing will be moving. I've looked at car hire too, but that's silly money. Flying is our only option, and the flights aren't cheap either, probably because everyone who would normally go by train is doing the same as us.'

I sigh. 'Just book it. I tell you, the bloody ship had better wait for us in Livorno. I can't afford to carry on at this rate.'

'At least it's stopping there for two nights. Gives us twice the chance of actually catching it.'

A few minutes pass while he navigates his way through the booking process. 'All done,' he announces as he shoves his phone back into his pocket. 'Let's find a taxi. I can feel the shower calling me.'

The hotel turns out to be on the other side of Cannes from the cruise port, so the taxi takes us along the coast and I study the view as we drive. After a short while, we come across a long sandy beach. Even though it's early evening, it's still busy with families and the after-work crowd. There are people playing beach volleyball, and the sea is full of bobbing heads.

'That looks amazing,' I sigh. 'I'd love a swim in the sea.'

'We could stop,' Cameron suggests.

'Nice thought, but I don't have my swimsuit with me. Do you?'

'No, but we could improvise. Just swim in your bra and pants.'

'Absolutely not. For a start, this is Cannes, and everyone else out there is looking effortlessly chic in swimsuits that probably cost a fortune, so I'm going to stick out like a sore thumb in my mismatched bra and pants. Second, I'm wearing white cotton knickers. What do you think happens to those when they get wet?'

'No idea.'

'They go pretty much transparent. I'll come out of the sea looking like I've been skinny dipping, and I don't even have a towel to wrap round me.'

'Hmm.' Cameron pulls out his phone again and fiddles with it for a couple of minutes, before leaning forward to speak to the driver.

'*Pardon monsieur, pouvons-nous aller à une autre destination s'il vous plaît?*'

'*Bien sûr, où aimeriez-vous aller?*'

'*La plage de la batterie.*'

The driver looks sceptical. '*Vraiment? Êtes-vous sûr?*'

'*Oui. Merci.*'

'Where are we going?' I ask Cameron as he settles back into the seat.

'It's a surprise. You'll see.'

After a short drive, the taxi pulls into a petrol station and I look at Cameron quizzically.

'*Par là, monsieur. En bas des marches,*' the taxi driver tells him, pointing at a set of steps on the other side of the road as Cameron pays the fare.

'What is this place?' I ask as we descend the steps and walk through a tunnel.

'It's a beach where nobody will worry about your mismatched underwear,' he tells me cryptically.

As we emerge from the tunnel and I glance around, the reality of what Cameron has done suddenly dawns on me. I'm reminded a little of one of those seal colonies that you see on nature documentaries, inasmuch as all the best sunbathing spots are occupied by basking bodies. The difference is that these bodies are both human and completely naked.

'Cameron,' I ask in a horrified whisper. 'Have you brought me to a nudist beach?'

'The only nudist beach in Cannes,' he tells me proudly. 'It was your remark about skinny dipping that gave me the idea.'

'I'm not taking my clothes off in front of you, and I'm certainly not taking them off in front of a bunch of strangers!'

'Nobody's forcing you to do anything, but if you fancy a dip in the sea, this is probably the only way.'

'I'm not that desperate. You can go if you want. I'll wait for you here.'

'Are you sure?'

'Yes. Thanks, but no thanks.'

He starts peeling off his clothes, placing them in a neat pile on the ground, before marching completely naked towards the water. I don't know what takes me aback more: Cameron's brazen self-confidence, or the complete lack of interest the other people on the beach take in him. I can't help watching as he walks into the sea, seemingly without a care in the world. Having felt how solid he is both at Alejandro's and when we hugged earlier, I'm not surprised to see that he's a very nice shape. His shoulders are broad, with just the right amount of muscle. The eye travels easily down his back to a pleasantly pert bum, under which his thigh muscles flex attractively as he wades deeper. Forcing myself to stop staring at him and glance around, it's like I've stepped into some alternate reality. The beachgoers are engaging in all the things you'd see on the main beach down the road. They're sunbathing, sitting under umbrellas reading, swimming in the sea, or chatting over a glass of wine. But none of them is wearing a stitch of clothing. It's a literal smorgasbord of human flesh. I sink onto the sand, overwhelmed.

'*Excusez-moi, mademoiselle.*' The voice comes from above me and I glance up, only to wish immediately that I hadn't. I'm literally face to face with a flaccid penis, surrounded by a few wisps of greying pubic hair. It's obviously spent a lot of time in the open air, as it's deeply tanned. I wrench my eyes upwards, past an equally tanned hairless pot belly that's shining in the sunlight like it's made of polished mahogany. I'm reminded momentarily of a Buddha statue before my gaze finally meets the face of the speaker. He's bald, probably in his early sixties, with an impressive grey moustache.

'*Si vous voulez rester ici, vous devez vous déshabiller,*' the man tells me.

'*Pardon. Je ne parle pas Français,*' I explain, dredging up my best schoolgirl French and silently cursing Cameron for both bringing me here and abandoning me.

'If you want to stay here, you have to take off your clothes,' the man says, switching seamlessly to accented English. 'It's the rules, I'm afraid.'

'Of course. I'm sorry,' I tell him as I feel the heat of embarrassment flooding across my chest and up my neck. What the hell am I going to do now? My initial hope that he'd wander off and leave me alone after delivering his message is dashed when he settles himself on a rock next to me.

'Your friend is enjoying the water,' he observes, pointing at Cameron, who is floating in the sea. If I were capable of projecting a death ray with my eyes, I'd be incinerating him right now. My new companion is looking at me quizzically, seemingly oblivious to the fact that I'm willing him with all my might to go away. Unfortunately, my powers of telepathy seem to be severely misfiring as, not only does he not get the message, but we're joined by an equally naked woman.

'*Salut, Philippe. Qui est ton ami?*' she says as he stands and embraces her warmly.

'*Je viens d'expliquer à cette jeune femme anglaise qu'elle doit se déshabiller si elle veut rester ici,*' he tells her.

'She isn't going to undress with you watching her,' the woman says with a laugh. 'Where are your manners?'

'You are right. My apologies. *A bientôt, Claudine.*' To my relief, Philippe gets up and wanders off.

'Is this your first time?' the woman I now know is called Claudine asks me. I'm trying hard to stay focused on her face, but I can't help taking in the rest of her. Her ample, deeply tanned breasts have no hint of a bikini line but, unlike Philippe, she's sporting an impressive bush of pubic hair.

'Yes. My friend brought me,' I tell her, pointing at Cameron, who is still floating happily in the sea. Maybe he'll get swept away by a freak wave, or eaten by a shark.

'There is nothing to be embarrassed or ashamed of,' she says. 'Come. Take off your clothes and join him in the sea. The water is the perfect temperature today. You will love it. It's easiest if you cover yourself with a towel to begin with. Do you have one?'

'No.'

'Follow me. I will lend you a towel. Bring your friend's clothes.' She takes me by the hand and leads me down the beach to a spot where an umbrella has been set up, with two chairs underneath and a cool box. One of the chairs is occupied by Philippe but, after the initial shock, seeing him again is less difficult. Claudine reaches into a bag and pulls out a beach towel.

'Put that around yourself while you undress. Then, when you're ready, I will count down and *voilà.*'

I'm still deeply uneasy, but something about Claudine's manner reassures me, and I wrap the towel around me as I wriggle out of my clothes, piling them neatly on the ground.

'Are you ready?' she asks.

'No,' I tell her honestly.

'Just go for it. Drop the towel. I promise you the world will not end. I will count down. *Trois, deux, un, allez!*'

I fix my eyes on her, trying desperately not to think about what I'm actually doing, as I tug the towel away from my body.

'There you are. That wasn't so difficult, was it?' she says encouragingly as I drop the towel on the ground. I daren't glance down; although the soft breeze playing on parts of my skin that never normally experience it is firing messages to my brain that I am, in fact, naked, I think visual confirmation of the fact would be too much.

'It is a nice sensation, hmm?' Claudine says. 'But you must be careful with the sun. You do not want to burn. Do you have lotion?'

'In my bag,' I tell her.

'It is evening now and the sun is *moins fort*, so you will be OK if you don't stay out for too long. Do you want to go and find your friend in the sea? The sensation of swimming without clothes is *incroyable*.'

I look around, expecting to see the eyes of everyone on me, but nobody is taking any notice at all. Nevertheless, the idea of walking past so many people to get to the sea is overwhelming. Claudine evidently senses my anxiety.

'Shall we go together?' she asks gently.

'Please.'

She takes my hand again and gently leads me down to the water's edge. I can't believe I'm doing this, and I'm tempted to drown Cameron as soon as I get within reach of him, but the murderous thoughts are extinguished as soon as the cool water envelops me. I've heard people waxing lyrical about how wonderful skinny dipping is, but this is my first experience of it. The sensation of the water brushing against my bare skin is both soothing and exhilarating at the same time.

'You like it?' Claudine asks.

'It's incredible,' I tell her as I start to giggle uncontrollably.

'What is so funny?'

'I was just thinking what my friend Sam would say if she could see me now.'

'She would think what a brave, confident young woman you are, I think.'

'I'm not so sure, Claudine. I think she'd probably have a fit.'

21

'You decided to join me then?' Cameron asks as I swim out towards him. Having guided me into the sea, Claudine has tactfully retreated and is sitting under her umbrella, chatting to Philippe. They look like an old, albeit naked, married couple, but I got the impression from the way they greeted each other that they were just friends. I wonder what the real story is there?

He's floating on his back, which I rather wish he wouldn't, as it's hard to ignore little Cameron bobbing in the water. I resolve to stay firmly boobs down. No point in giving him more of a view than he needs.

'Isn't the water amazing?' Cameron continues. 'Have you ever skinny dipped before?'

'No,' I admit. 'But then I've never been to a nudist beach before, either. What about you?'

'I will confess to skinny dipping once with Ellie, but it was night-time and there wasn't anyone else around. This is my first experience of a nudist beach though. Who was your friend?'

'Claudine. She came to my rescue after her pal Philippe told me off for wearing clothes.'

'Sorry. I thought you'd be OK where you were.'

'It's fine. I think I'd prefer it if you warned me in advance before pulling any more stunts like this, though.'

He smiles. 'You'd have said no if I'd told you.'

'Of course I would!'

'OK. Serious question. Now that you're here, do you honestly regret it?'

I consider his question for a moment before answering. Would I have willingly come to a nudist beach? Definitely not. Do I regret it though? I do feel weirdly elated, like I've confronted a taboo and overcome it. Sam will never believe I've done something like this either. Neither will Em or Jono, come to that. The more I think about it, the prouder I feel of myself.

'Do you know what? I don't,' I tell him. 'Although I am a little worried that something might swim up inside me. Does that happen, do you think?'

'I reckon Frou-Frou is safe,' he says with a smile, although it takes me a moment to work out what he's talking about.

'What about those fish that swim up your urine stream and latch on?' I persist.

'I think you only find them in the Amazon, not off the coast of Cannes. But, if you're worried about it, probably best not to pee.'

I quite fancy rolling onto my back and floating, like Cameron is, but I'm very conscious that that will give him a full-frontal view of me, and I'm not comfortable with that.

'Confession time,' Cameron says, as if picking up on my train of thought. 'I watched you walking into the sea, so there won't be any surprises if you want to turn over and float.'

'You know what you are? A dirty voyeur,' I tell him as I pluck up the courage and roll. I do feel very exposed, but it's a lot more comfortable.

'OK, I'll take that on one condition.'

'Which is?'

'You tell me, hand on heart, that you never so much as glanced at me.'

'I was anxious. I needed to know where you were.'

He laughs. 'Nice try.'

As we float together, my self-consciousness begins to ebb away and I focus on enjoying the water. It really is the perfect temperature, and crystal clear. After a while, Claudine gets up from her chair and wanders into the sea.

'Ça va?' she asks as she joins us.

'*Ça va bien. Merci, Claudine,*' I reply, stretching my schoolgirl French to its limits. 'This is Cameron, my friend. Cameron, Claudine.'

'*Enchanté.*' She nods at Cameron. 'Are you staying long in Cannes?'

'Just one night,' Cameron tells her. 'We're actually on a cruise and missed the ship.'

'Ah. *Quelle domage.* Tomorrow night we will be having a drinks party and barbecue on the beach. I was going to invite you. My friend Philippe is a butcher, and he cooks the meats perfectly.'

A mental image of Philippe barbequing sausages naked flits into my mind. It's not a nice picture and I push it out again as fast as I can.

'Forgive me,' Cameron asks. 'But isn't barbequing without clothes a little... dangerous?'

Claudine laughs. 'He wears an apron. What did you think? Anyway, we will miss you. Maybe you will come back one day?'

Cameron smiles. 'Maybe.'

After around half an hour of floating and swimming, I've had enough so I start to summon the courage for the walk from the shore to Claudine's umbrella and the safety of my clothes.

'I'm going in,' I tell Cameron.

'Good idea. I think I'm starting to burn a bit, so I'll come too.'

If walking into the sea with Claudine took courage, walking out of it with Cameron is in a different league. It's not just that he's a man, it's that I can't help surreptitiously checking him out, and it follows that he must be doing the same to me. I can feel myself blushing again. When we reach Claudine and Philippe, I quickly wrap myself in the beach towel, grateful for the covering. Cameron appears to have no such qualms and happily perches himself on a rock next to Philippe. Claudine reaches into her cool box and pulls out four bottles of beer, which she opens and passes round.

'You need to take the towel off,' she whispers with a smile as she hands me the bottle. 'You will dry better in the breeze, and Philippe will tell you off again if you don't. He's very strict about the rules.'

I peel the towel off reluctantly, earning myself a nod of approval from Philippe. I'm relieved to note that his glance is purely cursory before he turns back to continue talking to Cameron. To begin with, I feel acutely self-conscious, but after a few minutes I can feel myself relaxing. Claudine proves to be excellent company, chatting away happily about everything and nothing. As the sun starts to dip in the sky and the heat goes out of the day, we help Claudine and Philippe pack up, before clambering back into our clothes and heading back through the tunnel to the main road. Claudine is wearing a brightly patterned kaftan, and I'm struggling to reconcile clothed Philippe, looking smart in his dark blue shirt and light trousers, with the naked man who loomed over me earlier.

'Claudine?' I ask. 'I need to buy a change of clothes and some underwear, not too expensive. Where is a good place to go?'

'You need the *hypermarché*,' she tells me firmly. 'They have everything there. I will take you.'

'You don't need to do that. Just give us the address and we'll get a taxi.'

She laughs. 'How many taxis can you see around here? You will wait a long time, I think. It is no trouble. I will take you to get what you need and drop you afterwards at your hotel.'

Sensing that further resistance is futile, we follow her meekly to her car, an ancient and battle-scarred Renault. We say our goodbyes to Philippe before she whisks us at breakneck speed across town to an enormous supermarket, where Cameron and I manage to secure everything we need for a surprisingly reasonable price.

'I definitely need a shower now,' I tell Cameron as we make our way up to our room after saying goodbye to Claudine and checking in. The hotel is rather smarter than I'd realised, and I did detect a few curious glances from other, better dressed customers as we made our way across the lobby to the lifts.

'I know what you mean,' he agrees. 'I feel distinctly salt-encrusted, and I think I might have a touch of sunburn in, umm, unusual places.'

'Oh, no,' I say, giggling. 'Is little Cameron a bit singed round the edges?'

'Stop it,' he says, but he's smiling.

'Just know that I'm not rubbing cream into him. You're strictly on your own there.'

'Did I ask?'

'No. Just setting the boundaries, that's all.'

'You're a bit pink yourself,' he observes. 'I think the sun was a little stronger than we realised.'

The room, when we reach it, is large and dominated by the enormous bed. Cameron sprawls on it as I unpack my shopping and head for the bathroom, where I discover a walk-in shower big enough for both of us, not that we'll be testing that out. I will admit to having enjoyed looking at Cameron naked, but that's as far as it's going to go. I step under the rainfall head, surprised by how much my skin stings under the warm water. Having washed my hair and rinsed away every remnant of sweat and salt, I wrap myself in one of the huge white towels the hotel has provided. It's only when I wipe away the steam from one of the mirrors and see myself that I gasp in horror. My face and shoulders are bright pink. I carefully peel away the towel to reveal a similar story for the rest of me. Shit. Never mind all-over tan, I have all-over sunburn. Thankfully, we did buy a bottle of aftersun lotion at Claudine's suggestion, but it's in the other room.

'Bloody hell,' Cameron observes when I come out of the bathroom. 'Is that...?'

'Yup. The same all over. And no, I don't need your help rubbing cream into it.'

He laughs. 'I wasn't offering. Although you might need me to do your back.'

'OK. I'll take you up on that. You'd better get in the shower yourself and then we'll know what we're dealing with.'

When he emerges a while later, also wrapped in a towel, it's clear that his extra time in the sea has come at a price, as he's even redder than me.

'Right. Take the towel off and come and lie down on your front,' I command him, reaching for the bottle of aftersun lotion. When he drops the towel, my eyes fall to his manhood and I can't help laughing.

'What on earth have you done to poor little Cameron?' I ask. 'He looks like a frankfurter.'

'Perhaps I should have spent less time floating on my back,' he admits.

'I did tell you.'

'That wasn't about sunburn. You said he was distracting you.'

'Yeah, well you'd better keep him covered up once you've treated him. You could use him as a beacon to guide shipping looking like that. Come on. Lie down.' I pat the bed next to me and he carefully lowers himself onto it.

'This will feel cold,' I tell him as I squeeze some lotion onto his back and he flinches. I carefully move round so I'm straddling his naked buttocks and begin to massage it into his skin. I can feel the heat coming off him through my thighs.

'You are seriously hot,' I tell him.

'Why, thank you,' he says, laughing.

'I meant hot temperature hot,' I clarify as I squeeze a little more lotion out of the bottle and start to work it into his skin. His muscles are firm underneath my hands, and I'm totally unprepared for the effect massaging him is having on me. As I work down his back towards his buttocks, I'm starting to feel distinctly flustered. It's a long time since I've touched a man like this, and it's doing things to me.

'I'm going to do your bum and the backs of your legs, OK?' I tell him as I shuffle down, being careful to tuck a fold of towel between my legs to prevent me coming into direct contact with him. I don't think I'd be able to cope with the sensation of that at the moment.

'Yes, fine.'

If massaging Cameron's back affected me, rubbing the lotion into his buttocks is far worse. As I run my hands over them, I have to reluctantly admit to myself that I'm actually quite turned on. I shake my head, trying to dispel the feeling and regain some control before hastily moving on to the backs of his thighs and calves.

'You're done,' I tell him hurriedly, clambering off before I do or say something I'll regret. I wonder if he felt it too. He certainly seems in no hurry to roll over. Is it wrong that part of me hopes little Cameron is giving him trouble?

'Thank you. That feels miles better already,' he murmurs, and I listen carefully to his tone of voice to try to detect if he feels anywhere near as hot and bothered as I do.

'Are you OK there?' I ask him after a minute or so.

'Yes, absolutely. Right. Towel off and lie on your front. It's my turn.'

Oh, shit.

22

I have no idea how I got through Cameron's massage without jumping on him, but I just about managed to maintain my composure, thank goodness. The downside is that I had an incredibly filthy dream about him and woke this morning still feeling distinctly flustered. Thankfully, the bed was wide enough that there was no possibility of a repeat of erection-gate, as I don't think I could have been held responsible for my actions. One thing is in no doubt: I'm looking at Cameron in a totally different light today. Despite my best efforts, however, I can't work out whether he feels it too; if he does, he's doing a good job of concealing it. It's probably for the best. This is a temporary hormonal setback, nothing more. If I'd given in to temptation, it would have undoubtedly been fun in the moment, but it would also have led to a morning of incredible awkwardness and regret. I like him. I fancy him even. But I can't cope with the mess of what that would mean in reality if we acted on it.

We're now back at the airport, waiting to catch our flight to Paris. We're still pink, but the lotion has done a good job of soothing the worst of the sunburn, and I'm feeling much more human, having had a long shower and dressed in clean clothes this morning. I'm just about to switch my phone to flight mode when it pings with a message. It's from Sam, and my heart sinks.

If she's going to tell me something's gone wrong and they're not docking in Florence, I might react badly.

> GOOD NEWS! We're docked in Livorno, and we're here for two nights so you've got plenty of time to make it here. Robin and I are off to visit Florence today, but really hoping we'll see you later. Sx.

The relief is intense as I turn the phone and show Cameron the message. 'All we need now is for the flights to behave and we're home and dry,' I tell him.

'Don't jinx it,' he warns me. 'Bad luck comes in threes, remember, and we've only had two doses so far.'

'You're a barrel of joy this morning,' I observe. 'Did you get out of bed on the wrong side?'

'Sorry, I didn't mean to be negative.'

'Yeah, well, I'll be blaming you if we get stuck in Paris.'

'There are worse places to be stuck,' he remarks.

'Paris is probably even more expensive than Cannes,' I retort. 'Not being funny, but I have a fully paid-for cabin that I'd like to get some value for money out of.'

'It has been an adventure though, hasn't it? Can you believe we've only been away from the ship for two nights?'

'Is that really all? So much has happened that I can't believe it was only the day before yesterday that my phone was stolen in Barcelona.'

'I know it's been a faff, but we haven't actually missed out on anything, have we? In fact, we've done better because we got to see some of Cannes, which nobody on the ship did. Do you think you'll keep in touch with Claudine?'

'I don't know. She wasn't going to let me go without getting my number but what have we actually got in common?'

'Who knows, when you're a fully-fledged member of the nudist community in the UK, you might want to invite her and Philippe over.'

'That's not going to happen. It was strictly a one-off, under duress.'

'If you say so.'

Thankfully, further debate on the subject is prevented by the announcement that the flight is ready to board. Annoyingly, we had to leave the toiletries behind at the hotel as they wouldn't have been allowed in the cabin, so our hand luggage consists of a single carrier bag with a few clothes in it. On the plus side, this allows us to sit back and enjoy the spectacle of the other passengers, most of whom are trailing wheelie cases, jostling for position so they can get on first and secure the all-important overhead locker space. By the time we wander down the jetway to the aircraft, pretty much everyone else has boarded and there's carnage as the cabin crew try to explain to the unlucky passengers who weren't quick enough that their bags will have to go in the hold.

'But I've *paid* to have bloody hand luggage,' one particularly irate English-sounding man is practically yelling at a stewardess. 'It's my *right* to have my bag with me.'

'Uh-oh,' I murmur to Cameron. 'Angry Brit alert. Why is it always us?'

'*Monsieur*,' the stewardess explains, remarkably patiently in my opinion, as the rest of the cabin goes quiet to listen. 'The aircraft is full. There is nowhere for your bag to go. Either you can let me put it in the hold, or you can get off and try a later flight. Shouting at me is not going to change anything.'

'This is an absolute joke,' he rants, unmollified. 'That man there had two bags. Why aren't you getting him to put one of his in the hold?'

'Because he has one in the locker and one under the chair in front of him. He's not taking any more locker space than anyone else.'

'For fuck's sake. This is totally ridiculous. I demand you find me a space for my bag.'

'There is space. In the hold.'

'I don't want it in the fucking hold. I've got meetings when I get to the other end. I haven't got time to wait around for your lazy-arsed baggage handlers to come off whatever strike they're currently on and load it onto the wrong sodding carousel, like they always do. And that's assuming the useless bastards haven't lost it first. I've specifically paid to have hand luggage, and it's not my fault your aircraft doesn't have enough storage. Piss off and find me a solution.'

'*Certainement, monsieur*,' the stewardess tells him before marching up to the front of the plane, where we all watch agog as she engages in conversation with one of her colleagues. A few moments later, a stern-faced woman wearing a badge identifying her as the cabin manager approaches the man.

'*Monsieur*,' she begins in a steely tone of voice. 'My colleague informs me that you have been abusive to her. I must ask you to leave the aircraft at once. We do not tolerate this behaviour.'

'I haven't been bloody abusive,' the man retorts, turning an even darker shade of purple. 'I merely explained to her that I've paid to have hand baggage, and therefore it's the airline's responsibility to find space for it.'

'*Monsieur*,' she repeats in an even more dangerous tone. 'You have reduced one of my staff to tears. I have no interest in what you believe to be your rights, and you are welcome to take that up with the airline once you have disembarked. I do, however, have a great deal of interest in the wellbeing of my crew, who are responsible for the safety of everyone on board during this flight. I cannot and will not allow them to be subjected to abuse. I will therefore ask you once more to leave the aircraft immediately, taking your belongings with you.'

'Yeah, well, good luck with that, darlin',' the man says, adopting a mutinous tone. 'I'm not going anywhere.'

'So, just to be clear. You are refusing to disembark, yes?'

'I haven't done anything wrong.'

'I see.' Again, we all watch as she marches up the aisle and disappears onto the flight deck. Moments later, the captain's voice comes over the intercom.

'Ladies and gentlemen, I'm sorry to inform you that there will be a short delay to our departure this morning. My cabin manager has explained to me that we have an abusive passenger on board who is refusing to disembark. I've spoken to our ground crew and we're just waiting for the police to come and remove him. As soon as that's done we'll close the doors and be on our way.'

'He'd better not make us miss our connection,' I say to Cameron. Entertaining as the exchanges have been, the seriousness of the situation is now becoming clear.

'What did I tell you about bad luck coming in threes?'

'Stop it.'

It takes around ten minutes for the gendarmes to arrive. There's palpable tension on the plane as the cabin manager points the man out to them and they advance down the aisle.

'Please come with us, *monsieur*,' one of them says to the man.

'Why? What have I done?'

'We will discuss that in the terminal building once you have disembarked.'

'I'm not going anywhere.'

'*Monsieur*. Either you come with us or we will remove you by force.'

The man sits there for a moment, evidently considering his options, before yanking off his seatbelt and getting up.

'Fine,' he says furiously, grabbing his bag and setting off up the aisle with the gendarmes behind him. He's just by the door when he suddenly turns.

'This is a *joke fucking airline*,' he yells loudly enough that the whole cabin can hear. 'I'm *never* flying with you bastards again, and I'm going to tell everyone I know not to fly with you either. You're fucking *scammers*.'

As the gendarmes bundle him off, the cabin manager gives a small farewell wave, and a ripple of relieved laughter runs down the cabin. The main door is closed and, to my relief, the pushback starts very soon after that.

'We're half an hour behind schedule,' I murmur to Cameron as we finally climb into the air. 'Are we going to have enough time?'

'It's going to be tight. We might need to run.'

'I'll bloody sprint if I have to.'

* * *

In the end, the captain managed to make up a bit of time, even though it was a short flight, so we were able to transfer to our connecting flight without breaking into anything more than a brisk walk.

'We've bloody done it!' I say to Cameron as we touch down in Pisa late that afternoon. 'All we need now is a taxi, and we're back in business.'

'I don't know whether to be pleased that we've made it or miffed that you didn't fancy spending a night in Paris with me,' he says with a smile.

'Another time, perhaps,' I tell him with a grin.

'I'll hold you to that.'

As the taxi makes its way towards the port, Cameron's words are echoing around my head. Did he mean what he said? Is he expecting us to actually schedule a whole trip to Paris, just the two of us? I mean, I like him and everything, and I'd like us to keep in touch after the cruise, but a weekend away in the self-proclaimed 'city of love' seems a bit intense. A scenario forms in my mind, and I let it play. Cameron and I are in a hotel room very similar to the one we stayed in last night, except we're in Paris, obviously. I'm lying face down on the bed and he's massaging my back, my buttocks, as well as the backs of my thighs and calves. I close my eyes, remembering the sensations from last night and feeling myself becoming aroused again. However, the fantasy isn't finished with me. With a sigh of pleasure, I roll over and he begins to massage my shoulders, working down to my breasts, lowering his head to kiss them...

'We're here,' he announces, puncturing the daydream and causing me to snap open my eyes. Although the fantasy was extremely pleasant, the reality of seeing the *Spirit of Malmö* up close in the flesh again is even better.

'I can't believe it,' I murmur as we pass through security and walk up the airbridge. 'We've made it.'

'Yup. I don't know about you, but I'm going to have a long shower and then head up to the pool for a well-earned drink.'

'I think I'll join you. For the drink, I mean. Not the shower, obviously.'

'Obviously,' he agrees, looking at me quizzically. 'Are you all right, Ruby?'

'Yes, fine. Just, umm, overcome by finally being back on board. See you shortly.'

I turn and flee in the direction of my cabin, blushing furiously. The idea of sharing a shower with Cameron was way more attractive than it had any right to be. I need to get this situation under control, and fast.

23

'Oh, thank God. You made it!' Before I even have a chance to put down my drink, Sam has sprinted over to my sun lounger and enveloped me in a massive hug. 'I've been so worried,' she murmurs into my hair, holding me so tightly it's actually a bit of a struggle to breathe.

'Relax,' I tell her with a smile. 'We're absolutely fine.'

'I've been such a terrible friend,' she continues, ignoring me. 'I dragged you onto this cruise, then abandoned you before leaving you to fend for yourself in a foreign country. I'm so, so sorry, Ruby. How can I make it up to you?'

I gently detach myself so I can look her in the eyes. She does look genuinely contrite and, for a moment, I'm tempted to milk the situation a little, but I can't do that to her.

'I wasn't left to fend for myself,' I tell her gently. 'Cameron was there. And, although I wouldn't have chosen things to turn out the way they did, we have had quite an adventure.'

'Of course he was.' Sam turns to Cameron, looking at him as if he's some kind of comic book hero. 'Thank you so much for looking after Ruby, Cameron.'

Cameron smiles. 'We looked after each other,' he says diplomatically.

'That isn't strictly true,' I correct him. 'It was Cameron who got the chief of police on side in Barcelona, and he's taken care of all the arrangements since, some of which were more surprising than others.' I smile at him and he grins back. He knows exactly what I'm talking about, and I'm enjoying the connection between us.

'Hey, guys, great to see you back!' The American accent is familiar, and I look up to see Brad and Gail coming over from the bar. 'You gave us all quite the fright. Barry will be particularly pleased to see you. I don't think he's ever lost a couple before, and he hasn't really known what to do with himself.'

'Barry's going to have to wait in line,' Sam tells him. 'Cameron, is it OK if I borrow Ruby for a while?'

'Umm, I don't think you need my permission, Sam. It's up to Ruby.'

I'm torn. On one hand, I'd quite like to stay here with Cameron, who's frankly been a much better friend to me on this cruise than Sam has. I'm sure Brad and Gail are going to want a blow-by-blow account as well, and part of me feels it would be a lot easier if we stuck together during this phase, so we can limit the number of times we have to tell the story. On the other hand, I can tell I'm not going to get any peace until I've given Sam what she wants.

'Will you be OK?' I ask Cameron.

'I'll be fine,' he says with a laugh. 'Go.'

Sam doesn't need telling twice and practically drags me to my cabin, closing the door firmly behind us.

'Start from the beginning and don't leave out a single detail,' she commands.

She listens open mouthed as I tell her about my phone being stolen and Cameron using his police ID to jump the queue at the police station.

'Don't you think that's a little suss?' she asks when I explain how Alejandro got my phone back. 'I mean, if this guy is in the habit of stealing from tourists, he should be in jail, shouldn't he? Sounds like this Alejandro guy is in cahoots.'

'I don't think so,' I tell her. 'What's in it for him, for starters? He seemed genuinely concerned for the welfare of the boy and his mother. Anyway, he couldn't do enough for us, even insisting we stayed the night with him and his family.'

Sam looks horrified. 'I'm sorry. You've only known this guy for five minutes and you *stayed the night* with him? He could have been a kidnapper!'

'Again, unlikely. One, he was the chief of police—'

'That could have been a fake. I'm still not ruling out him being in cahoots with the phone thieves.'

'Hard to pull off, given that we literally met him in his office, in the police station, and all the other people there seemed to know who he was. And two, before you interrupted, what would he gain by kidnapping us? We're hardly ransom material.'

'Hmm. OK, maybe he's legit. I still think it's risky though. Didn't your mother ever warn you about going off with strangers?'

'Referring you back to the part where he's the chief of police. Anyway, we met his wife and children, had a lovely meal and then stayed in their spare room. She took us to the airport the next morning. They were all really nice, actually. You wouldn't get hospitality like that in England. It was quite shaming in a way.'

'Whoa, back up.'

I sigh. 'What now? Are you going to suggest that Gabriela, his wife, was also some kind of master criminal? I know, maybe she was smuggling drugs in her baby's nappy. Or she was going to use us as drug mules, before she realised that we didn't have any luggage to conceal the gear in. Or, just possibly, she was also a nice person who took pity on a couple of strangers like her husband did.'

Sam flaps her hand dismissively. 'No, I'm sure she was lovely. I'm more interested in the spare room.'

'Why? It was perfectly ordinary.'

'And you both slept in there? I take it he was on a couch, or the floor or something.'

'No. We shared the bed. We are grown-ups.'

'You shared a bed. With Cameron,' she repeats slowly.

'Nothing happened.' I've decided not to tell her about erection-gate.

'Mm-hm. It's still a big thing. When was the last time you shared a bed with a guy?'

'Move on, Sam. There's nothing to see here.'

'Fine. So you platonically shared a bed with Cameron and then this lovely lady, who isn't a criminal and definitely didn't want to use the two of you as drugs mules, drove you to the airport. Then what?'

'Then we flew to Nice and got a taxi to Cannes, just in time to see the ship leaving without us for the second time.'

'Didn't you get my message?'

'Yes, but we were already on our way, so it made sense to continue to the port and see if anything could be done.'

'And did you pick up any random strangers to spend the night with?'

'We did meet some people, but we stayed in a hotel.'

'Separate rooms or same room?'

'You're getting a bit one-tracked here, Sam. Same room, if you must know. It was cheaper.'

'And the people you met?'

I bite my lip. Do I tell her about the nudist beach or not? At the time, I was certain I was going to tell her, because it's the last thing she'd have thought me capable of and I wanted to see her face. Now, with her trying to tease out a sexualised interpretation of my every move, I'm not so sure. And we haven't even got to the aftersun lotion story yet, which I would actually appreciate her view on. After hesitating for a moment, I decide to take the plunge and fill her in. To my delight, the expression on her face makes it completely worth it.

'No!' she exclaims when I've told her all about meeting Philippe and Claudine, and my skinny dip in the sea.

'What are you doing?' I ask as she begins rummaging through the pillows on the bed.

'I'm looking for my friend Ruby. It's clear that you're some kind of impostor.'

'Knock it off,' I say, laughing.

'Seriously, though. Skinny dipping? Prancing round in the nude with people you've only just met?'

'I can assure you there wasn't any prancing. We had a swim, we sat and chatted, and we got horribly sunburned.' I pull down my top a little to show her.

'Ouch.'

'Yeah.' I steel myself and prepare to tell her the bit of the story that I know is going to send her off the deep end. 'And this is where things got a bit weird. I'd value your opinion, actually.'

I can see her mentally shifting gear into serious mode. 'OK. I'm listening,' she says.

'So, like I said, we got burned.'

'Yes, I can see that.'

'When we got back to the hotel, we doused ourselves with aftersun lotion.'

'Sensible. I'd have done the same.'

'I offered to do Cameron's back, so he lay face down on the bed and I started rubbing the ointment into him. I, umm...'

'Yes?'

'I liked it. Rubbing the ointment.'

She narrows her eyes. 'Did you like it, or did you *like* it?'

'I *liked* it. And then, when he started rubbing the ointment into me... Dear God.'

'You *liked* that too.'

'It was all I could do not to raise my hips off the bed and offer myself to him.'

'So why didn't you?'

'I'm sorry?'

'You were obviously feeling it, and I'm going to hazard a guess and say he was too. Why not go with the flow?'

'You have no idea how tempting that idea was in the moment, but I had just enough presence of mind to realise that it would have complicated everything massively.'

'Not necessarily. As long as you were both clear that it was a one-night stand, no harm would have been done.'

'I can see that, but I'm not a one-night stand person, Sam, and I'm pretty sure Cameron isn't either.'

'He's a man, and there's one thing all men have in common. When they get an erection, all the blood from their brain is redirected to their penis. They completely lose the power of rational thought.'

'All the more reason not to get carried away. Thinking of which, how's Robin?'

'He's OK. Stop trying to change the subject. What are you going to do about this thing between you and Cameron?'

'I'm not sure I'd call it a thing, and I'm certainly not going to do anything about it. He's a friend, no more.'

'Do you fancy him?'

'He's good looking.'

'That's not what I asked. I've fancied men who looked like the inside of a bin in my time. The two things don't necessarily correlate.'

'Fine. I fancy him, but I'm still not going to do anything about it.'

She studies me for what feels like an age, and I can feel the heat spreading across my chest and up my neck as she gazes at me.

'OK,' she says eventually. 'I don't get it, but it's your choice.'

'That's it? No shining a light in my face and acting like the Spanish Inquisition?'

'I know you, remember? I've pushed as far as I can and I can see you're shutting down.'

I sigh with relief. 'Tell me about Robin.' Although I wanted her opinion, she hasn't said the things I wanted to hear, so distracting her will hopefully get me off the hook.

'What do you want to know? We're in a good place. He's invited me to stay for the weekend at the end of the month.'

Now it's my turn to let my jaw drop. 'So you're taking it into the real world? What about him being a vicar?'

'It's not ideal, but I get why he didn't tell me to begin with. If I'd known he was a vicar from the outset, I wouldn't have gone anywhere near him, and I'd have missed out on getting to know what a wonderful, funny and kind person he is. The vicar thing is just something we have to work around.'

'What about the whole "no sex before marriage" gig? How are you going to cope with that?'

She smiles. 'Without going into too much detail, it turns out there's quite a lot you can do without actually having sex. It's surprisingly fulfilling. I don't think either of us feels short changed at the moment.' She lowers her voice. 'Truth be told, I've had more orgasms with Robin in the last couple of days than I've had with anyone before.'

'Is that allowed?'

'It's probably not strictly in the spirit of the law, but no penetration is taking place. Well, not with a penis, anyway.'

'What if you get carried away?'

'Robin's very matter-of-fact about that. His view is that he'd prefer us not to have actual sex before we get married, but he's also honest about the fact that he's a man and not a virgin. He had girlfriends before he felt the call to ordination, so this isn't his first rodeo. We've agreed to take joint responsibility to try not to let it happen, but not to beat ourselves up if it does.'

'Wait. You're talking about marriage already?'

She laughs. 'Only as a construct. Don't worry, I haven't hurled myself off the deep end just yet. Anyway, the good news for you is that I've blown him out for tomorrow so I can spend the day with you, just the two of us, like we were supposed to before I turned into a selfish cow.'

'You're not a selfish cow. You just fall hard when you fall.'

She smiles. 'Thank you, but I think this holiday has shown me that I kind of am. However, I'm resolved to do better, so where shall we go? What does it say in your little book of plans?'

I smile at her, but the truth is that I'm conflicted. I was expecting to spend the day with Cameron tomorrow, but I'm not sure how to tell her that without sounding ungrateful. Turning down Robin would have been a big thing for her.

'What?' she asks, frowning.

'Sorry?'

'Something's off. Are you still mad at me?'

'Not at all. It's just...'

Her face clears. 'You want to spend the day with Cameron, the guy you're secretly desperate to hump but are determined to be just friends with.'

'Do you mind?'

She laughs. 'Not at all. Can I make one request though?'

'Of course.' At the moment, I'd happily give her anything for being so understanding.

'Can Robin and I tag along?'

'Hmm. Can I interrogate him about his intentions towards my best friend?'

'If you must.'

I grin. 'Then you'd be most welcome.'

24

Brad wasn't wrong; you'd think we were risen from the dead, the way Barry carried on when Cameron and I strolled into the Nautilus lounge last night. Thankfully, he was distracted by two more couples taking advantage of the fact that it was the penultimate night of the cruise to swap their badges for red ones.

'I love each and every one of you so much,' Barry had gushed. 'I've never had so many new couples on a cruise. I expect invitations to all your weddings, do you understand? My contact details are in your packs.'

Sam, Robin, Cameron and I had grabbed a table together for dinner and, after a certain amount of negotiation, we agreed that we'd join the organised tour to Pisa today. I was a little disappointed to begin with because I was looking forward to seeing Florence and visiting the Uffizi gallery. Although Sam and Robin had said they were quite happy to spend another day in Florence, it seemed a waste of their time, and the fact that the Uffizi was sold out when I checked online sealed the deal.

'Did you know it's not just the tower that's leaning in Pisa?' Sam asks, her nose in a guidebook as the bus makes its way towards the city. 'According to this, both the cathedral and the baptistery are also sinking.'

'What's a baptistery?' I ask.

'They generally date from the early church, when lots of adults wanted to be baptised into the rapidly growing Christian faith,' Robin explains. 'You'd often have an area where people would make their vows, before being led into the central chamber where they'd undergo full immersion baptism. Sometimes, baptisteries would be incorporated in the main church building, but they were often separate structures, like the one in Pisa.'

'Who needs a guidebook when I have you?' Sam remarks.

'It is kind of my area of expertise,' Robin replies with a smile.

'Of course it is.' She pats his knee and leans across to give him a kiss. Normally, a public display of affection like this would make me slightly uncomfortable, but they seem totally at ease with each other, and she's not simpering in the irritating way she was the last time we saw them together. I have tried to imagine him wearing a clerical shirt and a dog collar, but I can't see it.

'Are you OK to chat to Sam for a bit today?' I ask Cameron quietly. 'I think things between her and Robin might be getting serious, so I'd quite like to find out a bit more about him.'

'Are you sure that's a good idea?' He looks dubious. 'She might not thank you if she thinks you're sticking your nose in.'

I smile. 'Let's put that to the test, shall we?' I turn to Sam. 'Sam, you don't mind if I steal Robin for a chat, do you?'

'Knock yourself out,' she replies. 'Of course, that means I'll have to entertain Cameron. How do you feel about that?'

'I have no secrets,' I tell her before turning to Cameron and whispering, 'Don't tell her anything.'

'I'm not sure there's much to tell that she doesn't know already,' he murmurs back.

'Just be careful, that's all. Sam's a Rottweiler if she thinks there's hidden information.'

He laughs. 'Oh, and you're a pussy cat, I suppose. Robin's not about to be grilled to within an inch of his life at all.'

'I just want to check he's on the same page as Sam, that's all.'

To his credit, Robin seems completely relaxed as I fall into step next to him. Sam and Cameron are ahead of us and, from what I can see, their conversation is flowing naturally. I'm slightly anxious, knowing that they're probably talking about me, but I make a conscious effort to focus on Robin.

'It sounds like you and Sam are serious about each other,' I begin.

'I hope so,' he replies. 'I'll confess that I didn't have particularly high hopes of meeting a match when I was persuaded to sign up for the cruise, but she and I just seemed to click from the start.'

'You know she's not churchy though, don't you? How do you see that working out?'

He smiles. 'That's one of the things I like most about her. You probably think I should be on the lookout for a clichéd vicar's wife, don't you? Someone a bit blousy, who's an expert baker and feels her ministry is serving cups of coffee and running kids' clubs.'

'That does seem a more natural fit,' I admit.

'Don't get me wrong,' he continues. 'Many of my colleagues are married to people exactly like that, and they're lovely, but I'd feel stifled. Being a vicar is intense; it's not like your average nine-to-five job.'

'Don't you only work on Sundays?'

He laughs. 'I wish. It's a six-day-a-week job and, if some of my parishioners had their way, I wouldn't get a day off at all. I've got three parishes, which means three of every type of meeting on top of all the pastoral visiting and occasional offices.'

'Occasional offices?'

'Sorry, church speak. Weddings, baptisms, funerals. Any service that falls outside the regular schedule, basically. The point is that it's full-on.'

'OK, but surely a churchy wife would be an asset in that scenario? I'm not marrying you and Sam off, don't worry. I'm just pursuing this to its logical conclusion.'

'I get where you're coming from, but if my wife was churchy as well, we'd be at risk of the church dominating every aspect of our lives. The last thing I want is to spend my precious downtime talking about the latest scandal in the flower arranging group, or whatever.'

'Sam's not a bad flower arranger.'

'Yes, but she also has what I would describe as a healthy fuck-offness to her. She doesn't stand for any shit, and that's incredibly attractive. Let me give you a scenario, and you can tell me how Sam would react.'

'OK.'

'I come home from a meeting of the church leadership team. Someone's made an anonymous complaint about something I've said in a sermon.'

'Does that happen?'

'Oh, yes. Anonymous complaints are a church speciality. So a traditional wife would probably trot out something Biblical about turning the other cheek. What do you think Sam would say?'

'She'd say that someone who wasn't prepared to put their name to a complaint isn't worth the time of day and you should tell them to fuck off.'

'Exactly. OK, here's another one for you. It's my day off, but I'm mulling a tricky parish situation.'

'She'd probably let you discuss it, give you a robust assessment and then expect you to move on. If that didn't work, she'd probably get naked to distract you.'

He laughs. 'I'll have to remember that. Forget the flowers and chocolates. If I want to get Sam naked, hit her with a tricky parishioner. The point is that someone like Sam would help me to stay balanced. I don't want the church to dominate my marriage; it already has the rest of my life.'

I turn and study him. 'OK, I get why she'd be good for you. Why would you be good for her?'

'Ooh. Tough question, and one she's probably better placed to answer than me. I like to hope, to use her words, that I'm not a dickhead at least. I'd do whatever I could to make her happy, does that count?'

'I don't think you're a dickhead,' I agree, 'and I don't think anyone could ask for more than someone who wants them to be happy. In fact, I think you'll do very well, Robin.'

'So I passed the test?'

'With flying colours, not that it matters.'

'It does matter. You're Sam's best friend, so it would be awkward if you didn't like me.'

'Trust me, my opinion carried absolutely no weight when it came to her previous boyfriends. Thinking of which, how do you feel about the fact that she's not exactly pure as the driven snow?'

He grins. 'Do you want the Biblical answer or the Robin answer?'

'Both.'

'The Biblical answer is "let he who is without sin throw the first stone".

Even if I didn't have a sexual history myself, there's plenty of other stuff you could hold against me. Wearing a dog collar doesn't give me the moral high ground, whatever some people might believe.'

'Nice. And the Robin answer?'

'I couldn't give a shit who she's been to bed with in the past. It's hardly unusual, is it.' He lowers his voice and smiles. 'I mean, if she was on Only Fans or Pornhub, that might be tricky, especially as I'm fairly sure a couple of my congregation are voracious consumers of that kind of thing and would recognise her. Is there anything like that I need to know about?'

'You're quite safe there,' I tell him with a laugh. 'Sam's very open minded in lots of ways, but not that. Are you sure you're a vicar though? Swearing and adult websites don't seem very holy to me.'

'Just because I love God doesn't mean I don't live in the real world.'

'I'll bear that in mind.'

* * *

'Did you get everything you needed out of Robin?' Cameron asks once we've returned to the ship and taken up our positions by the pool.

'I liked him very much. He's a fascinating mixture of holy and worldly. How did you get on with Sam?'

'She's full-on, but she obviously thinks the world of you. She had some pretty strong opinions.'

'She always does.'

He lapses into silence, and I take a sip of my drink. Over by the bar, Brad and Gail are also in their usual spot, evidently engaged in a heart to heart, if their facial expressions are anything to go by.

'Last night of the cruise,' I observe. 'Can you believe it? It feels like it's flown by.'

Cameron smiles. 'The fact that we missed two nights of it probably didn't help. Barry's Bonanza in Malta feels like ages ago though, doesn't it?'

I consider his point and he's right. Although time seems to have sped up since we rejoined the ship, our adventures in Barcelona and Cannes make the early part of the cruise feel like they happened a lifetime ago.

'How do you feel about going home?' he asks after a while.

'I'm ready, I think. You're right that it does feel like we've been away for ages, so I'm looking forward to getting back to the bookshop, even if I'm slightly worried about what I'll find at the flat.'

'Your sister Em?'

'Not her so much as her boyfriend, Charlie. She swore he'd improved, but he's one of those people whose perception of their cooking ability often outstrips reality. If my kitchen has escaped unscathed, I'll be happy.'

'And then there's Samson. I expect he'll be pleased to see you.'

'Once he's finished punishing me for going away, yes. Em will have spoilt him rotten, which won't have helped. What about you? Looking forward to getting back to your guns?'

He stares at me for so long without speaking that I start to feel uncomfortable.

'Hello?' I try eventually. 'Earth to Cameron?'

'Sorry, I was thinking about something.'

'Are you going to share?'

'How do you feel about coming clay pigeon shooting with me? There's a really good ground near Paddock Wood. It's a bit of a flog from you, but I could collect you first thing and we could have a pub lunch afterwards. Make a day of it.'

'Are you inviting me on a date?'

'No. Absolutely not. Sam told me you'd run a mile if I so much as mentioned the D word. No, this is two friends enjoying a day out together, nothing more.'

'Sounds awfully like a date to me.'

'Let me put it this way then. We're friends, right?'

Now it's my turn to fall silent. What are we, exactly? Friends seems a bit anodyne given that we've shared two beds, been skinny dipping together and massaged each other's naked bodies, even if only from behind. Our relationship feels like we've reached a deeper level of intimacy than just friends. But we're not dating, and we're not heading that way either. What is the correct term for more than friends but less than lovers?

'I wasn't expecting that to be such a difficult question,' Cameron remarks, and I can hear the slight tone of hurt in his voice.

'Sorry. Of course we're friends,' I assure him.

'Right. And, unless the world has changed dramatically and nobody has told me, friends do stuff together from time to time.'

'Doing stuff' conjures up an image of us massaging each other, and I'm momentarily distracted again by the thoughts of where that could have gone.

'Are you all right, Ruby?' Cameron asks.

'Yes, yes. Sorry.'

'You seem a little distracted. Is there something on your mind?'

'No, nothing. What were you saying?'

'I was trying to invite you to come clay pigeon shooting with me without it being a date, but I suspect that you hate the idea and you're trying to buy time to think of a way of letting me down gently. Forget I said anything. I just thought it would be nice to have something in the diary, but I don't want you to feel pressurised.'

Shit. I've properly upset him now. Why am I making such a meal of this? I mean, I'm not sure about the whole shooting thing, but I know it's important to him and I want to understand it. He's not inviting me to move in with him. Come on, Ruby. Make a decision.

'Do you know what?' I tell him. 'Friends do do stuff together from time to time, and I'd love to come shooting with you. As your friend.'

'Great. Let me check my diary once I'm back and I'll text you some dates.'

He settles back on his sun lounger, evidently happy, but I'm in turmoil. Part of me wants so much more than friendship from him, and I think he probably wants that too, but that would involve opening myself up to him and being vulnerable. I've protected myself for so long that I'm not even sure I'd know how to do that, even if I wanted to, which I definitely don't.

You don't do relationships, I mentally remind myself. *Your life is perfect as it is. Don't mess it up.*

The problem is that I suspect I've already messed it up by allowing myself to fancy him. And, to make matters worse, the real reason I don't do relationships is the one thing I definitely can't talk to Sam about.

25

It really does feel like I've been away for ages as the taxi pulls up outside our home. Most of the other people in the Marco Polo group went straight from the ship to the airport, but I was glad that Sam and I had booked an extra night in Rome, as it meant we had time to do a little more exploration including the all-important visit to the Sistine Chapel. Although I missed Cameron more than I expected to, and Sam was definitely missing Robin, it was nice to spend some time together, just the two of us. She had, typically, continued probing to try to find out whether there was more than friendship between Cameron and me, but I'd managed to shut her down.

'Here we go then. Back to reality,' she sighs as she pulls her case up to the front door and rummages in her bag for the keys. No sooner has she pushed open the door than Em appears, wearing a party hat and blowing on one of those extending whistles. I glance into the living room to see that she's decorated it with balloons and a huge 'Welcome home' sign.

'This is all very elaborate,' I observe cautiously. 'What are you trying to cover up?'

'Nothing! No need to be so suspicious. I just wanted to welcome you back in style.'

'I think it's lovely, Em,' Sam tells her, giving her a hug as I stick my nose into the kitchen.

'There's nothing to worry about in there,' Em says. 'Everything's absolutely fine, I promise. Even the shop is still in one piece.'

'Where's the boy?' Sam asks, looking around the sitting room for Samson.

'Ah.' Em does look a little sheepish now. 'I did tell him you were coming home and he ought to be here to welcome you, but he seems to have ignored me and gone out.'

As if on cue, the cat flap bangs and Samson nonchalantly saunters in. When he sees us, he stops in his tracks and flicks his tail in mild irritation, before stalking straight past us, jumping up onto the sofa and curling up, watching us warily.

'Don't be petulant. We're home now,' Sam says as she sits down next to him and starts to stroke him. After a while, he begins to purr softly. It's not his full-on road drill purr; he's obviously holding back, making sure we know that we're not forgiven yet, even if he is enjoying the attention.

'You should go away more often,' Em remarks as she settles on the arm of the sofa and takes over from Sam, causing a marked uptick in the volume of the purring. 'We've had a grand old time, haven't we, Samson?'

'And Charlie?' I ask.

'Has an interview for a job in London next week,' she says happily. 'We're not counting any chickens, but it's a start. Anyway, did you have an amazing time?'

'Sam's dating a vicar,' I tell her.

'A vicar?' Em's eyebrows have shot up so far they're practically in her hair line. 'I thought you were off churchy people after that place you went to where they made you feel like the whore of Babylon.'

'Bit strong, Em,' I admonish her.

'But Biblical,' she replies with a smile. 'And therefore topical, no? Charlie found it in the book of Revelation.'

'What was he doing rootling around in the Bible?'

'It was a project he set himself, to read the Bible from end to end. He was doing quite well until he got bogged down in Numbers, so he skipped to the last book. There's some pretty spicy stuff in there, I can tell you. He read the whore of Babylon bit out loud to me; it talks about "the abominations and filthiness of her fornication". It just reminded me of the way those people were with you. Anyway, I reckon you'll outrank them all if you rock up with a bona fide vicar on your arm. Is that the point?'

'No,' Sam tells her. 'I didn't even know he was a vicar to begin with.'

'He's really nice,' I add.

'Ruby made a new friend too,' Sam tells her, causing her eyebrows to shoot up again.

'Just a friend,' I clarify.

'The type of friends that share a bed and go skinny dipping together,' Sam continues, seemingly determined to take the focus off her by throwing me under the bus. 'And that's before we get to the raunchy massages. Make of that what you will.'

'Raunchy massages?'

'She's exaggerating,' I explain, shooting Sam a warning look. 'We got sunburned and had to rub lotion into each other's backs.'

'Of course you did.' Em giggles. 'Was this after the skinny dipping? An all-over massage to counter the all-over sunburn? Was there a happy finish?'

'You have a dirty mind.'

'Why, thank you.' She bows. 'I'm just getting it all out of my system before I go back to Mum and Dad's. It's been so liberating staying here, I tell you. And Jono is such a sweetie. I'm going to miss working with him in the shop.'

'You're always welcome to come and help out.'

'Are you paying?'

'No.'

'I don't love it that much. Anyway, I'd better get out of your hair and let you get settled in. Welcome home.'

* * *

Although it's nice to be back at work, it's not long before it feels like I've never been away at all. Em has done a great job of stock control, and I was both amused and grateful to see a table set out with 'Em's Gems'; with everything that happened on the cruise, I didn't make even a small dent in my reading list so I don't have any new 'Ruby's Recommendations'.

The text arrives on Wednesday, and I'm surprised how pleased I am to hear from Cameron.

> Hope you're settling back into normal life OK. If you still fancy it, we could go shooting a week on Monday? Let me know if that day is no good, and I'll choose another one, assuming you haven't gone off the idea completely. Cx

'Shooting?' Jono exclaims, horrified, when I tell him.

'It's his thing,' I explain.

'That's as maybe, but it's not yours. Seems a little emotionally illiterate if you ask me. When you organise a date for someone, you're supposed to show how important they are to you by choosing something they enjoy, not doing your own thing and expecting them to tag along.'

'It's not a date. We're just friends.'

'You tell yourself that if it helps, sweetie. All I'm saying is that if it walks like a duck and quacks like a duck...'

'Are you saying we can't be friends, just because we're the opposite sex? Who's being emotionally illiterate now?'

'I'm not saying you *can't* be friends, honey. I'm just questioning whether you *should* be friends. Does he look like the back end of a bus? Smell? Eat with his mouth open?'

'No, no and no.'

'Gay?'

'No.'

'You sound very certain.'

'His last partner was female.'

'OK. So he's male, heterosexual, reasonable looking, without any obvious character flaws. He evidently likes you and, in case you need reminding, you're pretty hot yourself, even though you're not my type.'

'What's your point?'

'Two attractive single people who like each other. Friends? I don't think so.'

'Friendship is all that's on offer.'

'Do you fancy him?'

'Objection, your honour. I've already stated the boundaries of the relationship.'

'Overruled. Do you think he fancies you?'

'Irrelevant, given my previous answer. Move on.'

Jono laughs. 'Oh, Ruby, my love. You're so full of shit it's a miracle your eyes aren't brown.'

* * *

On the day of our shooting trip, I'm feeling distinctly jittery as I get ready. I've given Cameron my address and he's collecting me at nine, but I've been up since half past six, and that's only partly because I have no idea what I'm supposed to wear for a trip like this. Having experimented with a variety of different looks, I've gone for jeans with a fitted jersey top. The weather has turned distinctly cooler, so I've also dug out a gilet that Mum and Dad gave me a few Christmases ago. It's really not my style, but I reckoned it would be perfect for shooting as it would keep me warm while leaving my arms able to move freely. At least, that's my theory. I'm totally at sea here.

The main reason for my anxiety, however, is seeing Cameron again. I'm not so worried about Jono's predictions that we can't be friends; I'm confident I can manage that. My primary concern is whether the easy friendship we enjoyed during the cruise will translate into the real world. It's going to be a difficult day if our conversation proves to be awkward and stilted.

'Interesting,' Sam observes when I show her my outfit before she leaves for work. 'If you're going for garden centre Barbie as your vibe, you've totally nailed it.'

'I'm not sure that's the look I'm going for. I was aiming for practical for being outdoors, with a hint of chic when I take the gilet off for lunch.'

'Oh. Well, that works too, I guess. Underwear?'

'Yes.'

'No. What type?'

'Why does that matter? He's not going to be seeing it.'

'You sure? He's seen an awful lot more in the past. I've just had a thought. This isn't some nudey shooting gig, is it? I mean, you do have history in that department.'

'Behave.'

'OK, well, I'm running late so I'd better go. Have fun and I'll look forward to hearing all about it when I get home. Don't do anything I wouldn't do.'

She's barely out of the door before the bell rings. The knot of stress in my stomach as I open it is only slightly alleviated when I see that Cameron is also wearing jeans and a gilet over his shirt.

'Snap,' I say awkwardly as I step aside to allow him to enter the flat.

'I like your thinking,' he says with a smile. 'Although you might prefer the one I've got for you in the car. It has a built-in pad to stop the gun bruising you.'

As Cameron steps into the living room, Samson opens his eyes and watches him warily from the sofa.

'This must be the famous Samson,' he says, approaching slowly and holding his hand out for the cat to sniff. 'You're just as handsome as I was led to believe.'

Having decided that Cameron is not a threat, Samson starts up his loudest purr and headbutts his hand, demanding attention. Watching how natural Cameron is with him eases the tension in my stomach a bit more.

'You've got a fan there,' I tell him. 'Did you want a coffee or anything before we go?'

'I'm good. I've got our guns in the back of the car, so I can't really leave them. I only came in because I wanted to meet this chap. Are you ready?'

'As I'll ever be,' I tell him with a smile as Samson stretches luxuriously and headbutts Cameron's hand again. 'I'm not sure Samson is though. He'd happily let you keep that up all day.'

'Sorry,' Cameron says, gently withdrawing his hand, much to Samson's evident disgust. 'Maybe later.'

Cameron's car turns out to be a bright red, sporty-looking hatchback, and I can't help smiling as 'Everybody Wants to Be a Cat' from *The Aristocats* comes out of the speakers when he starts the engine.

'I'd love to tell you that I spent all of yesterday compiling a Disney playlist for today,' he tells me. 'But the reality is that this is the playlist I keep for whenever my niece is in the car. I did remember to cue up your favourite though. Do I get points for that?'

'Absolutely,' I tell him with a grin.

As we potter through the inevitable queues of traffic trying to get out of the town, I'm relieved to note that our conversation flows just as easily as it did on the cruise. Silence does fall when we reach the dual carriageway, but it's comfortable, and I take the opportunity to stare out of the window and watch the view.

The further we go, the more I can feel my anxieties dissipating. We're knocking this just being friends gig out of the park.

26

'OK, this is probably the best place to start,' Cameron tells me as he leads me towards a stand. I'd imagined clay pigeon shooting would involve standing in a muddy field with lots of other people, but this seems positively high tech. There are neat paths between the stands, some of which are occupied by people dressed similarly to us. At Cameron's suggestion, I've swapped my gilet for the one he brought which, as well as the padding he mentioned, seems to have a ludicrous number of pockets.

'I'm going to release a clay and I want you to watch what it does,' he continues as he inserts the device he was given at reception to activate the trap. 'It's going to fly more or less straight up, pausing briefly before it falls to the ground. When it pauses, I want you to imagine it's got two little legs hanging off the bottom, and I want you to shoot those legs off.' He presses a button and a clay disc shoots up, doing exactly what he described.

'Don't I just point the gun at the clay and fire?' I ask.

'You could do that, but you'll never hit it. Because it's moving, you need to shoot where it's going to be when the pellets reach it rather than where it is when you pull the trigger. Trust me.'

He hands me a pair of ear defenders and carefully loads one of the guns.

'Keep it pointing at the ground and away from your feet until you're ready,' he explains. 'Then, if it goes off accidentally, you'll make a hole in the ground but nobody will get hurt.' He flicks a button on the side of the gun. 'Now press it firmly into your shoulder and look along the barrel. When you're ready, say, "Pull," and I'll release the clay, OK?'

I'm definitely not ready, but I do as he says and try to remember everything he told me. The first clay catches me by surprise, but not as much as the kick of the shotgun as I pull the trigger. Unsurprisingly, I don't hit it.

'That was your practice,' Cameron tells me with a smile as he reloads the gun. 'This time, you should be prepared. Remember, wait for it to pause and then shoot its imaginary legs off.'

He hands back the gun and I repeat the process. This time, I know what to expect and I focus on keeping the clay in sight down the barrel. As soon as it pauses, I shoot just below it and it shatters into tiny pieces.

'Well done! Now do it again.'

Somehow, I manage to hit eight out of the next ten clays and I have to admit that it's supremely satisfying. The recoil of the gun when I pull the trigger is still a bit of a surprise, but it's not putting me off any more.

'Right. Time to move on to something a little more challenging,' Cameron suggests when I've demolished another ten clays. 'Let's go and try one that goes from side to side. You'll need to put your gun a decent distance in front of the clay and keep swinging as you pull the trigger.'

If the first stand was fairly straightforward, this one seems impossible, to begin with at least. I just can't work out how far in front of the clay I need to be, and I only hit one of the first ten. Cameron is endlessly patient, suggesting different ways of looking at it.

'It's impossible!' I complain as another clay pigeon escapes my gun unharmed.

'It's just a different technique.'

'You do it then.'

He shows me how to operate the trap and loads the gun he brought for himself.

'Pull!' he calls, and I press the button. Irritatingly, he hits it square on, as he does with the following nine I give him.

'Show off,' I grumble as he loads my gun for me to have another go.

'It's just practice,' he tells me encouragingly.

'Can we go back to the other stand? I was good at that.'

'You'll be good at this one too. You just need your brain to have its Eureka moment. I tell you what. We'll do another ten here and, if you still don't get it, we'll move on and try something else. OK?'

Incredibly, something does seem to have clicked while I was watching Cameron, and I hit just over half of the next batch. By the time we pack up to head off for lunch, I've tried five different stands with varying degrees of success.

'I think I get why people enjoy this,' I say to Cameron as he slides the guns into their cases and loads them into the boot of the car. 'Although I'm going to have a bruise tomorrow.'

'You might be a little tender, but hopefully you won't bruise. You did really well. Would you come again?'

'Absolutely, if I'm invited.'

'Oh, you're invited.'

I'm in a good mood as he pilots the car into a nearby village and pulls into a pub car park. To my surprise, he pulls the cased guns out of the boot and hands one to me.

'Are you planning to hold up the pub?' I ask, slightly bemused. 'Most people find it easier to simply pay for their lunch. It involves less jail time on the whole.'

'Very funny. We're not allowed to leave these in the car, so we have to take them with us.'

I feel incredibly self-conscious walking into the pub with a gun over my shoulder, even if it is in a sheepskin case. I'm half expecting the lady behind the bar to take one look at us and demand that we leave but, to my surprise, she doesn't so much as bat an eyelid as Cameron leads me over to a table and we lean the guns against the wall.

'This is quite a popular pub with the people who shoot down the road,' Cameron explains quietly. Sure enough, as I glance round, I notice that a number of the other patrons also have gun cases stacked neatly by their tables.

'Let's just hope nothing kicks off,' I murmur back. 'With all these people packing weaponry, it could get ugly really quickly.'

'I think we're quite safe,' he replies with a smile. 'This is Kent, not the Wild West. Plus, the guns should be empty so, unless they were planning on beating each other to death with them, they're pretty harmless. What would you like to drink?'

'I'll have a glass of white wine, please. I think I've earned it.'

I watch him as he wanders up to the bar to place our orders. He seems completely at ease in this environment, and it's obvious this isn't his first time in here from the friendly banter he's exchanging with the woman behind the bar. A few minutes later, he walks back with two glasses and a couple of menus.

'How many other people have you brought here?' I ask suddenly, surprised by the pang of jealousy that just shot through me.

'I'm sorry?'

'You obviously come here a lot,' I tell him. 'I just wondered if this was somewhere you brought many people.'

He thinks for a moment. 'Actually, I don't think I've brought anyone here before. I've met people here, and groups of us have come up here for a bite to eat after a morning's shooting, but you're the first person I've actually brought here as a guest. Why?'

I feel foolish. What does it matter who he's been here with, and why? He's just a friend; I don't have any claim on him.

'Sorry. I was just curious,' I murmur, burying my head in the menu to hide my embarrassment. 'What's good then?'

'It's all good,' he says, seemingly unperturbed by my sudden inquisition. 'The fish and chips is excellent, as is the burger. It's made on the premises and the meat comes from a local farm. However, I'm going to have the steak and kidney pie, because it's my absolute favourite.'

'Hmm. Not a huge kidney fan. I'll try the burger.'

'Good choice.' He returns to the bar to place our order, and I take the opportunity to tell myself off for overstepping the boundary. When he returns, I make a point of keeping the conversation on neutral topics and, by the time the food arrives, everything feels back to normal. Cameron hasn't undersold the burger, which turns out to be delicious, and I surprise myself by letting him talk me into a sticky toffee pudding for dessert. As he turns the car back towards Margate, I feel full and pleasantly drowsy; the monotone humming of the engine and tyres on the motorway soothes me even more, and it's not long before I'm fast asleep, dreaming of confidently shattering clay pigeons coming at me from all directions.

'Wake up, Ruby,' Cameron's voice says gently. 'We're here.'

I open my eyes with a start to see that the car is stationary outside my flat. I do a quick, and hopefully subtle, drool check before turning to face him.

'Sorry,' I tell him. 'All that excitement this morning and then a big lunch.'

'No worries.' His eyes crinkle as he smiles.

'Did you want a cup of tea or something before you head back?' I ask.

'I would,' he says. 'But there's something I need to say before we get out of the car.'

His suddenly serious expression unnerves me and I can feel my heart starting to thud uncomfortably in my chest. My usual response to situations like this is to defuse them with a joke, but nothing is coming. I raise my eyes to meet his and there's a fierce intensity there that I haven't seen before. I can't maintain the eye contact, and I let my gaze drop to my lap. I feel incredibly uncomfortable all of a sudden. The silence feels oppressive. I want him to speak, but I'm also afraid of what I think he might be about to say.

'What is it?' I breathe eventually. My mouth is completely dry. Please let it not be what I think it is.

'The fact is, Ruby, that I can't carry on like this,' he says bluntly. 'I know what you've said about friendships, and I know what Sam said about never mentioning the D word, but I can't help the way I feel. Do you remember what I told Barry, after we won his Bonanza prize?'

'No.' My worst fears are coming true, and I can't wait to escape.

'I said I'd spotted you at the Singles Mingle event but was too shy to talk to you. I said how much I'd enjoyed spending time with you and that I was excited to see where things might go.'

'Yes.' I seize the lifeline. 'But we were hamming it up, to give Barry what he wanted.'

'I wasn't,' he says simply. 'You blew me away from the moment I first set eyes on you, and I couldn't believe my luck when you agreed to spend time with me. The better I got to know you, the more I liked you.'

'I like you too,' I say lamely. Please, God, make this stop.

'And then, of course, we missed the ship. I know it was stressful, but it was also one of the happiest times of my life, because I was with you. I meant what I told you about not looking for another relationship, and part of me hoped today would go differently, I promise. I wanted the attraction I felt towards you on holiday to have faded so we could just be friends, but spending this time with you has just reinforced the way I feel. The fact is, Ruby, that I've fallen for you. Hard.'

He stops speaking and the silence falls like a dark cloud. My mind is in turmoil, trying to work out whether I've led him on in some way. Yes, there was the whole massage thing, but I managed to keep that PG in the end. I've always been perfectly clear with him that friendship was all I had to offer. Why is he doing this? I can feel the tears rolling down my cheeks and dropping off my chin. This has been such a lovely day, and it's all ended in flames.

'I'm so sorry, Cameron.' I gulp through my tears as I reach for the door handle. 'I can't.'

Before he has a chance to say anything else, I yank open the door and get out of the car, shutting it firmly behind me. I've already got my key in my hand by the time I reach my front door, but a quick glance shows that he hasn't followed me. Once I'm safely inside the flat, I watch through the net curtains as he sits there for what feels like an age, before starting the engine and driving slowly away. Only once I'm sure I'm alone do I allow the full floodgates to open, collapsing on the sofa and sobbing my heart out. I feel exactly the same as him, of course I do, but I can't let myself go there. I just can't.

27

By the time Sam gets home, early in the evening, I'm all cried out; I just feel empty and desperately sad. Even Samson has been no comfort as, having initially taken my sobbing as an opportunity to get attention, he evidently decided after a while that I was becoming altogether too needy for him and went out instead.

'So. How was it?' Sam asks enthusiastically. 'Are you hooked on shooting now or was it Dullsville, Arizona?'

'The shooting was good,' I tell her, trying to summon some of the happiness I felt earlier today. 'I hit quite a few, actually.'

'Really?' She looks sceptical. 'I didn't have you down as the field sports type. This isn't the top of a slippery slope, is it? If you start foxhunting, I'll take a dim view.'

'Foxhunting is illegal, and it's not the top of a slippery slope. In fact, there is no slope at all.' My mask crumples and the tears start to fall again.

'What on earth happened?' Sam is on the sofa next to me in an instant, wrapping me in a hug.

'Nothing,' I murmur into her shoulder.

'Nonsense. Something happened, otherwise you wouldn't be so upset. Come on, spill the beans.'

I pull away from her and look her in the eye. 'You'll think I'm stupid.'

She grins lopsidedly. 'I'm sure we've both thought each other stupid many times over the years. That doesn't mean we have to hide stuff from each other. Come on, Ruby. Tell me what happened. Maybe I can help you with it.'

'You can't help.'

'It won't stop me trying. Even if I can't help, it will make you feel better. A problem shared and all that.'

In spite of myself, I laugh through my tears. 'You know that isn't true, don't you? Sharing a problem doesn't halve it at all. All you've done is bring someone else down, and you're no further forward than you were when you shared it.'

'I know I've said this before, but you, my lovely, are such a cynic. I'm sure you never used to be like this when I first met you.'

'Yeah, well, I have a lot to be cynical about.'

'Are you going to tell me what happened to make you so upset, or are you just going to retreat inside your shell and refuse to come out?'

'Not going to lie. The shell sounds pretty attractive at the moment.'

'You're being ridiculous now. This is me you're talking to. If you can't talk to me, who can you talk to?'

I sigh. 'You've got a point there. I did try talking to Samson, but it turns out he's not cut out to be a therapist.'

'Samson has many qualities, but empathy isn't among them,' she agrees.

'He's still the handsomest cat in Margate.'

'And you're trying to change the subject.'

I sigh. 'Fine. Cameron told me he likes me.'

For a moment, her face is a mask of incomprehension before the penny obviously drops. 'You mean, as in *like* like?'

'Yes.'

'Fuck.'

'Exactly.'

'What did you say?'

'I told him that I couldn't give him what he wanted, and then I dashed in here and hid until he drove away.'

She thinks for a while, evidently digesting the bombshell. 'And you're sure you didn't get the wrong end of the stick? He wasn't, for instance, just saying how much he'd enjoyed spending time with you and you maybe read more into it than there was?'

'I didn't get the wrong end of the stick, Sam. He told me he'd fallen for me. In fact, he said he'd fallen hard. I think that's pretty bloody clear, don't you?'

She thinks a little more before her face hardens. 'Here's what I don't get,' she says suddenly. 'I've always accepted your no dating rule as just a part of your adult personality. You're happy with your life as it is, etcetera etcetera. But if that's all it is, you would have just told him that you were sorry, that's not your vibe but you were happy to be friends, and moved on. There's more to this than you've told me.'

Shit. I should have known she'd see through me. I can practically hear her brain whirring.

'Now I come to think about it,' she continues after a while, 'you've also said you didn't intend to be single forever. So, if that's the case, and Cameron is falling at your feet, why turn him down? I mean, we know you like him, and we definitely know you fancy him. He's a decent guy and you seem to have a lot of fun together. What am I missing?'

It's like she's found a loose end on a knitted jumper and is pulling on it. The more she tugs, the more the carefully crafted self-defence I've hidden behind for so many years starts to unravel. I'm just not sure I'm ready to bring the truth back out into the open, let alone share it with her. Apart from the people involved at the time, I've never told a soul what happened; I can feel myself filling with shame and embarrassment just thinking about it. The problem is that, having suppressed my feelings for so many years, it feels a bit like I'm shaking a mental Coke bottle full of memories. Any moment now the cap is going to burst off and they'll all come flooding out, making a hell of a mess in the process.

'Something happened,' Sam continues thoughtfully. 'You were never short of boyfriends at school. Then you went away to uni, went out with Olly, and nothing since then. You dumped Olly, broke his heart, but you've never dated anyone since. Oh, shit!'

She turns to me with her eyes wide. 'He didn't, you know, lose his shit and harm himself or something, did he? I mean, I know you broke his heart and everything, but was it worse than that? Is this a guilt trip thing?'

The Coke bottle in my mind explodes, and I suddenly need to be alone. I dash into the bathroom, plonking myself on the loo and resting my head in my hands as I let my mind transport me back. Now that they're free, the memories are running amok and it feels like it all happened yesterday.

'Ruby.' Sam's voice comes from the other side of the door. Her tone is gentle and full of concern. 'Are you OK?'

'I'm fine,' I call. 'I'll be out in a minute.'

What the hell am I going to tell her? With the benefit of hindsight, my reaction to the events back then seems totally disproportionate, but it didn't feel disproportionate at the time. Do I really want to rake over the implosion of Olly's and my relationship again? Do I actually have a choice? Maybe it's time to come clean, with Sam at least. The prospect both drains and terrifies me, but I'm not sure I have the energy to keep up the lie any more. Time to face the music.

'Blimey, you look like you've seen a ghost,' Sam observes when I eventually rejoin her in the living room. 'Do you want a glass of water?'

'Please,' I whisper. If nothing else, it will get rid of her for a few more moments so I can carry on trying to put my whirling thoughts in order. While she's gone, I perch on the sofa with my legs curled up underneath me and my arms wrapped round my chest. As my therapist would have observed, my body language is full-on self-protection.

'Here you are,' Sam says, setting a glass on the table next to me.

'Thanks,' I reply, taking a sip. The water is cold and very welcome, and it's all I can do not to swallow down the whole glass in one go.

'So...?' she prompts after I've had a few sips.

I sigh. 'You're partly right,' I tell her. 'It does stem from my break-up with Olly. But the story I've always told you isn't quite true. I didn't break his heart. He broke mine. In fact, he didn't just break it. He smashed it into smithereens and stamped on the broken shards.'

She looks confused. 'So why didn't you say that all along?'

'I, umm, didn't take it very well.' That's the understatement of the year. The memories are fully formed now. 'The truth is, I had a bit of a breakdown.'

'You? But you're the most together person I've ever met.'

'I am now, thanks to shit tons of therapy.'

'What happened?'

'It was just before our finals; I was already under a lot of pressure, but I was handling it well, or so I thought. Olly and I were planning our future after university, and the idea of that kept me going. And then...' I dry up.

'And then?' she prompts again.

'And then he called me one afternoon and asked if he could pop by to see me. He sounded totally normal, so I didn't suspect anything. I thought maybe he was bored revising, like I was, and needed a bit of distraction. Ha. I couldn't have got that more wrong. As soon as I opened the door to him, I could tell something was up. He had this look on his face that I'd never seen before, and he actually dodged when I tried to kiss him. I asked him what was wrong, and it all came tumbling out. He was seeing someone else; he didn't want a future with me after all. He called me clinging and needy, said having sex with me had become a chore. He told me I was draining him, holding him back. He said he hadn't realised, and I quote, how "utterly fucking miserable" I made him until he'd started seeing this other girl.'

'Bastard!' Sam exclaims. 'And you didn't have a clue this was coming?'

'Nope. I was completely blindsided. And you know what the worst part was? He actually seemed to be enjoying trashing me. Here was this boy that I loved with all my heart, that I thought I was going to build a life with, maybe even marry, being so cruel and looking like he was getting pleasure from it. I don't know how long he spent sitting there telling me all the ways in which I wasn't good enough for him, but it felt like I was standing in a boxing ring while he punched me in the face over and over again. And then, when he was done, he simply got up and walked out. I felt like my world had been torn apart, but that was just the beginning.' Now that I've started to tell the story, the words are pouring out of me like a torrent. I couldn't stop them if I tried.

'When the initial shock started to wear off, I tried to call him, to reason with him, but he'd blocked my number already, so I went round to his house.'

'Uh-oh,' Sam murmurs. 'I have a suspicion I know where this is going. She answered the door, right?'

'Close. He answered, but she was right behind him. It looked like I'd disturbed them in the middle of sex. So not only had he seemingly taken pleasure in ruining my life, he'd hotfooted it straight back home for a celebratory fuck with my replacement.'

'What did you do?'

'I completely lost it. I screamed, I called him every name under the sun, I think I called her a few choice things too. None of it made any difference, of course. They just stood there while I ranted and, when I paused to draw breath, Olly smiled – the bastard actually smiled – and said, "You're making a fool of yourself, Ruby. Go home," and closed the door. I realised I'd played right into his hands. Bastard probably got a power kick out of it. If he wasn't fucking new girl before I arrived, I'd lay money that he fucked her after I left. I was totally humiliated.'

'Where is he now?' Sam asks. 'I'm going to find him and kill him.'

'I don't know. My therapist and I agreed it would be best if I didn't look for him. Anyway, you'd think that would have been the end of it, wouldn't you. I go away, lick my wounds and eventually move on. But Olly wasn't having that. He was enjoying my humiliation far too much. He knew my regular haunts, my routines, and he made sure he and his new girlfriend were in my face wherever I went. It was like he was taunting me. In the end, I stopped going out unless I absolutely had to. I got paranoid about seeing them, convinced they'd be round every corner. I was on a downward spiral. I even contemplated suicide at one point. I stockpiled paracetamol and bought a big bottle of vodka, but thankfully that was as far as I went.'

Sam's reaction is instant. She pulls me into her as the tears start to fall once more. 'You poor, poor baby,' she soothes, stroking my hair. I really want to stop telling the story now, but I'm not done. Now I've started, it all has to come out. I gently pull away from her and take another sip of my water.

'It was Helen, one of my housemates, who decided to intervene. Without telling me, she rang my mum and said she was worried about me. Mum arrived the next day, took one look at me, and that was that. By that stage, I wasn't even washing, just hanging around in my pyjamas when I wasn't lying in bed feeling sorry for myself. Apparently, and I only found this out a long time later, I absolutely stank. Mum sent me straight upstairs to shower and wash my hair, laid out clean clothes for me and then took me out and made me eat a proper meal. She obviously found the vodka and the pills because I noticed they were gone when I came down from the shower, but she never mentioned it. She was brilliant. She dropped everything and stayed with me while I sat my finals. As soon as the last exam was done, she took me home and enrolled me with a therapist.'

'Thank God for Helen and your mum,' Sam says. 'Why didn't I notice any of this?'

'You went off travelling immediately after you finished uni,' I remind her. 'I deliberately hid it from you because I knew you wouldn't have gone if you were worried about me.'

'Of course I wouldn't have gone!'

'Which is why I didn't tell you. And then it just became easier not to tell you, so I changed the story and told it for so long I actually started to believe it myself. Anyway,' I say, suddenly exhausted by letting this all out, 'the therapist helped me to regain my perspective before eventually signing me off. I started to move on, but not before I'd made a solemn promise to myself.'

'No more men,' Sam murmurs.

'No more men,' I agree. 'And it was working just fine until Cameron fucked it all up this afternoon.'

28

After my revelations, Sam and I sat on the sofa together in silence for a long time. I was immersed in my memories, and I imagine she was digesting what I'd told her. At some point, Samson had wandered in and curled up between us. It was obvious that neither of us was in the mood to cook, so Sam ordered a pizza for us to pick at and we're now back on the sofa, nursing two enormous glasses of white wine. She doesn't seem at all upset about the fact that I've lied to her about something so big for all these years, and I'm incredibly grateful for that. I feel raw, and dealing with her hurt and anger would have been very hard on top of everything I've shared this evening.

'Can I ask something controversial?' she asks, puncturing the silence.

'You can ask whatever you like. I don't have anything left to hide.'

'Do you think it might be an idea to go back into therapy for a bit?'

I'm caught by surprise. 'Why?'

'I was just thinking it all through. You've ruled out another relationship because you're scared you'll lose control again if it all goes wrong, correct?'

'It's not that, so much. I'm not that person any more, and I'm not under the same pressures, but I guess I've protected myself for so long that it's become second nature.'

'But I hope you'd agree that you can't carry on that way forever. You have so much to give in a relationship, and you deserve to be happy. And this is me talking, by the way. I think we can both agree that I have a master's degree in failed relationships, so I know my stuff.'

I smile weakly. 'You do have a strong dickhead count,' I agree. 'But now you've found Robin, and I think we can agree that I actually hold the top trump card for dickheads, don't I?'

'Yes, but here's the thing. I don't think it's the dickheads you're scared of, not that Cameron is a dickhead. It's how you re-programme yourself to let your guard back down. That's why I asked about therapy. It seems to me that your previous therapist helped you to close the door on Olly, and that's good. But, in the process, you've closed the door on everyone, and it's been closed for so long that the lock has rusted up and you've lost the key.'

I take a slurp of my wine. 'Maybe I'm like Sleeping Beauty. I just need the right prince to cut down the jungle and force open the door.'

'That's a shit analogy, because the right prince was here today with his garden shears and you sent him packing. Unfortunately for you, no prince is going to be able to fix this. You have to fix it yourself.'

I sigh. 'I'm not sure I know how. I may not be that person any more, but the idea of being that vulnerable again still terrifies me.'

'Which, again, is why I think a therapist might be a good idea. Someone to carefully help you find the key, lubricate the lock and open the door an inch at a time. I'm confident that you'd never go back to the dark place you were in at uni, but it doesn't matter what I think. Until you believe it, you're always going to be stuck.'

'Mm. It's hard though, because why rock the boat when I've survived quite happily for the last seven years?'

'Because the reality is that, deep down, you want your happy ever after just as much as I do. If you were truly content as you are, you wouldn't have got in such a mess when Cameron told you he liked you. The fact here, whether you're ready to hear it or not, is that you like him just as much as he likes you.'

'I think I shot that particular horse this afternoon, didn't I?'

She grins. 'A field sports reference. Interesting.'

'Stop it, Freud.'

'OK. I'm not sure you have shot the horse though. I would suggest that Cameron is feeling confused and embarrassed right now. He knew that he was overstepping the boundaries when he told you how he felt about you, and he probably thinks he's blown it. He might even be having a very similar conversation to ours with his best mate. My question to you is this: If you could fix this, would you? Could you see a future with Cameron? Do you want one?'

'I don't know. I've never allowed myself to think like that.'

'Let's try it the other way around then. The horse you shot is dead and you're never going to see Cameron again. How does that make you feel?'

'I hate that idea,' I tell her. The thought of it makes fresh tears start to fall. I've cried so much today, I'm frankly surprised I have anything left.

'That's your answer then.'

'I'm not sure it's that simple.'

'It really is. Look, I can't promise that you and Cameron will end up growing old together. There's no safety net where love is concerned. It's not a savings account with a guaranteed return. It's risky, like riding the stock market. But, like the stock market, people do it because the rewards are immense if you get it right. There's no "try before you buy" option either; you have to throw yourself in and hope for the best. Do you trust him?'

'Yes, absolutely. That's not the problem here. The problem is me letting myself open up to him.'

'OK, let's go back to the alternative for a moment. If you reject Cameron, who's really won here? Is it you or is it Olly? Every time you run away from a chance of happiness, you're letting Olly control you again. Is that what you want?'

'No, of course not.'

'Then change the narrative. Put yourself back at the centre of your story. Olly is past history. He's a narcissist who did you an immense amount of damage, but he doesn't get the last chapter. You do.'

'You make it sound so easy.'

'It's not, which is why I suggested a therapist. But if you don't kick any residual trace of Olly and what he did out of your life, you're never going to be free to be the person God designed you to be.'

'Did you just bring God into this?'

She blushes. 'Sorry. It was something Robin said to me and I liked the image.'

'And how is the dashing vicar?'

'Nuh-uh. We're not changing the subject until we have a plan. What are you going to do?'

'I guess I need to talk to Cameron.'

'Yes, you do.'

* * *

I'm lying in bed reflecting on our conversation and trying to think what to say to Cameron when my phone pings with a message. It's from him and there's only one word.

> Sorry.

I stare at the screen for ages, prodding it to stop it going dark. I'm stupidly pleased to hear from him, but I can't work out how to respond. I start several messages and delete them before deciding to bite the bullet.

> You have nothing to be sorry for.

The ticks go blue immediately and I can see he's typing.

> I overstepped the mark.

> And I ran away! Not exactly adult behaviour. I'm sorry too.

I can see he's read it, but there's a delay before he types his response.

> Can we be friends?

How to reply to that? I know that's not what he wants, and after my conversation with Sam, I know it's not what I want either. But this isn't a conversation we can have via text. I need to explain why I acted the way I did. If he thinks I'm a basket case and runs a mile, then I'll just have to deal with it, but we can't go forward unless I'm completely honest with him. Eventually, I type:

> When are you next in Margate?

> Friday. I'm seeing a man about a 12 bore at 3.

> Why don't you drop by the shop afterwards? We could go for a drink.

> OK. See you then.

I review the messages a few times before setting my phone back on the bedside table. I feel better now that I'm back in contact with Cameron and I know I'm going to have a chance to try to set things right. I think Sam will be pleased with me too.

* * *

I was right about Sam being pleased. Despite her continued assertions that I'd do well to book a therapist to work some stuff out, she's been happy enough to role play various scenarios with me, and I'm starting to get some clarity about how I want to approach things when Cameron arrives later this afternoon. We've agreed what I will tell him about Olly, sticking to the bare bones and leaving out the whole breakdown bit. We've also tested various ways things might move forward, from him declaring his feelings again (and me being a little more encouraging), to me having to bring it up. What this time has shown, if it were in any doubt, is that I do feel more than friendship towards him, and the idea of not having him in my life is not one I really want to contemplate. I just have to find a way to let go of seven years of learned behaviour, allow myself to open up and trust him.

The downside of him visiting today is that I won't have Sam on hand for a debrief later, as she's hotfooting it straight from work to spend her first weekend with Robin. She's tried to play down how excited she is out of sensitivity to me, but I can tell she's positively fizzing. When we haven't been working on my issues, we've been raiding her wardrobe to choose things for her to wear. The hardest one proved to be her Sunday outfit. I thought she looked smart in dark blue jeans with a jacket, but she fretted that jeans were too casual for church and Robin's parishioners would look down on her. We both felt that a full-on dress was too formal so, after trying a few skirt and blouse combos, we settled on a pair of fitted chinos with a white shirt and a dark blue jacket. Sexy but elegant.

'Are you sure you're all right?' Jono asks as I glance anxiously at the clock again. 'I've never seen you with such a bad case of the fidgets. He's just a man, we're nothing special.'

I've told Jono about Cameron's visit, but not given him any details. I've just told him that we had a spot of miscommunication and he was coming over to sort it out.

'I'm fine, thank you, Jono,' I reply, a little more tersely than I meant to, and I see a brief look of surprise cross his face.

'If you say so. He'd better be worth it,' he retorts before retreating back behind the coffee bar.

Is he worth it? In moments like this the doubts still creep in, but I hastily start repeating the mantra that Sam and I put together in my head.

He's not Olly. He thinks the world of you. He's a good man. Trust him.

It does succeed in soothing me, and I manage to focus on my work until the bell rings to announce that another customer has entered the shop. It's only when Samson leaps down from his chair and swaggers over to greet the newcomer that I lift my eyes and see him.

Cameron is wearing a simple white shirt and blue jeans, with brown brogues underneath. His expression is uncertain, which makes him look curiously vulnerable. I'm aware of Jono sizing him up from the other side of the shop, but for once I'm not interested in what Jono thinks. My heart fills as I look at him and my final doubts vanish.

Yes, Olly did a phenomenal amount of damage and I have a list of trust issues as long as my arm because of it. But this isn't Olly; it's Cameron, the man who has had my back without fail since I met him. The man who caused frankly obscene reactions within me with a simple back massage. The man who remembered my favourite Disney song and had it ready to play when he picked me up. And, I'm reminded as Samson weaves affectionately round his ankles, the man my cat took an instant liking to.

As I step out from behind the counter to greet him, I can feel my face breaking into a smile. Being careful not to tread on a furiously purring Samson, I wrap my arms around him and pull him close.

'It's so good to see you,' I tell him.

'You too,' he replies.

Sam's right. Why should I let Olly set the narrative any more? I want this. I want Cameron. Time to step out from the shadows into the light and set myself free.

29

Something's not right. I hope it's just nerves, but there's no sign of the easy conversation that Cameron and I are used to as we set off towards the pub. The further we go, the more I begin to convince myself that I've misread the situation and he no longer feels the same way about me. How can he, when he's barely spoken a word to me since we left the shop? His expression is sombre as we make our way along the pavement.

'I really am sorry, Ruby,' he begins eventually.

'I'm the one who should be sorry,' I tell him. 'It wasn't very mature of me to run away like that.'

'I know I've probably ruined everything, but if there was a way to salvage a friendship from this, I'd like to try. That's assuming you want it, of course.'

This is it. Decision time. I could take the easy route and say yes, of course we can be friends, but I know that's not what I want. The problem is that I'm no closer to knowing whether he still wants more or whether my reaction last time has put him off. I need to know how he feels before I say my piece. I may be ready to open up and be vulnerable, but not if he's changed his mind.

'Let me ask you a question,' I begin. 'On Monday, you said you'd fallen for me. Is that still true?'

'How the hell am I supposed to answer that?' he exclaims. 'If I say yes, then you'll run a mile, and if I say no...'

'If you say no...' I prompt him.

He sighs, stops walking and turns to face me. 'I'd be lying. I'm sorry, Ruby, but I can't help how I feel. What I can help is what I do about it. If friends is all we'll ever be, I'll take that. It's still better than not having you in my life at all.'

I'm almost overwhelmed with relief. He still feels the same. Somehow, however, I still can't quite bring myself to open my heart to him.

'Hardly fair on you, though,' I point out, trying to buy time. 'So I would get to skip about, waving the "just friends" flag, while you had to bury your true feelings just to give me what I want? That doesn't sound very healthy to me.'

'That's my issue to deal with,' he says firmly, ramming his hands into his pockets. 'I ruined everything on Monday by being selfish. You were always clear that friendship was all you wanted, and yet I still pushed for more. This is all my fault. You have no idea how much I wish I'd never said anything.'

He looks crestfallen. Shit. This is going in completely the wrong direction now. I need to rescue the situation fast.

'No,' I tell him just as firmly. 'You should never hide your feelings. That's not healthy either.'

'So what do we do?'

I take a deep breath and prepare to bare my soul. 'I have an idea, but I need to tell you a few things first, so you understand what you're getting yourself into, OK?'

* * *

Thankfully, the story proves easier to tell the second time around, helped by the fact that Cameron listens attentively without interrupting. In the end, I don't leave anything out and, by the time I've finished, the pub is forgotten and we're sitting on a bench overlooking the sea. The light is fading and the wind is cold, so we're huddled together watching the waves in silence. Every so often, the rhythmic swishing from the beach is joined by the noise of a passing car or a burst of conversation as the early-evening guests arrive for dinner at The Mermaid, a little further up the road. I feel drained but safe with him by my side. I'd love for him to reach out and put his arm around me, but he's lost in his own thoughts. 'I don't know what to say,' he tells me after a while. 'I mean, there are so many things I want to say, but none of them are particularly helpful and most of them just sound trite. I completely understand why you were so spooked on Monday now, and I guess my only question is whether there's anything I can do. I mean, I know there probably isn't, but I could maybe track Olly down and have him arrested on some trumped-up charge, if you like.' His mouth lifts in the faintest hint of a smile, and it's all I can do not to reach out and trace the contours of his lips with my finger.

'Nice offer,' I reply instead, 'but I'm not sure that it's ethical.'

'I will say this then. It takes someone truly amazing to go through all of that and come out as strong as you have.'

This is enough to give me the courage I need. 'I don't know about that,' I tell him. 'But I'd like to return to the question I asked earlier. Given what you know now, do you still feel the same about me?'

'Of course I do, but that doesn't matter. It's about you, and I completely understand how you feel, and why you feel that way. I won't mention it again, as long as we can still be friends. Do you think that's possible?'

'I'm sure it's possible,' I tell him, feeling nervous as I prepare to come clean. 'But I'm not sure it's what I want.'

His face falls again. 'OK, I understand,' he interrupts.

'Let me finish. I'm not sure it's what I want, because Sam has helped me realise that it's time to leave the past behind. If you're prepared to be patient with me and put up with the occasional wobble, I'd like to see where this could go.'

'Are you saying...?'

'Yes, Cameron. I am.'

'Oh, wow.'

I smile. 'I think you're supposed to kiss me now. That's if you still want to, of course.'

He doesn't need telling twice, and relief floods through me as he leans over and brushes my lips with his. This is nothing like our kiss on the cruise. Even though his face is cold from the wind, the feel of his lips against mine is causing heat to flood through me.

'I think it's time to get out of here, don't you?' I ask him when we finally break apart, some time later.

As we get to our feet, he takes my hand in his and I can feel everything I said to him about being patient and going slowly melting away. I'm trembling with nerves and anticipation as we make our way back to my flat, and it takes me a couple of goes to get the key in the door. No sooner are we inside than Cameron takes me in his arms and kisses me again, this time more deeply. I'd forgotten how much I enjoyed kissing, and I'm starting to lose myself when Cameron pulls away.

'Is this OK?' he asks breathlessly.

'What do you think?' I reply.

'Sorry, I just don't want to overwhelm you.'

I laugh. 'Cameron, you're the first person I've kissed in seven years. Of course I'm overwhelmed, but in a good way. Can you shut up now and kiss me some more?'

'Absolutely.'

* * *

I may have asked Cameron to be patient, but that has gone pretty much straight out of the window. It wasn't long before our hands seemed to go into autopilot, unfastening buttons and zips until all that was left was our underwear. Now, his arousal is plain to see and I can't help reaching down and wrapping my hand gently around the bulge in his pants.

'Little Cameron seems pleased to see me again,' I say with a smile.

Cameron groans. 'Must you?'

'Come with me. I have plans for him.'

I lead him to my bedroom, where it's not long before we're completely naked. We're both so pent up that the sex itself is over fairly quickly, but it's satisfying nonetheless.

'Can I tell you something without you laughing?' I say afterwards as I run my hand lazily over his chest and down towards his stomach.

'Of course.'

'When you were rubbing the aftersun lotion into my back in Cannes, I found it a bit of a turn-on.'

He grins. 'Did you now? I'll have to remember that for future use. Although, if we're confessing things, I did too.'

'I'm so sorry I nearly ruined everything.'

'If anyone nearly ruined everything, it was me. Although, given how things have turned out, I can't say I'm sorry.'

Our heart to heart is interrupted by Samson mewing at the bedroom door. No sooner have I opened it than he leaps on the bed, settling himself between us and embarking on a prolonged grooming session. If there was any residual sexual tension in the air, a large cat noisily cleaning himself is guaranteed to kill the mood.

'Do you fancy something to eat?' I ask Cameron.

'Does it involve getting dressed?'

'If you don't want to be arrested in the Chinese takeaway for indecent exposure, I'd recommend it.'

He sighs and slides out of bed, and I shamelessly admire the view as he tugs on his pants. I know there's nothing there that I haven't seen before, but I'm appreciating it in a whole new light.

'The rest is in the hallway, I think,' I tell him with a smile as I put on my own underwear. I can feel his eyes on me and, if the new bulge in his pants is anything to go by, he's enjoying the view just as much as I was.

'You've recovered quickly,' I joke. 'You might need to wait until I've had something to eat though. I'm starving.'

His face suddenly clouds over. 'Are you OK? This isn't too much?'

'I'm fine,' I assure him. 'No regrets so far. You?'

'Not as happy as when you were naked, but I'm hoping we'll be able to do something about that later.'

The words fall out of my mouth before I have a chance to stop them. 'Do you fancy staying the night?' I ask.

'Are you sure?'

'I don't think I'm going to be triggered by sharing a bed with you, given our past form. One word of warning though. You'll need to be up early as I'm working tomorrow and, if you want sex, I'll expect more foreplay than just a couple of prods in the back from little Cameron.'

He smiles. 'Only the best for Frou-Frou.'

I burst out laughing.

'What's so funny?'

'I was winding you up. My vagina isn't called Frou-Frou. In fact, it doesn't have a name. I think naming your private parts is weird.'

'I did think it sounded unlikely, but, if you don't want it to stick, you might want to stop referring to my penis as little Cameron.'

'I'm not sure I can.'

'Frou-Frou.'

'Fine. I'll try.'

* * *

By the time Cameron finally leaves on Sunday morning, I reckon I fully understand the meaning of the phrase 'dirty weekend'. Apart from the time I was working in the shop, we've barely left the bedroom, and I feel more relaxed than I thought possible so early in a new relationship. Although the physical side of things accelerated quickly, Cameron has been very careful to let me go at my own pace emotionally, so there haven't any been any rash declarations of love or anything like that. I feel completely comfortable with him though, which is the most important thing for me at the moment. I'm sitting on the sofa replaying some of the events of the weekend in my mind when Sam bounces through the door.

'How are you?' she asks as soon as she's thrown her bag into her room. 'Did you manage to sort things out with Cameron? I nearly rang you but I didn't want you to feel nannied.' She blushes. 'That and I was kind of distracted. It's been a slightly steamy weekend.'

'Mm,' I agree. 'It has.'

'*What?* What have I missed?'

'Let's just say Cameron and I have discovered we're very compatible in the bedroom.'

'Have you indeed? What happened to going slowly and all the stuff we talked about?'

'Yeah, that kind of didn't happen.'

'Well, congratulations. Are you happy?'

'Yes. Are you OK if he comes to stay next weekend?'

'Absolutely. In fact, that makes my life a bit easier.'

'Why?'

'Robin's invited me back next weekend. I didn't say yes, because I wanted to see how you were first, but it sounds like I might be surplus to requirements. So, if it's all right with you...'

'Yes, by all means go. How was your weekend, by the way?'

She sighs happily. 'Lovely. His house is gorgeous, although the garden could do with a bit of TLC. I met his cat too.'

'Oh, yes?'

'He's not as handsome as Samson, obviously, but he's still a good-looking boy. He's all black, apart from white socks on his paws, and he has the most enormous eyes. I could have stroked him all weekend, but Robin had other ideas.'

'I bet he did. And church?'

'Nothing like that one we went to, thank goodness. They were all really sweet, actually, apart from one woman that Robin reckons has the hots for him. She's got to be seventy if she's a day though, so I don't think she's serious competition. It was a little weird watching him doing all the holy stuff knowing what we'd been up to just a couple of hours previously. I guess I'll just have to get used to that.'

'It sounds like it's going well.'

'It really is. In fact, I'm starting to think he's the one.'

'I'm still struggling to see you as Mrs Vicarage.'

'I don't know. I'm starting to think I could pull it off. Anyway, tell me more about Cameron.'

By the time I've filled her in, her eyes are alight.

'You sound perfect for each other,' she says enthusiastically.

'How can you say that when all you have to go on is one, admittedly very dirty, weekend?'

'It's not the sex. It's the expression on your face when you talk about him.'

'It's very early days, Sam. Don't go choosing your wedding hat just yet.'

'We'll see. I have a nose for these things.'

I laugh. 'You so don't. If you did, Threesome Pete would never have made it through the door.'

What I haven't told her is that, despite trying to hold back and protect myself, I'm falling just as hard for Cameron as he said he'd fallen for me.

She's right that it's not about the sex; although that's very nice, it's the way he makes me feel when I'm with him. Now that I've let my guard down a little bit, I can see that my physical reaction during the massage in Cannes was in no small part due to the fact that I was becoming emotionally attached to him, even if I couldn't see it at the time. It may be early days, but I have a good feeling about him. Do I need a man? No. I'm a strong, independent woman and nobody will ever be able to do what Olly did to me again. Do I want a man, though? Oh, yes. I want this one very much indeed.

30

TWO YEARS LATER

'Are you ready, Ruby? We need to hit the road if we're going to be on time,' Cameron's voice calls from outside the bathroom.

'Two minutes,' I call back as I apply the finishing touches of make-up. 'Have you sorted Samson?'

'He's fed, watered and, I suspect, gone off to annoy Jono in the shop.'

By the time Sam moved out to marry Robin a year ago, Cameron was spending so much time at the flat with us that asking him to move in officially felt like a mere formality. It's taken a while for him to sell his house in Maidstone, but it finally completed a month ago, so we're starting to look for somewhere a little larger, perhaps with a proper garden for Samson, not that he'll appreciate it. I'm not sure he's actually noticed that Sam has gone as Cameron is definitely his favourite human being these days. I try not to be put out about that fact, but his lack of loyalty does rankle from time to time.

'I do get why Robin does these things on a Saturday,' I say as I shut the car door behind me, 'but it really doesn't suit those of us who work in retail.'

'Relax. Em knows what she's doing, and it was very nice of her to give up a day of her precious weekend to help you out.'

'You're right. Sorry, I don't mean to sound grumpy.'

'I think she enjoys it, particularly when Charlie's abroad like he is at the moment. It's got to be better than rattling around in their flat with nothing except marking to do.'

I smile. 'I still can't believe she's a teacher. She was always the class clown at school, according to Mum.'

'Poachers often make the best gamekeepers.'

'What?'

'If you want someone to understand the way the naughty children think, you need someone who was a naughty child themselves.'

'Mm. She still seems to have a unique talent for winding Mum and Dad up, so she hasn't completely changed her spots.'

We settle into a comfortable silence as Cameron turns onto the dual carriageway. This is a journey we've become familiar with over the last few months. Normally, we travel up on a Saturday evening and return after lunch on Sunday, but there's a special event on today.

'How many couples did Sam say there were going to be?' Cameron asks as we turn off the motorway, following signs for Dorking.

'Four, including us. The others are all local though.'

'I know I say this every time, but it is a hell of a trek, isn't it?'

'Yes, but we've only got to do it twice more after this.'

'You've been counting down.'

'Haven't you?'

He smiles. 'Maybe.'

The vicarage door is open when we pull onto the drive, so we walk straight through to the kitchen, where we find Sam sitting at the table with a cup of tea. As soon as she spots us, she starts to heave herself to her feet.

'Stay sitting,' I order her as I walk round the table to give her a kiss. 'Pregnant woman's prerogative.'

'Thank you.' She grimaces. 'The little bastard has been kicking me all morning.'

'Do you need a hand with anything? Just shout and I'll fetch and carry.'

'Nice try, but you're strictly punters today. Robin's been very strict with me about it. I've got a couple of ladies from the church coming to help out, don't worry.'

'And where is the vicar?'

'In his study, just making sure he's got everything he needs.'

As if knowing that we're talking about him, Robin wanders in to join us.

'Ruby, Cameron. Lovely to see you as always. You're the first to arrive. Are you ready for a day of wedding preparation?'

'As we'll ever be,' I reply. 'Although I'm still not sure what to expect.'

'Don't worry, it's nothing too intense. In the morning, we look at various common areas of marital conflict – money, sex, communication styles and all that. Then we'll look at the service itself this afternoon.'

'I'm not talking to complete strangers about sex,' I tell him firmly.

'You won't be,' he assures me. 'Nobody's marking your homework. We're just giving you space to think about different aspects of your relationship before you tie the knot.'

'Did you do this before you and Sam got married?' I ask him.

'We did a version of it, yes. Relax, it'll be fine.'

'There's nothing less fine than talking about sex with a vicar,' I remark.

'I don't know,' Sam pipes up from her seat at the table. 'You could be talking about it with your parents.' She winks at Robin. 'Or even doing it with a vicar.'

'That's true.'

'Anyway.' She strokes her baby bump affectionately. 'I think we can assume this particular vicar knows a thing or two where sex is concerned.'

'What's worse?' Cameron asks me quietly. 'Talking to a vicar about sex or thinking about a vicar having sex?'

'Something tells me today is going to be a long day,' I murmur back.

'It's not too late. We could cancel and book the registry office instead.'

'Apart from the fact that I don't think Sam would ever forgive us, we've put so much effort into this, what with all the back and forth to attend Sunday services to get our qualifying connection. Plus, I quite like the idea of Robin marrying us. It's more personal somehow.'

'You're right. And it's totally worth it if I get to marry you at the end.'

I smile and lean against him, giving him a surreptitious kiss. 'You say all the right things. I'm pretty excited about marrying you too.'

'Have you two sorted out your honeymoon yet?' Sam asks, breaking into our private moment.

'We have, actually,' I tell her. 'Despite my favourite travel agent moving to

Dorking, it turns out it's still possible to book holidays. Your colleague Janet helped us out.'

'Go on then, spill the beans.'

'We're going on a cruise,' Cameron tells her with a smile. 'Revisiting a few places and catching up with old friends.'

'We're on the *Spirit of Malmö* again,' I add.

'Try not to miss it this time,' she says, laughing.

'I'm sure we'll find ways to entertain ourselves if we do,' I tell her with a smile. 'I'll be expecting a massage, for starters.'

'I don't think we need to miss the boat for that to happen,' Cameron remarks.

'Okay, too much information,' Sam declares. 'Save it for marriage prep.'

'Talking of which, I think these are our other couples,' Robin announces as the sound of car engines filters through from the open front door. 'Shall we find out if you're ready to get married?'

I glance at Cameron, who smiles crookedly back at me. I already know the answer to that question; I am so ready to marry him.

* * *

MORE FROM PHOEBE MACLEOD

Another book from Phoebe MacLeod, *The Do-Over*, is available to order now here:

https://mybook.to/TheDoOverBackAd

ACKNOWLEDGEMENTS

Thank you so much for reading this book, and I hope you enjoyed Ruby and Cameron's story.

Setting a book on a cruise ship was a challenge, having not been on a cruise myself, but my friend Sharon gamely stepped up to the plate to fill me in on all the port protocols, sail-away parties and everything else. Thank you! Thanks also to Neal, who filled in a couple of blanks while I was writing and Sharon was away on a cruise...

Thank you to Paddock Wood shooting school and the instructors there, who were a mine of information about different clay pigeon shooting techniques. Cameron is based on a real-life firearms enquiry officer, who surprised me with his genuine enthusiasm for shotguns that I tried to carry across into the book.

Massive thanks as always to my editor, Rachel. There's been a lot going on during the writing and editing of this book and I'm grateful for all the support and encouragement you've given me. Thank you also to Cecily for copy editing again, and Jennifer for proof reading. I also want to say thank you to the rest of the amazing Boldwood team for the incredible work you do to connect my books with readers. I know I say this every time, but you really are the best publisher to work with.

Final thank yous, as always, go to my family, who could not be more supportive and give me time to write. Thanks also to Bertie the Labradoodle – we may not be walking at the moment, but I'm sure you're still helping somehow!

ABOUT THE AUTHOR

Phoebe MacLeod is the author of several popular romantic comedies including the top ten bestseller, *The Fixer Upper*. She lives in Kent with her partner, grown up children and disobedient dog.

Sign up to Phoebe MacLeod's newsletter to read a bonus deleted scene from The Do-Over!

Follow Phoebe on social media here:

facebook.com/PhoebeMacleodAuthor
x.com/macleod_phoebe
instagram.com/phoebemacleod21

ALSO BY PHOEBE MACLEOD

Someone Else's Honeymoon

Not The Man I Thought He Was

Fred and Breakfast

Let's Not Be Friends

An (Un)Romantic Comedy

Love at First Site

Never Ever Getting Back Together

The Fixer Upper

My Not So Perfect Summer

Too Busy for Love

The Do-Over

Hook, Line and Single

LOVE NOTES
LOVE IN EVERY CHAPTER

WHERE ALL YOUR ROMANCE DREAMS COME TRUE!

THE HOME OF BESTSELLING ROMANCE AND WOMEN'S FICTION

WARNING: MAY CONTAIN SPICE

SIGN UP TO OUR NEWSLETTER

https://bit.ly/Lovenotesnews

Boldwood

Boldwood Books is an award-winning fiction publishing company seeking out the best stories from around the world.

Find out more at www.boldwoodbooks.com

Join our reader community for brilliant books, competitions and offers!

Follow us
@BoldwoodBooks
@TheBoldBookClub

Sign up to our weekly deals newsletter

https://bit.ly/BoldwoodBNewsletter